2/94

P9-CLX-530

NO ESCAPE

All Arianne wanted to do was escape.
Escape from Lord Galen Locke and his
insufferably arrogant offer, and from the
terrible temptation that his unthinkable
proposal presented.

When the baron was forced to slow his
horses because of a tangle in traffic,
Arianne saw her chance. She gathered up
her skirt and her courage and leapt from
his phaeton.

"Where the devil do you think you're
going!" Locke shouted after her.

Arianne wanted to scream in return. She
wanted to stamp her foot and throw a
tantrum. Most of all, she wanted to fling
herself on the grass and cry until her heart
broke. That such an impossible man could
bring her to this state was not logical—
but logic had nothing to do with the
emotions careening through her right
now. . . .

PATRICIA RICE was born in Newburgh, New York,
and attended the University of Kentucky. She now
lives in Mayfield, Kentucky, with her husband and
her two children, Corinna and Derek, in a rambling
Tudor house. Ms. Rice has a degree in accounting
and her hobbies include history, travel, and antique
collecting.

Artful
Deceptions

by

Patricia Rice

A SIGNET BOOK

SIGNET
Published by the Penguin Group
Penguin Books USA Inc., 375 Hudson Street,
New York, New York 10014, U.S.A.
Penguin Books Ltd, 27 Wrights Lane,
London W8 5TZ, England
Penguin Books Australia Ltd, Ringwood,
Victoria, Australia
Penguin Books Canada Ltd, 10 Alcorn Avenue,
Toronto, Ontario, Canada M4V 3B2
Penguin Books (N.Z.) Ltd, 182–190 Wairau Road,
Auckland 10, New Zealand

Penguin Books Ltd, Registered Offices:
Harmondsworth, Middlesex, England

First published by Signet, an imprint of New American Library,
a division of Penguin Books USA Inc.

First Printing, August, 1992
10 9 8 7 6 5 4 3 2 1

REGISTERED TRADEMARK—MARCA REGISTRADA

PRINTED IN THE UNITED STATES OF AMERICA

BOOKS ARE AVAILABLE AT QUANTITY DISCOUNTS WHEN USED TO PROMOTE
PRODUCTS OR SERVICES. FOR INFORMATION PLEASE WRITE TO PREMIUM MAR-
KETING DIVISION, PENGUIN BOOKS USA INC., 375 HUDSON STREET, NEW YORK,
NEW YORK 10014.

1

HOLDING HER BREATH and biting her lip, Arianne Richards gently removed the oddly situated backing from which a piece of canvas protruded. Many old paintings had unusual frames and odd bits of paper and board tacked to the reverse, but this particular painting was neither very old nor very valuable. Actually, she considered the insipid portrait on the other side one of the artist's poorest works. Her mother could not possibly have looked that vain even twenty years ago, and she certainly had never been the frail and porcelain beauty the artist had thought to make of her. Perhaps that kind of beauty had been as fashionable then as it was now, but Arianne knew quite well that her mother was as tall as she, and had always enjoyed robust good health.

Until these last few years. Frowning, Arianne pried painstakingly at the backing. If she listened carefully, she could hear her mother's cough in the rooms above, but here in the workroom she tried to shut out this reminder. Her father had brought in no new commissions lately, and there was nothing to be done down here, but Arianne had used the excuse of cleaning one of their own portraits to escape for a while into this solitude.

Not that she minded tending to her younger brothers and sister, or even cared that the major part of the housework fell on her shoulders now that her mother's coughing spells had become more frequent. Her family had been all her life for twenty-one years. She knew little else. But the constant worry of the hacking cough gnawed at fears Arianne didn't wish to confront.

She could remember a time when she had run through the wild grasses of Somerset, free and laughing as only a child could be. She had been too young to remember the death of her first baby sister, but she could remember the time after the fever, when her new baby brother had been carried off on angel's wings, as her mother had explained it. It had been then that the laughing summer days had dwindled to a permanent winter.

Her mother had been a long time recovering from the fever. Her father's genial absentmindedness had become more distracted. Bits and pieces of their heavy old carved furniture had begun to disappear: the lovely chair with the faded tapestry of lions and Romans, the massive walnut sideboard with so many intricate carvings that Arianne used it as a hiding place for her smallest treasures, even the golden candlesticks with the dragon heads that breathed fire when the candle was lit. Along with these fantasies of the past disappeared Arianne's childhood.

They had removed to London by the time Lucinda was born. Even as a six-year-old Arianne had taken the responsibility of looking after the infant, rocking her cradle when she cried, keeping her amused when she was awake so her mother could rest and get strong again. It seemed a natural progression of things that her mother's "best little helper" should be the one to watch the toddler when she began to walk, to set the table and clear the dishes on the maid's night off, to stir the custard when the kitchen was a flurry of activity.

Arianne breathed a sigh of relief as the backing finally came loose from the frame. She knew no one minded when she came down here to get away for just a little while. Her father had encouraged her habit of slipping away to watch him work as he cleared centuries of dirt and grime from the rare and valuable oils brought to him from the collections of the wealthy. He had even allowed her to help him on less valuable pieces, until she knew the best chemicals to use for which oils and could work patiently without his guidance while he went out to obtain more business.

It was because his own collection was so extensive that Ross Richards was consulted by royalty and aristocracy seeking to keep their family treasures or newly acquired ones in good repair. Arianne wrinkled her nose in frustration as she thought of the fortune in paintings adorning the walls of this rather humble abode. The paintings were almost all they had left when they had moved to the city, and her father refused to part with even the least of them, even if it meant not taking a much-needed trip to Bath or Brighton to improve her mother's ailing health.

It was the one subject on which she and her father were at odds, and it wouldn't do to dwell on it now. Her father's passion for art supported them, while her parents' aristocratic relations gave them the connections to the world necessary to provide that support. They seemed content with that, and Arianne knew it wasn't her place to interfere.

But as the backing slipped away to reveal a palette of colors that shouldn't be there, Arianne gasped and felt a flutter of hope somewhere deep inside, hope hinged on keeping this discovery a secret from her beloved father.

Arianne didn't bother to look in the mirror as she tied the ribbons of her eminently practical buckram-stiffened bonnet over her heavy chestnut hair. She had no lady's maid to cut and comb and tease and curl the thick lengths into a fashionable coiffure, and she had no patience for it herself. By pinning her tresses carefully into a heavy chignon, she managed to keep them in control enough to fit a bonnet over them. That was all that was necessary under the circumstances.

Tightening her generous mouth and catching a glance of the result in the mirror, Arianne sighed as the knocker sounded below. She had been watching for the carriage and had hurried to make ready as soon as it had turned down the narrow street, but it would be completely indecorous to run out before Melanie's footman had even knocked at the door. Thinking of Melanie, she sighed again. Melanie had the pouty bowed lips of fashion. Why couldn't she at least resemble her fashionable cousin in this one small respect?

Hurriedly pulling on her gloves, Arianne hastened toward the hall stairs, but she had no chance of escaping without notice. Fifteen-year-old Lucinda came bounding out of the upstairs parlor, and from the sound of running footsteps, she would be followed closely by their brothers.

"Rainy, Melanie is here! Could I go too? Please, Rainy? Just this once? I've never ridden in a carriage through the park before. Please, Rainy?"

Arianne didn't hesitate, though her heart tugged at her sister's plea. Were it not for their cousins, she would never have seen the fashionable world from an elegant carriage either, but this carriage ride had more importance than a gay outing.

Smiling up at her sister, Arianne called, "Another time, Lucy, I promise," before hurrying through the door held by Melanie's footman.

Her cousin practically bounced with eagerness as Arianne sat beside her on the velvet squabs. Melanie had lost both her parents, leaving her in the somewhat whimsical care of her twin brothers, Gordon and Evan, but aside from that one unhappy circumstance, Melanie Griffin had everything that Arianne had not.

The Griffins were wealthy and moved in the fashionable circles of their grandfather, the Earl of Shelce. At eighteen Melanie had been presented to court under the auspices of her brother Evan's new wife, and she was now enjoying the Season she had been denied after her father's death.

But it wasn't so much Melanie's wealth and fashion that Arianne envied as her cousin's blond, petite beauty and sunny disposition. Melanie practically glowed with charm and laughter and seemed totally unaware that heads turned to watch her wherever she went. Beside her, Arianne felt the veriest dull horse, but then, she wasn't here to charm anyone into anything.

"Tell me now, Rainy!" Melanie clasped Arianne's gloved hand and turned blue eyes burning with curiosity to her elder cousin. "Tell me or I shall die of suspense. What is it that actually has you sending for me for a change? Usually it is I who must seek you out. Have you found a beau, Rainy, and wish to meet him secretly? Is Uncle Ross to become curator for the Regent? It must be something vastly exciting to stir you from your busy hearth and home."

Arianne smiled briefly at her cousin's overindulgence in romantics. It was widely recognized among the family that Arianne was the practical one while Melanie was an incurable dreamer. Before the late Viscount Griffin's untimely death, Arianne had been much in Melanie's household simply as a balance against the younger girl's high spirits. They had been tutored together until Arianne was too old for tutoring and was needed too much at home to be spared. It had been several years since she'd enjoyed the freedom of the Griffin household but Melanie hadn't allowed their friendship to fade with time.

"How can I tell you my poor secrets after hearing those wild dreams? Art curator for the Regent! As if Prinny weren't far enough in debt, my father would have the whole of the monarchy up the River Tick in no time."

Melanie giggled at this solecism from her solemn cousin. Arianne seldom smiled, and it was difficult for strangers to know whether she was serious or not, but Melanie knew her sharp wit well enough. "I should like to see that. Do you think they might sell the crown jewels, then? I rather have a fancy for that ruby coronet. Wouldn't I look grand?" At Arianne's lifted brow, she grinned again. "And you have not ruled out a beau, Rainy. I wish you had allowed Gordon to bring you out with me. Some of these entertainments are deadly dull without you along to prick all those puffed self-esteems."

Arianne shook off her annoying bonnet within the

privacy of the carriage's closed confines and smiled at the memory stirred by her cousin's words. "The Puffed Self-Esteem, a rare bird, as I remember. One wouldn't want to prick one, would one? Now, the Haughty Snuff-Snatcher, there's a common one, put salt on his tail if you like. He'll not likely know the difference."

"He will if the salt lands in his snuffbox! Oh, I had forgotten that, Arianne. You should never have encouraged me so. I don't think there was one of the twins' friends who did not avoid us after that."

"Oh, p'raps one or two. They weren't all lofty fellows. I rather suspect some of them had a good laugh at their clubs that night. 'Twas a pity I hadn't told you pepper worked better, but I had no notion you would take it into your head to salt our imaginary birds."

Melanie swallowed a chuckle. "I don't suppose the poor fellow ever figured out why I chose to salt him. But the stairwell wasn't a very good hiding place. Even if the lid of the salt cellar had not come loose, someone would have seen me as soon as he began choking on that awful snuff. I must have appeared quite the goose."

"Feather-Headed Guinea Hen," Arianne affirmed readily. "But by now I'm certain all is forgiven and you have bevies of suitors at your doors."

"Straitlaced Sapsuckers and Peafowls by the dozen." Melanie dismissed them airily with a wave of her hand. "Now, what is it that you need my advice for? It is such an unusual occasion, that you cannot hope to distract me from your request for long. If you have not found a wealthy suitor, have you some notion of persuading Uncle Ross to part with his precious paintings?"

To Melanie, all of life was a game to be laughed at and played with an abundance of cheer. Arianne had to smile at her wild assumptions. It was much easier to feel good about her decision when there was someone to urge her on. "In the absence of suitable beaux and the silver tongue required to persuade my father of anything, I have done something quite despicable. I have stolen a painting."

That startled the laughter from Melanie's lips, and she sent her cousin a hasty look of concern before realizing the ever-practical Arianne had made another joke. Relieved, she sat back and joined in the game. "You have spirited his Gainsborough from above his desk and hidden it in the garden."

Arianne did laugh at this mad suggestion. "The house and grounds would have been leveled by now in his search had I done so. No, nothing nearly so dramatic or valuable. You know I have been helping him with cleaning the paintings that have been brought to him?"

Melanie made a face. "All those smelly oils and turpentines. I don't know how you abide it."

"It is great fun. You must persuade Gordon to bring in some of your family portraits sometime. All those years of dirt and grime from wood smoke hide so many of the true colors. I enjoy watching a musty old ancestor become a colorful rogue or dashing lady once the colors are revealed."

"I doubt that we have a single interesting ancestor between us worth uncovering, but what does any of this have to do with your stolen painting? Surely you have not stolen someone else's painting?"

The horror in Melanie's voice rang more with drama than anxiety, and Arianne ignored it. With some difficulty she explained the discovery of the hidden painting and her decision not to tell her father of its existence. "For I know he will spend more money to have it framed and hung on a wall where no one but his clients will see it and where no good can come of it at all. But if it could be sold, even for a few pounds, I might persuade Mama to spend a few days in country air. The physicians say she should spend time at Bath or Brighton, but the expense is enormously prohibitive. But I thought just a few days somewhere quiet, out of the stench of belching chimneys and flowing sewers . . ."

Melanie wrinkled her nose in distaste. "Enough! I

have never thought of London that way, but if Aunt
Anne's lungs are delicate, then I suppose you are
right. We should remove her from the city at once.
But why must you sell your musty old painting to do
so? I'm certain Evan wouldn't mind if she stayed at
his place in Devon."

Arianne had been afraid that would be the approach
Melanie would take, and she stiffened her resolve. "If
I remember rightly, the estate actually belongs to the
earl, and he and my father have never been on the
best of terms. It is better this way, without argument
or damaged pride."

The slightest trace of a frown briefly marred Melanie's cheerful features, and she tapped her fingers
lightly on the carriage side as it turned into the park
drive. "I really cannot believe that Grandfather would
care one way or another. It is your father who will
not accept his help. They are both quite perverse in
their pride, but I suppose you're right. There would
only come an argument of it. I don't think Grandfather ever forgave my father for marrying into your
family. Old people are quite silly sometimes."

"The fact that my family has no particular title and
certainly no amount of wealth could have something
to do with your grandfather's opinion," Arianne replied wryly. "But that is neither here nor there. We
would never suit in society, so we are happy as we
are, were it not for Mama's health. But I think the
painting is some solution."

Melanie remained dubious. "If it was hidden behind
another canvas, how could it be very valuable? Someone thought little enough of it to hide it like that."

Arianne clenched her fingers together. "The painting it was hidden behind was that terrible portrait of
Mama, one of Lawrence's very early works. I am almost certain it is another Lawrence, an even earlier
one. No one could hope to duplicate his style, and
just the fact that it is nailed behind one of his . . ."

Melanie's eyes grew wide. "I heard his portraits cost
a hundred guineas now. How much would one of his
early portraits be worth?"

"I do not know. The style is not so polished as his current works. It is very lovely, though. It shows a woman and a little boy, and they look so incredibly happy. She has lovely dark hair, her coloring is darker than most, but she is extremely handsome just the same. The landscape behind them is rather rugged, so I know it must be nearer Bristol than London. I would think it ought to bring a good price, but there is the problem. How would I go about getting the best price, and where? I daren't take it to anyone who knows my father."

Glancing out the window, Melanie gave a sudden start; then, bouncing merrily again, she pounded on the box and ordered the driver to pull over.

Arianne followed her cousin's glance and discovered to her surprise that they were already caught up in the fashionable crowds of Hyde Park. Quickly donning her bonnet, she wondered what her cousin could be up to now. Elegant landaus and old-fashioned barouches vied for a place among the dashing thoroughbreds with their silk-hatted riders. Beside them strolled pedestrians showing off their fashionable walking attire, the ladies in their delicate gowns on the arms of gentlemen in padded coats and knee-high boots. Arianne had no desire whatsoever to descend into that public arena, where the only purpose of existence was to see and be seen.

But Melanie had no such reservation. Tugging Arianne's arm, she indicated the footman opening the door, waiting for them to descend. "Hurry, or they will be gone. I should have brought an open carriage. Out!"

Bewildered, Arianne descended to the grass. People turned in curiosity, but finding nothing of interest in a tall woman in dowdy brown broadcloth and unadorned bonnet, they moved on. Melanie's appearance stirred interest, but she seemed to take no notice of it as she brashly caught Arianne's arm and brought her around the vehicle into view of the road.

Garbed in a rich yellow silk topped by a white eyelet spencer and wearing a matching bonnet trimmed

in roses, Melanie rivaled the rarest bird in this aviary
of peacocks. Her wave at two gentlemen setting a
reckless pace in a shining new high-perch phaeton
could scarcely be ignored. Arianne gasped at her cousin's forward behavior, but the phaeton instantly
slowed, and its occupants looked more than pleased
at being thus signaled.

As the driver of the other vehicle expertly steered
his horses from the road, Arianne tried not to stare,
but she was very much reminded of the god Apollo
steering his chariot across the skies. Tall and golden-
haired, he had a smile remarkably similar to Melanie's, but she knew he was not one of her cousins.
The resemblance failed to go beyond the smile and
hair coloring. Whereas Melanie was petite and small-
boned, this gentleman towered well over six feet and
his large frame made languid elegance an impossibil-
ity, although the excellent cut of his coat showed off
his broad shoulders to perfection. The smiling eyes
were clear gray and direct, taking in not only Melanie
but also her angular and awkward cousin.

"I don't suppose I may do anything so dashing as
rescue a lady in distress, may I?" The golden-haired
driver dropped to the ground beside them.

The man with him did not remove from the carriage
with the same physical swiftness, but at a leisurely
pace that belied the sturdy stockiness of his frame.
When he came across the grass, Arianne could see
that he limped, but the quiet darkness of his eyes and
the wide intelligence of his brow endeared him to her
without a word being exchanged. Here was a man
who could defy society, everything about him said. His
clothes were not of the first fashion, and he wore them
with a casualness that said he did not care. Closer, he
could be seen to have worn spots on his cuffs, but his
linen was as immaculate as his companion's. His gaze,
however, fell only on Melanie.

"Yes, you most certainly may, but not in the manner in which you are thinking," Melanie laughed in
reply to the driver's question.

The large gentleman slipped Melanie's hand through

his arm with an insouciance that contained as much amusement as pleasure, then turned questioningly to Arianne. "My lady, will you join us also? It's a lovely day for a stroll, and I can see Melanie means to bend our ears for a while."

Melanie's laughter pealed beside him. "Galen, don't you remember Arianne? Honestly, we have been in and out of each other's houses forever. Surely you have come upon each other before."

Surprised gray eyes swept upward from Melanie's pert face to the solemn young woman in a spinster's rags. Eyes of a deeper blue than her cousin's met his gaze gravely, and Galen fought a twitch of his lips as he remembered just exactly where he had seen those eyes last. "Let us pretend to ignore her, Miss Richards," he replied, slipping Arianne's hand through his other arm. "Melanie is spoiled beyond redemption and fails to remember that she has not deemed London worthy of her presence for these last two years or more. And even then, if I remember rightly, she was but a schoolroom miss not worthy of my attention. But you, Miss Richards, I do remember. You had a decided propensity for showing up in your cousin's library at the most awkward of times."

Arianne was not accustomed to blushing, but she felt a warmth in her cheeks now as she finally remembered the identity of this imposing man. It had been years, when she and Melanie were but girls hiding from Melanie's governess, since she had last encountered him, and he had been little more than a gangly Oxford student. The heat in her cheeks increased as she remembered what he had been doing then.

"I trust the maidservants have learned to stand out of your way since then, my lord," she managed to retort, before removing her hand and turning to the unknown gentleman watching this tableau unsmilingly.

Melanie gave her tormentor a triumphant smile and made the introductions. "Arianne, may I introduce you to Rhys Llewellyn, a dear friend of my brothers. Mr. Llewellyn, this is my cousin Arianne Richards.

You and she will have much in common, and cutting Galen will be the least of it."

Mr. Llewellyn made a perfunctory bow, but a twinkle could be discerned beneath his indecently long lashes as he noted his friend's rather astonished expression. "A pleasure to meet someone who is not overpowered and tongue-tied by Galen's imposing visage, Miss Richards. Have you been saving that retort for him ever since his juvenile infraction?"

"He all but boxed my ears when I informed him the maid would almost certainly be put off if he continued what he was doing." Arianne dared a brief glance to the man who had grown from the irate youngster, and noting he only grinned at this recitation of the tale, she managed a smile. "And since he and Melanie are so very much alike, I cannot be terribly impressed. I know Melanie's foibles too well to expect Lord Locke to be of any better character."

"Unfair!" the maligned lord complained. "To be tarred with the same brush as Melanie is patently ridiculous. You must give me time to redeem my character, Miss Richards."

Melanie tugged the crook of his elbow and steered him farther from the road. "We do not have eternity, dear Galen. You may salvage what you may by giving us some aid with your expertise." She threw a swift look to her cousin to be certain she and Rhys were following. "Arianne, despite appearances, Galen is an expert in the field of art. He apparently means to rival the collection of the Duke of Devonshire in his old age."

Galen turned in time to catch the look of interest in the eyes of the prim-and-proper Miss Richards. He remembered her as a beanpole of a girl with a thick braid and a frown of disapproval upon her face, but circumstances might have influenced his memory. From what he could see beneath her long-brimmed bonnet, she wasn't frowning now, and the long braid had become an abundance of rich chestnut. Beside Melanie, she was awkwardly tall, and the unadorned brown round gown she wore did little to enhance this impression, but he knew the difficulties of height himself, and he disregarded society's opinion in the matter. She certainly wasn't a beanpole any longer, and his eyes crinkled in a sudden smile at the thought.

"Undoubtedly that old age is just around the corner in Melanie's eyes. Will you lend me your shoulders for support, Miss Richards, so I might dodder over to yonder bench?"

Melanie beat his arm with her fist, but with much laughter and teasing they managed to acquire the bench, Melanie promptly appropriating the seat and placing her cousin beside her so that the gentlemen must stand and admire them while they spoke.

"Do be serious for a minute, Galen. We have very important business to discuss. Arianne has a painting she wishes to sell. How does one go about selling paintings? And how can she be certain to receive the best price?"

"Pretty ladies have no business worrying over such things. I'm certain Miss Richards' brothers or father will be able to take care of it. I will be happy to give them what little advice I might have at my disposal. But in the meantime, you must tell me if you mean to attend the Rawdons' soiree tomorrow. For you I will attend, but otherwise I would rather dine at White's than be subject to those minuscule inedible objects that pass for food on Rawdon's table."

Both men had a glimpse of flashing eyes before Miss Richards rose stiffly from her seat. "Melanie, I must be on my way. Mother will need me. Gentlemen, if you will excuse me . . ." She made a brief sketch of a curtsy and turned to leave.

"Arianne, don't be a goose!" Melanie called after her. "Galen can be made to be sensible when he wants. Come back here right now. You aren't going to walk home from here. Rhys, stop her, will you? She has a terrible temper sometimes, but I must say, she's justified this time." She turned a scathing look to the indolent lord lounging before her. "Galen, when will you grow up? Arianne's brothers are barely out of knee breeches and her father must never learn that she means to sell one of his precious paintings. You know my Uncle Ross. He is a positive miser when it comes to his collection. He would give away his last penny, but he could not be parted from those wicked pieces of canvas for love or money."

Lord Locke leaned against a nearby tree and crossed his legs lazily as he watched Rhys catch up with the wayward miss and talk her back to reason. Rhys had a way with words, mostly written, but he could make use of his tongue when required. Within seconds the dark pair were returning to the bench, Arianne's face turned eagerly to watch the intensity of the Welshman's eyes as he spoke about some subject that obviously fascinated them both. Locke tapped his shining black boots with his stick. "I had forgotten Mr. Richards. Forgive me, my dear. She definitely has a problem if she means to pry one of those oils from his hands. How does she suggest to do it?"

By this time the other pair had returned. Arianne gave Locke a cold nod, then seated herself beside her cousin. Melanie squeezed her fingers and explained the situation as hastily as she could, before Arianne and Galen could freeze each other to death. It was too late now to remember that Galen and Uncle Ross had had words over the authenticity of one of Galen's artworks. She only prayed that Galen was too much the gentleman to allow an old argument to influence his reaction to a lady's need for help.

She held her breath when she was done, waiting while Galen frowned at his boots. When he finally looked up again, the smile was back on his face, and he held out his hand to help Melanie up.

"Where can we see this fine painting?"

2

ARIANNE FRETTED at her gloves, wondering how it had come about that she be the one to sit beside Lord Locke in his fashionable phaeton while Melanie and Rhys tooled in the carriage back to Griffin House. She knew Melanie had asked Lord Locke to look at her painting, but it didn't have to be done this minute, while Melanie was running late for some appointment requiring her to go in one direction while Arianne went in another. It could have waited. But no, nothing was to be done but send his lordship haring across town with Arianne in tow to see her infamous painting.

She tried to look calm and accepting as she directed the golden gentleman to the narrow house on the narrow street in the less-than-fashionable section just off St. James's, but her heart thudded with a nervous beat every time he whipped the reins and set the horses to their paces. She had no place in this expensive and ludicrous vehicle beside a man who possessed not only a title but also the demeanor to go with it. Galen Locke was at home in the houses of dukes and earls, not the middle classes of men who must work for a living.

Still, there was no sign of distaste upon his serene features as he handed Arianne down from the carriage in front of the unprepossessing house that she called home. The fishmonger gawked at sight of the phaeton, and she could hear sashes being thrown open in windows all up and down the street, but there was naught to be done about it now. Taking a breath and throw-

ing back her shoulders, she advanced upon the front
door.

Inside could be heard cries of "Rainy's back!
Rainy's back!" echoing in various keys from the top
floor to the bottom, but that was only to be expected.
Galen Locke was well aware she was not an only
child. What he probably wasn't aware of was the ex-
plosive energy about to be unleashed upon him. Undoubtedly Lord Locke would come of a household
where children were kept behind closed doors or on
tight reins with governesses to mind them. Arianne
smiled slightly to herself as the door flew open without
any need to touch it.

"Rainy! Can I ride in the gig? Can I? Please?"
Without further hesitation the pleader pushed past the
couple on the doorstep and flew down to offer carrots
to the mettlesome thoroughbreds in the street.

As Lord Locke turned to put a halt to this danger
from the freckled schoolgirl, another figure came
flinging out the door on her heels without so much as
a plea or a by-your-leave. Fortunately, Arianne was
fast enough to catch this culprit by the collar and drag
him back while calling over her shoulder to the other.
"Lucinda, you come back here right this instant and
apologize to Lord Locke. Such behavior is inexcusable."

The girl offered up the last carrot and patted the nose
of the nearest horse before throwing back her braid and
glancing over her shoulder. Seeing that her sister
meant what she said, she resignedly dragged her feet
back to the entrance. "I never get to go anywhere,
Rainy. Can't I just pet them?"

By the time Arianne coaxed Lucinda into the house
and unloosed David with an admonition to take his
younger brothers back up the stairs where they belonged, the downstairs hall had taken on the appearance of a crowded street. A mobcapped maid came
chattering out of the back to shoo the children away,
a low-slung dog with long black hair dangling in its
eyes came over to sniff the intruder, and a weary-eyed
woman appeared on the stairs to ascertain the cause
of the commotion.

Upon being introduced to Lord Locke, she smiled tentatively, whisked a ginger cat from the stairs before it could follow the dog, murmured an apology for the manners of her children, and disappeared into the nether regions of the house after the cries of the little urchins deprived of their treat.

Before Arianne could even suggest that they make a hasty retreat to the parlor, where she might bring him the painting, a door to the rear of the hall opened and she groaned in dismay. With a quick, beseeching look, she took Lord Locke's hand and shook it firmly. "So kind of you to see me home, my lord. I will not impose on your time any longer. Convey my gratitude to Melanie, if you will."

Dazed by their lavish reception and the equally abrupt departure of the small creatures inhabiting the household, Galen tried to maintain the calm equilibrium of a well-bred English gentleman. He had not forgotten his reason for being here, but Miss Richards' rather direct hint indicated his curiosity was not to be satisfied immediately. Still, he didn't intend to fall apart under attack like Boney's armies at Waterloo. He, too, had seen the far door open, and Locke waited with the expectancy of a man about to meet his nemesis.

Fate had not assigned him a particularly imposing nemesis. The man emerging from the far room was tall, but in a stoop-shouldered manner that disguised his height. His hair had receded to a circle around the back of his head and above his ears, and what there was of it was disheveled and improperly cut. The spectacles perched on the end of his nose threatened to fall off when he abruptly straightened at the sight of the stranger in the hall, but it was apparently an expected occurrence, for he reached to catch the wire rim and tuck it into the pocket of a supremely disreputable and rumpled coat.

"Arianne, you're home. I needed you to make a minor purchase for me today. Are the shops still open? No, of course they're not. Excuse me, sir, have I had the pleasure of your acquaintance?" His tone did not change with any of his various comments or questions, but his open expression reflected curiosity and approval while it was focused on the visitor. But distracted by Arianne's reply, he began hunting for something in his pockets and Lord Locke was momentarily forgotten.

"Father, this is Lord Locke, a friend of the Griffins. Lord Locke, my father. I apologize for your wild welcome, but the children are not accustomed to my being gone for any length of time. I'm sorry you had to come so far out of your way to bring me home. Perhaps we may meet again someday."

The steely hint remained in her voice, but Galen was too intrigued to depart immediately. For years he had harbored a grudge against the critic who had dared to declare his Rubens a fraud, but he had never met the man. Now, meeting Ross Richards like this, with his anxious daughter at his side, he could find nothing of the coldly intellectual cynic he had expected to find.

Richards turned an engagingly conspiratorial smile to the silent young man. "She's a tartar, no doubt, but I can't do without her. Pleased to make your acquaintance, my lord. Don't let her throw you out if you're not ready to go. I understand you have an eye for art. Would you be interested in seeing my collection?"

Arianne's eyes rolled heavenward as she removed her bonnet, but far from being dismayed by her reaction, Galen merely admired the sight uncovered and decided Rubens' ideal woman was not his. He rather enjoyed the combination of shadowed cheekbones and high-set brow. Somehow, they were extremely appropriate to this setting, although certainly not fashionable anywhere else.

"I would be delighted and honored, sir. Miss Richards?"

"I've heard Father's lecture before. You're on your own. It's been a pleasure meeting you again." Arianne dipped a curtsy that emphasized the hypocrisy of her words and took herself off toward the stairway whence the remainder of the household had disappeared, leaving Locke to his own defenses.

Richards was already wandering back down the hallway by the time Galen lost sight of Arianne's slim figure in the dim recesses above. He hastened after his host in time to catch the last of his words.

". . . good girl, but headstrong. That's what comes of teaching them to use their minds, I suppose. Couldn't do without her, mind you, but I do recollect a time when women were dainty young things who spoke only when spoken to. Not certain at all that we weren't better off then."

Never having given the subject a thought before, Galen wasn't certain he was inclined to agree. Wit had its advantages, the least of which was to drive away boredom. Fencing with Miss Arianne Richards could turn out to be a delightful pastime.

Rolling up the canvas and tucking it beneath her practical cloak, Arianne cursed the weather, cursed the arrogant man who was her reason for going out in this damp, and cursed her cousin for introducing him into her life again. Then, taking Puddles on his leash, she escaped the house, where the children were still droning over their lessons, and made her way out into the still-wet streets.

Melanie should have known when she summoned her that Arianne had no maid to accompany her along these city streets. Although St. James's was the site of all the fashionable men's clubs and Almack's was only just around the corner, a lady risked life and reputation by venturing alone into this very male territory. Arianne knew the back streets that kept her away from the clubs and their nosy occupants, but Puddles was scarcely any protection should she be accosted along the way.

But surrounded by brothers and servants who cushioned her every step, Melanie would not realize that her cousin had no means of reaching Green Park without walking unaccompanied. It was no distance from where Arianne lived, and she had no difficulty traversing it, but she would appear the poor luckless cousin when she arrived at this fashionable gathering place on foot and with no maid in sight. Resolutely ignoring her sudden concern with appearance, Arianne turned to enter the elegant gates to the park.

The rain had stopped but the moisture-laden leaves still dripped continuously as she approached the assigned meeting place. Undoubtedly Melanie thought it highly dramatic to meet in secret for this uncovering of the hidden painting. Of course, Melanie would be arriving in a covered carriage with Galen to hold her parasol to keep her from the damp once she stepped out onto the paths. Arianne gritted her teeth and tried not to let her mood reduce her to the jealous smallness she felt at this moment. Life was what one made of it, not what one was given.

She gasped in surprise as a large male figure came around the shrubberies and nearly collided with her. A strong hand caught her elbow and balanced her, and she found herself staring up into Galen's smiling face.

"I suppose one might say the disadvantage of my size is that I am forever bumping into things, but then, I am very good at catching them before they fall. My apologies, Miss Richards. Are you all right?"

The little dog on the leash barked once, sniffed Galen's cuffs, then jumped excitedly to paw at his knee. Arianne winced as the once-immaculate buff breeches became marred with mud, but Lord Locke merely crouched to pat the dog and scratch behind its ears. Puddles wiggled in ecstasy and Galen glanced up quizzically at the dog's frozen owner. "You know, I have a dog just like this, but he's the most obnoxious piece of hound I ever hope to come across."

"You have a dog like Puddles?" Since the animal in question was little more than a hank of hair and a bit of bone, Arianne found it exceedingly hard to believe that this large and impressive man would possess any such creature, or be willing to admit it.

Galen grinned and straightened. "Belonged to my mother, but he kept biting my father's ankle and chewing his boots, so they banished the beast to London and my tender care. The animal does nothing but tear around the house barking his fool head off at every sight and sound until the servants would gladly pitch him out the door. Don't know what's the matter with the fellow."

By this time Melanie and her maid had joined them, and she was listening with great interest to this exchange. Arianne did her best to ignore the elegance of her cousin's silk pelisse and matching parasol as she hovered at Locke's elbow, but she did not seem able to control her tongue. With a sharpness she never intended, she replied, "A male dog? If you don't know what's the matter with him, then I'm not the one to tell you." With a slight nod, Arianne turned to greet her cousin.

Locke's look of astonishment and sudden roar of laughter brought a puzzled frown to Melanie's pretty features, but at the sight of the smile tugging at Arianne's mouth, she decided to smile too. "I am very glad to know that you and Galen are getting along so well, although I do wish you would explain to me what was so funny."

Locke choked, threw a pleading look to Arianne, and lifted his hands in abstention. In that moment Arianne almost liked him, and for her cousin's sake she vowed to do so. Pulling Puddles on a tighter leash so he could do no more damage to his lordship's trousers, she deftly avoided explanations. "We were merely discussing the habits of pets. I'm afraid Puddles has made rather a nuisance of herself."

"On the contrary, I might rather borrow Puddles for a while, if it means peace in the household. What are your feelings on the matter of puppies, Miss Richards?"

He was being scandalous, but since his talk went well above Melanie's head, Arianne could only hide the twitch of her lips and appear to frown disapprovingly. Locke's grin grew wider, and she knew she had hidden nothing. "My view of puppies has nothing to say on the matter. Puddles returns with me. You must do your own procuring. Did you wish to see the painting or did we come here merely to exchange pleasantries?"

Galen was choking on laughter again, but Melanie eagerly stepped in to fill the gap. "Oh, yes, where is it? I'm dying to see what you've found."

Melanie glanced around for some sign of the maid or servant who must be carrying the portrait, then realized the enormity of her error as Arianne removed a slender roll from beneath her cloak. Flushing in the sudden realization that she had forced her cousin to walk out unattended, Melanie grew quiet and took Puddles' leash without comment as Arianne unrolled the canvas.

Galen removed the unwieldy canvas from her hands to study it more closely, his gray eyes growing suddenly serious and intent as he absorbed the subject, the quality of the work and found the telltale signs that made it unmistakably a Lawrence. He held it out for Melanie's perusal, and after her enthralled exclamations, gently rolled the canvas again.

"You're quite right, Miss Richards. The work is undoubtedly an early Lawrence, but I cannot tell you how much it might be worth. I should think the subject of the painting would be most likely to pay the best price. Do you have any idea who it might be?"

Arianne shook her head. "It must have been done before my mother's, and that was done in Bristol. I very much suspect the setting is Wales, the woman has that sort of coloring. She and the child appear well-dressed, but it is doubtful that anyone from that background would be found here in London, and I have no means of going west to find them. I am well aware that the market for art is not great, particularly for contemporary art, but I do not need a great deal. My mother and I are very good at managing money. We can make a small amount go a long way."

Locke could tell from the braid on the let-down hem of her cloak how they managed their money, but he hid his frown. It was no business of his that Richards sat on a fortune in artwork while his family went clothed in the next best thing to rags. The market for art had only grown in these last years since Boney's war had emptied the coffers of Europe. Very few people as yet had an appreciation for the treasures on their walls. Richards' collection might someday provide a valuable inheritance for his young children, but in today's world it would merely put food on the table. He turned his attention to the problem at hand.

"I am tempted to make you an offer myself, Miss Richards. The portrait is one of the better examples of the artist's work and is certain to be valuable someday. But I cannot know if I am offering a fair price."

By this time Rhys had rambled up to join them, his cuffs stained with ink and an absent expression on his face. He gave a polite nod of greeting, shook his head at Galen's offer of the painting, and caught the tail end of their conversation.

"I thought about that last night," he intruded without preamble.

Arianne glanced to him in surprise. Melanie had mentioned that this new acquaintance had once been a soldier and was now writing for the local newssheets as well as on his own. She had not thought that he had taken any notice of her problem at all. She rather fancied that Melanie was his object of interest, as she was to most men who came into her sphere. To know that Mr. Llewellyn had given some thought to her problem was cause for surprise.

"Christie's has been doing a brisk business lately. They've sold some private collections at decent prices, I understand. They might be willing to take on a single piece in a general auction."

Arianne and Melanie stared at him in puzzlement, but Galen nodded approval. "You may have something, Llewellyn. What better way to determine a fair market price than at a general auction? They could display it for a few weeks while we mention the piece here and there and stir up interest. Perhaps even Lawrence himself will come."

Bombarded with questions, the men explained the purpose of the auction house on Pall Mall, how an auction worked, and the increasing reputation Christie's in particular was developing. Arianne looked dubious that a place where people's saddles and housewares could be sold to the public might also bring a good price for a piece of art, but she could offer no other alternative. She had thought in terms of a private sale such as her father so often negotiated on major works, but she had to admit that a portrait by Lawrence didn't rank in that same area. Who would wish to purchase a portrait of someone else's family?

Trying not to hope, Arianne surrendered her prize to the care of Lord Locke.

3

"I DON'T MEAN for you to grow to be an old maid looking after me and the children, Arianne. I'm quite young enough to look after myself. Now, go and join Melanie and have some fun. It's been too long since you've had a chance to enjoy yourself. 'Tis a pity Melanie's father had to die just before she had a chance to return to London for her come-out. But now that she's back, I'm certain she can use some of your practicality. Go along with you, now."

Thus dismissed by her mother, Arianne reluctantly turned to find her cloak and gloves in her own room. She was twenty-one to Melanie's eighteen, but the gap in ages was as nothing to the gap in their places in society. Under the auspices of her brother's new wife, Melanie was finally having her come-out, and her talk was filled with the excitements of the latest entertainment and the *on-dits* of the hour, subjects that could have no interest to Arianne. Even when Melanie discussed her suitors, Arianne could not show a suitable interest, for she had little or no acquaintance with the gentlemen.

Except for Mr. Llewellyn and Lord Locke. And those two gentlemen came in for much discussion when Melanie was about. Arianne was surprised to note that her young cousin should even notice the dark-and-silent writer next to his lordship's intoxicating golden charm, but Melanie had known her own mind from an early age. With two older brothers to flood the house with all the gallant gentlemen of London throughout her formative years, she was no stranger to the vagaries of their characters. Arianne had to smile at the aptness of some of her observations.

Arianne was the innocent when it came to men. Being the eldest, she saw her brothers as only wild creatures to be kept corralled. Her father's work occasionally brought home elderly gentlemen, who paid her little mind. Beyond that, her only experience was with shop clerks and, upon rare occasions, Melanie's older brothers. Since she had last met her male cousins before the war had usurped one and his grandfather's estate claimed the other, she couldn't even claim to have known them well enough to do more than call them cousin.

To be suddenly thrust into the company of Mr. Llewellyn and Lord Locke at every turn seemed rather hard to endure, particularly since both gentlemen appeared well-taken with Melanie. Shrugging, Arianne donned her only pair of kid gloves, straightened her bonnet with the help of a mirror, and descended the stairs just as the knocker sounded.

Mr. Llewellyn waited to aid her into the elegant landau, where Melanie and Lord Locke already sat. If Arianne felt dowdy in her unfeathered bonnet next to Melanie's beribboned and adorned confection, she had only to turn her gaze to Mr. Llewellyn's patched elbows and worn stock to feel at home. As if acknowledging his lack in comparison to Locke's exquisite frock coat and elegant cravat, the writer gave her a conspiratorial grin and squeezed her hand before he let it go.

"You two needn't look so smug," Melanie said crossly, observing this exchange. "Galen has already told me I will look a peacock among the quail. No one told me I must wear rags to visit an auction house."

Galen rolled his eyes heavenward rather than insert his finger any further into that pie, but Rhys wasn't so reluctant. "Evan would turn you over his knee for that remark, young lady. Now, behave yourself, or I shall enlighten him as to the toploftiness of his sister."

Melanie's already ruffled feathers bristled further as she glared at the man in the opposite corner as the carriage pulled away from the curb. "You have no right to speak to me like that, Rhys Llewellyn. You're not my brother, much as you like to pretend you are. I think you dress as you do out of spite. You know full well both Evan and Gordon would employ you in a far better fashion than your filthy newssheets."

Galen coughed politely and interrupted before the irate reply obviously burning Llewellyn's tongue could be loosed into the fray. "That is an enchanting hat you are wearing, Miss Richards. How is it that we have not seen it before?"

Arianne touched her hand to the bonnet from which she had viciously severed the long-billed brim before lining it with a bit of rose muslin left over from the gown she had made and wore now. It was obvious to her that the hat had been mutilated from the old one, but she was becoming accustomed to Lord Locke's mockery. He used it on himself as well as everyone and everything that he encountered.

"You have not only seen it before, but will see it again in one of its many transformations should you advance our acquaintance, my lord. I had a mind for pink today. Tomorrow it might be blue. Do you approve?"

He studied the shorter hat frame and the angular face beneath before replying. "I approve. Just do not transform it back into that long-beaked thing again. Perhaps in its next reincarnation you could make it invisible."

Rhys removed his battered hat and polished the crown against his sleeve before holding it out to Arianne. "Can you transform this into something that might meet my lady's approval? I'd rather not have pink, if you don't mind."

Even Melanie came out of her sulk as Arianne resorted to a brief flashing smile at this acceptance of her limited wardrobe. The foursome laughed and chattered and turned heads all along the way as the carriage maneuvered around the square and into Pall Mall. If any were to wonder why two peacocks of fashion such as Lady Melanie Griffin and Lord Locke were accompanied by two such plain wrens, there was none to mention it when they climbed down from the carriage before the residence housing Christie's auction house.

"Gainsborough used to live there." Galen nodded to the house next door. "Does that not foretell good fortune for any artwork passing this close?"

"For Gainsborough, mayhap, unless he possessed some fairy dust that fills the air in his vicinity, even years later. Did they truly hang my painting in here?" Arianne attempted the same dispassionate temperament as Lord Locke always displayed, but she could scarcely contain her excitement. If the painting sold for even twenty-five guineas . . . It wouldn't be much, but it might persuade her mother to consider a short journey to the country.

"Where all can see it. I talked to the manager this morning. He says there has been considerable interest in it already. He's framed it quite ably, as you will see." Locke took Melanie's arm and guided her through the doorway, leaving Arianne and Rhys to bring up the rear.

He led them directly to the room where the painting was housed, and Arianne gazed in satisfaction at her artwork's position in the center of the wall. So immersed was she in her contemplation that it was some minutes before she noted her companion's stunned reaction to this first sight of her discovery.

Rhy's hand clenched her elbow with a ferocity that bruised, while a curse of astonishment whispered across his lips. Startled, Arianne felt him release her arm, but before she could question, he was already limping forward, his gaze fixed intently on the woman serenely smiling down from the wall. Melanie and Galen were more interested in an assortment of jewelry displayed in a glass case and took little notice of Rhys's reaction.

Arianne hastened to his side, anxious that she had done something to disturb him in such a manner. "What is it? Do you know the lady?"

Rhys reached to touch the golden ring on the woman's finger, an action that would have sent Arianne's father into fits and lectures on the proper care of oils. But his touch was so reverent that Arianne could neither reprimand nor correct the motion.

Instead of replying, Rhys turned abruptly away from the painting and took Arianne's arm. "Let us get out of here. I find it suddenly stifling. Would you object to my company if I walk you home?"

"No, of course not." But she certainly should. She had scarcely known Rhys Llewellyn for a week. Although he was not of the same imposing stature as Lord Locke, he was still her better by half a head, and the strength in his broad arms was not to be denied as he pulled her to where the others were laughing and playing.

"Miss Richards and I mean to walk back and perhaps take an ice along the way. Would you mind if we excused ourselves now?"

Melanie looked startled at this defection and Galen's smiling features turned thoughtful, but there was no denying Rhys's demand. Arianne found herself hurrying to keep up as he headed for the door. For a lame man, he moved swiftly.

"I apologize for my abruptness," he said as they stepped into the sunshine, but there was no apology in his voice. He fell silent for several paces as they started down the street.

"The painting has disturbed you. I wish you would tell me why." Despite her commonsensical reservations about being shepherded down the street by a near-stranger, Arianne felt no real fear of Mr. Llewellyn. He had always behaved as a gentleman despite his rough appearance, and she sensed a deep passion and pain behind the dark eyes he turned to the world. She felt more empathy with this man than with the charming Lord Locke, and she found herself wishing he was not so attached to her cousin.

"I went to Oxford before I joined the cavalry, you know," he replied irrelevantly, slowing his pace to a more sedate walk as they encountered the fashionable crowds closer to St. James's Street. He turned down a side street rather than walk past those windows of the gentlemen's clubs.

"No, I didn't know." Arianne didn't know what else to reply. She wasn't at all certain he was even talking to her, or heard her answer.

"Evan and I belonged to the Four-in-Hand Club. We were notorious whips. I think I learned to ride before I walked. Good horseflesh was as much a part of me as the foot I no longer have."

Arianne gave that appendage a covert glance, seeing no more than the boot to match the other. As brief as her look was, Rhys caught it, and his lips turned up wryly.

"Looks better than it did, I'll admit. Amazing what a little money and modern conveniences can disguise. There used to be only a peg there, until Evan objected vehemently and dragged me off to the surgeon. But that is not a matter to discuss with ladies. I have forgotten my manners."

"You and Evan were in the cavalry together, then?" Arianne tried to piece together the odd bits of information he was relating to her. Only wealthy gentlemen could afford Oxford and the cavalry. Wealth, at least, was a necessity, she believed. There were many in both places—despite their birth—who could not be termed gentlemen.

"We've been through everything together. We're of an age and attended the same schools right from the start. That is the only reason Melanie knows me so well."

Arianne remembered the furor raised in the Griffin household when it was decided to separate the twins and send Evan to school while quiet Gordon had private tutoring. But she could not see where all this led.

"Melanie was little more than a child when Evan went off to war. She couldn't have known you very well."

Rhys switched subjects abruptly. "Where did you find that painting, Miss Richards? Tell me everything."

"I have told you everything." At his swift frown, Arianne hastened to repeat all the details she had recited before, and perhaps some that had been left out in her earlier haste. None of them seemed very remarkable.

"Perhaps your father would know more of the portrait," he said when she was done.

"I think if he had known of it at all, he would not have left it where it was. You do not know my father. He is a connoisseur of fine art. He would have been horrified at such treatment of a piece of work as good as that. No, I believe the artist is responsible for stretching a new canvas on the reverse of the old. He would not wish to destroy a painting he had spent so much time on, but if he could not sell it, he would make best use of what he could, particularly if he had little money for new frames. I was fortunate that he did not just paint over it, as many have in the past."

"So am I." Rhys slowed his pace even more as they approached the door to her house. Catching her hands in his, he studied Arianne's face intently, from the wide, arched brows to the stubborn jut of her chin. "I know this is asking much of you, but could you ask them to wait before putting the painting up for sale? There are questions I need answered, and that painting is my only clue."

She wanted to ask why, but it was evident he didn't mean to tell her. Although they had been much in each other's company this past week, they had observed all the proprieties and could not claim more than a passing acquaintance. Acquaintances did not ask personal questions of each other.

But Rhys Llewellyn's request raised their relationship to some new level for which she was not prepared. Arianne frowned slightly and released her hands from his grip. "If it is so very important, I would like to honor your request, but I'm not certain that I can do so. Lord Locke has been dealing with the auction house for me. He would have to be the one to make the request."

"It will not create a hardship for you?" Rhys inquired anxiously, his dark gaze searching her face for any evasion of the truth.

Arianne gave a wry grimace. "We have waited this long, I cannot see that it matters if we wait awhile longer. When should I tell Lord Locke to make it available?"

Llewellyn's carved visage closed up again, as if anxiety and concern were no part of him any longer. Only a note of gratitude could be found in his words. "I will speak with him myself. You cannot know how much I am indebted to you, Miss Richards. Perhaps someday I'll be free to tell you."

"I would appreciate that. You have my curiosity all astir. Won't you come in to have some tea?"

Rhys hesitated, contemplating her bravely refurbished bonnet and the intriguing face beneath, sensing the first tentacles of interest drawing them together. But he had resisted stronger bonds than these, and for good reason. Making a polite bow, he murmured his excuses, and was on his way before he could change his mind.

"Rhys did that? I cannot believe it of him. I shall ask Evan of it. They know each other very well, but they're both as closemouthed as hermits. Do you think I should ply him with wine first?"

Arianne laughed at Melanie's reaction and shook her head. "Your brother would suspect something immediately if you were to cozen up to him like that. It really is none of our concern if Mr. Llewellyn doesn't wish to talk about it. Perhaps there is some sentimental attachment to the subject and he wishes to find the funds to buy it for himself."

"Rhys never takes his head out of his papers long enough to recognize the difference between a fly and a hole in the wall. I daresay you could cover his walls with paintings and he would think them wallpaper. No, there is a story here, and I wish to know it. He and Evan have always been very secretive about something. It makes me so angry, I could kick them." Melanie stomped her slipper-clad foot to prove her point.

That was a rather startling reaction for one who spent the better part of her life laughing and making light of most subjects, and Arianne raised her eyebrows slightly. But the momentary aberration had passed, and Melanie was already flitting about her brother's library, unleashing her abundant energy on her plotting.

"Evan joining the cavalry was to be expected. He thinks himself some kind of white knight dashing off to save the world. But it wasn't at all the kind of thing that Rhys would do. But it wasn't until they came back from the war that I noticed he was acting strangely. I thought perhaps it was the injury to his foot that made him so . . ." Melanie searched for an appropriate word and tried, "Aloof. Distant. Rhys didn't used to be so. He used to treat me as if I were a real lady, even when I was little. We would go riding together, and talk of books, and he would tell me the funniest stories. But then he came home from the war and everything was changed. He works and scarcely comes to the house anymore, and when he does, it is only to see Evan or Gordon. The only reason he has been with us this last week is that Galen insisted on it."

That was a dampening thought, but Arianne tried not to give it too much consequence. She couldn't blame Lord Locke for wishing to have Melanie to himself and insisting on a fourth to the party to aid in that endeavor. But it would have been pleasant to think that Mr. Llewellyn had joined them willingly.

"Since he must work to support himself, it is very possible that he didn't wish you to think of him as a suitor," Arianne answered slowly, in response to the frustration in Melanie's voice. "When you were young, it was permissible for him to be your friend. But now you are an eligible young lady, and it would not do to harm your reputation by encouraging someone who may not be quite suitable. It is possible that Mr. Llewellyn is trying to protect you."

Melanie brightened briefly at the thought that Rhys only meant to protect her, then drew her exquisite features into a thoroughly formidable frown as she understood the implications. "But that is just it, you

see! Evan would never have invited him to the house
if he were not of perfectly respectable family and consequence. I know Evan has thoroughly disreputable
friends among all sorts, but he introduces only the
most proper people to me. Rhys never went without
before the war, and I have met his uncle and know
his family is accepted by the *ton* and lacks for nothing.

"There is no reason I know of that he cannot dress
as respectably and live as comfortably as Galen. I
think I shall strangle him."

4

LORD GALEN LOCKE, sixth baron of that name, adjusted his impeccable gloves, picked up his ebony carved walking stick with the gold crown and the gleaming black beaver hat to be arranged on his golden curls, and strode out of the house. At peace with the world, he hummed a merry tune as he chose to enjoy the warm spring night and walk to the club where he had arranged to meet Rhys.

He liked to think of himself as an uncomplicated fellow, with no grudges to grind and no ambitions to distort his view of the world as a very pleasant place to play in. As an only child, he knew he would inherit fortune and title with his father's passing, and as he did not indulge himself to excess with wine, women, horses, or gambling, he had sufficient wherewithal to support himself very comfortably in the meantime.

Although many another gentleman in his idle position filled his time with the physical pleasures London had to offer, Galen's interests were more intellectual. Not that he didn't enjoy good horseflesh and an occasional bout of fisticuffs to keep in shape, but they weren't sufficient to stimulate his mind or senses. With the extra time and money he had on his hands while waiting for his father to surrender the operations of his estate, Galen found pleasure in the arts.

Again, he wasn't the first gentleman to follow his Grand Tour with a passion for collecting, but his tour had been limited by Boney's war, and his passion had been whetted by collections here at home. His father's estate had a fine gallery, and his interest had begun when pursuing a particular Turner landscape to complete one wall. One Turner hadn't been enough, and he had begun to search out other suitable examples when the available supply of Turners was exhausted.

In consequence, Locke had begun to meet the artists who produced the paintings he most enjoyed. Constable had not yet made a name for himself, but Galen was certain he would soon, and he patronized the artist frequently. He knew Sir Thomas Lawrence personally, although he wasn't any more fond of the man than of his paintings. But the acquaintance led him to new and different artists who in turn led him to learn more of the old and valuable art being sold for a song in the aftermath of war. His pursuit had become almost as much of a passion as he would allow himself.

For a proper English gentleman did not allow himself passions; they were upsetting to logic and the orderly running of things. Galen had been taught that at his father's knee and learned the lesson well. It was most likely the reason that he and his father seldom spoke now. The earl was a busy man and had taken time to lecture his son only when his heir had indulged himself in excess, whether it were of high spirits or liquor or song. Perhaps another man would have chosen to consistently indulge in excess in order to obtain his parent's attention, but Galen was made of stronger stuff. He was an only child, after all, and obedience was trained into him. Not for him were the romps in the haystacks with brothers and sisters, or wild races through the fields with neighboring children. His had been an orderly upbringing with the proper tutors and the right sort of amusements. And so after a while his father did not need to notice him at all.

And he had turned out quite excellently well. Galen grinned at the thought and pushed his hat to a cocky angle with his walking stick. His main fault was that he wasn't serious enough. Perhaps he would turn serious when he had an estate to run. Meanwhile, he found it amusing to watch people, entertaining to be the center of attention when he entered a room, and pleasant to drink wine, make love, and enjoy art. Not necessarily in that order.

But that was the order for tonight's entertainment. Galen knew he should be seriously considering marriage, but until he was ready to take that step, he had healthy urges that shouldn't be neglected. It had occurred to him upon occasion to set up a mistress, but as in wife-hunting, he had not found a woman that he was serious enough about to consider. So when the need came upon him, he met with some other cronies and went visiting.

The house he had in mind for tonight was not so delightfully stimulating as that of the Wilsons, but he had his company for the evening to consider. Harriet Wilson and her sisters were priced high, too high for Rhys Llewellyn to afford. So they would take their chances at one of the more respectable bawdy houses in Covent Garden.

The problem of Llewellyn caused a momentary frown to crease Locke's seamless brow, but not for long. He would ply the gentleman with good food and wine and an artless evening, and by morning he would know what was on the man's mind. Rhys was a good friend, but he'd never met a more stubborn man. What in hell could that painting possibly have to do with the fact that his family considered him a bastard?

Rhys met Locke at the club as planned and they ate and drank and amused themselves with tales of old, but by the time they were on the street again, the ex-soldier was more taciturn than ever on the subject that most concerned them.

"Devil take it, Llewellyn, I'll buy the painting myself if that is what concerns you. I meant to anyway. I just thought Miss Richards would receive a fairer price if it went through the auction house. You can hang the damn thing on your wall and contemplate your muse as much as you wish, or buy it from me when you're feeling flush, it makes no mind to me. I just don't see why you must make the lady wait for her money. You, of all people, must understand what it is like to scrimp and save. She could undoubtedly use the ready.''

"I would not wish to feel obligated to you if the painting commands a high price, that is all," Rhys answered stiffly. "Good intentions are well and good, but common sense would win out if the thing went higher than it is worth. And I really would not wish it to fall into other hands.''

"And you're not only not going to tell me why you want the damn thing, but you aren't going to tell me why in the name of Jupiter it should command more than the hundred guineas a portrait of Lawrence's brings currently?''

"No." The reply was simple and curt and brought them to the house they had meant to visit.

Galen cursed and knocked upon the door, and they entered to the usual fawning welcomes of delight. Glancing around at the garish taste of the decor and the flamboyant dress of their hostess and her "girls," Galen made a new resolve to begin a serious search for a wife in the morning. It would be much more suitable if one could meet an intelligent woman in impeccable dress in the quiet tastefulness of one's club and take her home to indulge these harmless needs. Why mankind made sex sleazy and tawdry was beyond his desire to imagine. It was high time he acquired a wife when he began to think like that.

Rhys wasn't any more communicative when sipping from a snifter of brandy with a half-dressed nymph wrapped around his shoulders than he had been at dinner. The girl was short and dark and perhaps a trifle too plump, but a mischievous urchin with a smile that teased. Remembering other smiles from other women, Galen began a methodical search through his memory for the ones that pleased him most. It gave him something to do while deciding which of the ladies to choose.

Undoubtedly Melanie's smile stood out from all the others. He'd known the chit since childhood. She had never been the whining sort of brat that many another of his friends' younger sisters had been. She was always pleasant and smiling and happy and well-behaved. Well, almost always. Her behavior on the way to Christie's the other day was an oddity he had not bothered to investigate. But she had become her usual self quickly enough, and Galen thought her usual self was all that a man could ask.

Yes, Melanie was very definitely the sort of girl for him. She would make a proper earl's wife when the time came, and in the meantime she would afford him much amusement. They knew each other well and she would know precisely what to expect from him. He really should have thought of this sooner, and he could have been going home to a laughing conversation with his wife rather than sitting in this disreputable parlor watching an overdressed, overweight hostess go in search of a better selection for him.

But even as Galen sorted Melanie out from all the others, his memory kept snagging on a barely perceptible winsome smile that appeared and disappeared so quickly as to leave no trace. Why he should remember that smile, he had no clue, unless it had something to do with the haunting enchantment of the Mona Lisa's. And he really didn't think he could classify Miss Arianne Richards in the Mona Lisa's company. Not to mention that she was much too prim and respectable to be in that dubious lady's company, but it would never occur to her to seduce a man with a smile. No, it must be just that she so seldom smiled, a man noticed when she did.

Satisfied with that decision, Galen gave a nod of agreement as the hostess led out a pleasantly blond young lady of pleasing proportions. The girl's smile showed healthy white teeth, and she clung to his arm quite agreeably. Galen set down his snifter, gave Rhys a nod, and set out in the direction of the stairs.

Rhys watched him go with a glare that had nothing to do with the company of the young woman presently trying to climb onto his lap. It didn't take a blind man to notice that Galen had chosen the one woman in this place that resembled Lady Melanie Griffin. Rhys wanted to reach up and grab the other man's collar and jerk him back for a serious blow to the jaw.

The irrationality of that thought brought Rhys to his senses. There was absolutely no resemblance between that prostitute and his best friend's sweet-natured sister. The fact that Galen had gone off with the best-looking whore in the house was scarcely unusual. Rhys had never particularly resented Locke's easy charm and wealth. Actually, he liked the man, as much as he could like the man who would no doubt marry Lady Melanie. Doubtless Evan and Gordon felt the same way. It was a damn good thing that he had no younger sister of his own. A damn good thing.

With that return of his own problem, Rhys abruptly set his disappointed companion back to the floor and rose. There was no point in wasting good coins tonight when he was only in a mood to punch and throttle. He would do better to clear his head in the night air.

It was a long walk back to his rooms near the market at St. James's, but he needed the exercise to work off his anger. Not that anything ever completely disposed of it. It was just that sight of that painting had stirred up old injustices and hurts, pains he had thought long since buried under acceptance. And after seeing that painting, he could never completely accept again.

He would have to do something about it. He could no longer go on believing what he had been told. When he was younger, it had been emotion that had led him to deny what they said, and their reason and logic and evidence had won out. But now there was one bit of evidence to support his soul's howling fury. One tiny little shred to give him the impetus he needed.

He had gone screaming off to war last time, but a quick and merciful death had been denied him. Now, faced with the reality of a long life stretching out ahead of him, a life that he had never expected to face, Rhys could not do it without knowing in his heart that it was the life he was meant to live.

He had learned to live without fine wine and elegant

food during the war. Uniforms had easily replaced fashionable clothes. And when they had become little more than tatters, anything at all had been comfort enough. So he fitted well enough into his life now, content with a full belly and a warm coat on his back. He could do it without complaint.

But the life that he had lost still nagged him. Remembering an enchanting face, a lilting smile, a soft hand, he groaned, and walked faster. There were women enough in the workaday world that he frequented now. Few had the charm and education that wealth could bring, but there were certain to be a few good sober women he could choose among. Supporting a wife might be some difficulty for a while to come. His writing might bring in an extra pound or two, enough for a wife. But of necessity, children followed acquiring a wife, and he would have to think about that for a while.

But he didn't have to think for long. His feet had already carried him past his lodging and into streets that he had come to know this week. As Rhys recognized where he was unconsciously heading, his thoughts took a relieved upswing.

He could ask for no finer lady. She was as sensible as he, had an eager intelligence that he craved, and she had no better expectations than he did. He had deliberately kept her at a distance, as he did with everyone now, but in this case there was no real need for it. She would not expect to be kept in grand style, nor would she look for a title. She might, perhaps, require an honest name, but he had a feeling Miss Arianne Richards might be a little more open-minded than the *haut ton*, even if his search could not provide one. She would give him the purpose that he needed to root out the truth. For her sake, he would find out once and for all who was the liar and who was the bastard.

A row appeared to be in the making when he knocked on the panel door to the Richards home. Rhys hesitated, but now that he had made up his

mind, nothing would stop him. He brought the knocker
down firmly, and was rewarded with an Indian war
whoop on the other side.

A moment later the door flew open and a carrot-
haired youngster gave what could only be a death cry,
but the vowels and consonants came together in such
a manner as to be almost a name. Or a chant. The
boy certainly didn't look to be in the throes of death
as he grinned and flew down the hall, leaving the door
open and Rhys standing on the step.

A stampede of feet clattered through some distant
room, a cat appeared and wrapped itself around his
ankles, and a lanky man wearing spectacles and a bemused expression on his face appeared at the rear of
the hall. Somewhat intimidated by this chaos after his
own quiet quarters, Rhys removed his hat and contemplated disappearing into the night. Only the fact
that the man in the hall had finally discovered him
kept him from carrying through his retreat.

Before the gentleman could come forward, a rush
of skirts sounded on the stairway between them, and
a pert brunette bounced a curtsy as she reached the
bottom. From above, a boyish voice piped, "I told
you so!" and the little lady suddenly turned hoyden
by sticking her tongue out at her unseen antagonist.

The gentleman finally made it close enough to replace his daughter and offer a proper greeting. "Good
evening, sir. How may I help you?"

Deciding this had to be the elusive father who was
never at home or never appeared whenever he had
come to the door, Rhys held out his hand. "Rhys
Llewellyn, sir. I know it is an improper time, but I
had hoped I might see Miss Richards for a moment.
There was a matter we were discussing earlier, and I
have come to give her the settling of it."

"Glad to meet you, Mr. Llewellyn. Arianne seems
to have a quantity of suitors at the door recently.
Won't you please come in? Llewellyn. Why does that
name sound familiar?" Vaguely making way for the
visitor but not indicating the direction of the parlor,
Mr. Richards puzzled over the name while his younger

daughter dutifully opened the room reserved for visitors and ran to fetch Rainy.

"I have had an article or two appear in the *Gazette* and the *Times*. Perhaps that is what you are remembering."

Richards made an indecipherable noise resembling "hmpf" and stood in the parlor doorway shaking his head. "Never read them. Useless lot. Well, it will come to me. Good to meet you. If you ever have any artwork you wish appraised or cleaned, remember me. Good evening to you." With that, he ambled out and back down the hall, leaving Rhys standing in bewilderment in the musty front parlor.

Arianne rescued him some minutes later. Wearing her chestnut hair in soft curls over her ears, undisguised by bonnet or hat, she had the fresh, clean-faced appearance that Rhys needed after his visit to the bawdy house. She hastily lit a few lamps until the room took on a respectable golden hue and sent dancing highlights through the rather daunting blue of her eyes. Rhys knew at once that he had made the right decision, and he gave a smile of relief as she welcomed him without question.

"I wish we were somewhere that I could take you walking through the gardens. It is a night not to be wasted, and it could only be enhanced by your presence."

Startled, Arianne studied her caller a little more closely. Rhys was obviously garbed for the evening. In his navy-blue long-tailed coat and white linen and gloves, he appeared every inch the gentleman, though the kind light of the lamp undoubtedly disguised the worn and mended places in his attire. But his swarthy face wore a look on it that she had never seen there before, and from the sound of his words she rather thought he'd had a little too much wine with his dinner.

But he did not seem at all dangerous, and she was more flattered than not. With a gesture of her hand she indicated the door. "Perhaps the night air would be refreshing. We are blessed with a small kitchen garden that promises a rose or two for future table settings, if you do not mind using the back door."

"I am no stranger to back doors, I can assure you. Shall we promenade around the walk, then?"

Rhys held out his arm and Arianne took it, and with all the dignity of a couple descending into an elegant ballroom, they made their way through the dark hall, past the butler's pantry and the back stairs to the kitchens, and out into the night.

Lacking any need for mews or carriage houses in this section of the city, the narrow alley between the buildings on one street and the one behind it had been converted to an assortment of uses. Someone had made a feeble attempt to erect a fence and convert this small patch of dirt into a living garden, not an easy task given the lack of light and air, not to mention arable ground. But in the dark, the attempt was successful enough, giving the impression of bushes in the rear and the scent of herbs underfoot. Arianne drew in a deep breath of air, trying not to cough as the wind carried a strong scent of sewage and coal smoke to fill the lungs.

"Have you ever lived in the country, Miss Richards?"

"For a while, when I was very young. My parents come from Bristol, but I was barely more than six when they moved here. City life is all I know. This garden is my mother's attempt to keep a piece of the country with her."

"You would not miss the hustle and bustle of the city should your parents decide to move back?"

"My father will never leave here, but I have always wished we could go somewhere where the air is fresh and clean for the summer months, as so many do. It must be nice to own the luxury of two houses. I would not wish the responsibility that accompanies them, I suppose. One household is more than enough to run." The dry tone of Arianne's voice indicated the difficulties involved.

"I would like to return to the country someday. It is a dream I might manage with a little hard work and time. But there is something I need to do right now, and it is going to take me out of the city for a little while. I have spoken to Locke about your painting, and he is to do with it as he thinks best. Whatever happens, will you allow me to call on you when I return?"

So many words at once from the taciturn writer. Arianne looked up where the stars ought to be, but they were eclipsed by roofs and houses. Perhaps his perception of the word "call" was different from hers. One paid morning calls, to be sure. But did a gentleman "call" on a lady to whom he did not mean to pay suit? She wasn't in society much, but it seemed there were many interpretations to the word. It was only her own longing for company that made more of it than it was.

"By all means, Mr. Llewellyn. How long will you be gone? Or do you know? I shall rather miss our meetings."

Those were encouraging words. Rhys couldn't see much of her face in this light, but her voice was low and pleasant, and he liked the welcoming sound of it. "I shall try to make it as short as possible so you do not forget me. I've not had time to say my good-byes to Lady Melanie, if you would forward them for me. "

Arianne turned to face him in the dark, hearing something much like wistfulness in his voice. He must be alone in the world. It would be a terrible thing to be alone. As much as she cursed her younger brothers and sister, she would not do without them. "I'll deliver the message with your regards. I'm certain she will miss your company also. Come back safely."

He hesitated, then daringly, letting the wine speak, Rhys said, "There are things about me that you don't know, that I can't tell you without bringing shame to those who were once dear to me. I'm hoping to rectify some of that situation with my journey. Do you think . . . ? Could you possibly . . . ? I am not a whole man, but you know that. Does the thought put you off?"

Silently Arianne contemplated the dark face turned in her direction. Her heart had begun an erratic beat, but her head remained clear. Still, her reply was not a sensible one. "Could you kiss me? I have never been kissed, you know. I would rather like to know what it is like."

Rattled by this announcement, Rhys took a step closer. A woman who had never been kissed was beyond the realm of his experience. But he rather liked the thought of it. And he definitely liked the idea that she had asked him to be the one to teach her. No shy miss, this. Miss Arianne Richards looked at the world through the same practical lens as he. She was overwhelmingly suitable and no doubt too good for a reprobate such as he. But he would try to earn her respect.

Gently Rhys touched a rough hand to her cheek, holding her safely in his palm while he bent to place an innocent peck on her lips. Her response was fluid and immediate, and he had some difficulty stepping away as a gentleman should when the kiss deepened into more than a promise.

When their lips finally parted, Arianne stared at Rhys blankly, feeling the heat and texture of him imprinted on her lips, absorbing the sense of wine and masculine musk and male linen. Men were very different creatures indeed, but she thought she might come to like the difference.

"Hurry back," she whispered.

"You will be the first to know." Not trusting himself more, Rhys whirled on his heel and started for the door. He had caused enough chaos for one night. Better to let it rest until he knew more.

5

THE FURIOUS POUNDING at the front door sent Arianne flying down the stairs. After the event of last evening, she wasn't at all certain that she was coming or going, but her heart pounded almost as loudly as the knocker when she ran to answer it. Perhaps Rhys had had second thoughts and returned to speak with her more freely. Perhaps he had come to ask her to fly away with him. Twenty-one years of secret romantic dreaming easily burgeoned into the improbable after one night beneath the stars.

Her shock at seeing both Melanie and Lord Locke at this early hour was nearly as great as it would have been had it actually been Rhys with coach and four waiting to spirit her away. Lord Locke's normally elegant composure appeared sadly ruffled. Although his clothes were of their usual excellent fashion, fitting superbly to wide shoulders and falling in uncreased lines to his exquisitely polished boots, his cravat was not quite correct, his hat seemed to be missing, and his waistcoat and coat were unbuttoned. There was the slightest indication of puffiness beneath his eyes, as if he had not slept long, and his hair was not its usual masterpiece of perfection. In fact, a blond curl fell rather awkwardly across his forehead.

Melanie, on the other hand, looked quite respectably put together, but the worry in her eyes told a story as loud as Locke's disreputable appearance. Arianne gestured them in, but Locke hesitated, glancing toward the stairway, where the sounds of racing feet indicated the household was up and stirring.

"Can you come away with us for a few minutes where we might speak in private?"

Anxious, Arianne bit her bottom lip and followed his glance upward. Her mother wasn't feeling at all well and the one maid they managed to keep had the day off. As if interpreting her glance, Locke interceded.

"I'm sorry, that was selfish of me." He turned to Melanie. "Perhaps we ought to take the children for a drive in the park?"

Melanie looked mildly alarmed as the whoops of laughter above grew louder, but bravely she nodded her head. Galen turned his head in time to catch the wisp of a smile flitting across Arianne's lips at her cousin's reaction, and he felt a jolt of remembrance, but now was not the time to contemplate the prior night's foolishness. Without compunction for the crisp muslin skirts of his fashionable companion, he ordered, "Bring them with us. The day is fair and they can run off their energy in the grass."

Knowing it was not at all fair to her friends to subject them to the wild spirits of her siblings, Arianne couldn't help imagining what a treat it would be for her younger brothers and sister to ride in a carriage. She hesitated over the decision too long. Davie pounded down the stair with two cats and a dog on his heels, heading straight for the doorway where their guests still stood. Galen caught the redhead while Melanie executed a swift maneuver to slam the door before the animals could make a break for the street.

Davie whooped at being flung toward the ceiling by the tall gentleman. The dog, upon once again discovering Galen's scent, leapt ecstatically up his leg. One cat ignored the commotion and took this opportunity to clean his paw, while the other found Melanie's skirts to her liking and purred around her ankles. It was only a matter of moments before the two youngest boys stumbled down the stairs to discover the source of Davie's joy, and on her best haughty-lady manners, Lucinda held herself aloof and above the noise by waiting on the stairs and giving the crowd below a disdainful look.

"Go fetch your bonnets and caps," Galen ordered, swinging Davie back to the floor. "Your sister says you might come riding with us today."

The shrieks of wild excitement ascended the stairs to include Lucinda, whose pose instantly disintegrated into childish glee as she raced to find her best bonnet. Arianne rolled her eyes heavenward, then regarded her guest with painful directness.

"You would have done better to tell me now than wait for the horde to descend upon us. What can you have to say that would be so terrible that you must submit yourself to this punishment?" A wretched thought occurred to her, and Arianne gave the fashionable pair a startled look. "Is it Rhys? Has something happened to Rhys?"

Melanie looked startled at her proper cousin's use of a gentleman's given name, but Arianne had focused on Locke's reaction. Clear gray eyes gave her a thoughtful look, and some small part of his usually languid aplomb briefly disappeared, but he reverted to normal swiftly enough.

"You'd best find that fetching hat of yours, Miss Richards, or your curls will be decidedly disheveled before we reach the park."

Arianne threw him a suspicious look, but retreated up the stairs after the required article. Undoubtedly it was bad news they brought, and she could always wait to hear bad news.

As Melanie led the children on a romp through the park, Galen took Arianne's gloved hand and led her to the nearest bench. Clasping his hands behind him, he stood before her, searching for the best words to use.

"It has something to do with the painting, doesn't it?" she finally broke the silence, making it easy for him.

"I'm afraid so." Galen tried not to imagine the pain that would soon fill those luminous blue eyes, but he could feel their impact as she waited patiently. Miss Arianne Richards was not the kind of laughing, lovely beauty he usually fancied, but there was something in her grave demeanor and intelligent face that gave him cause to look twice. What he saw was a woman fully capable of dealing with whatever came her way, and he breathed a sigh of relief. "The painting was stolen last night."

Arianne's eyes widened as she absorbed this information. "Stolen? How can that be? Who would steal a painting? It cannot be sold like diamonds or jewels. With all those other valuable things lying about, why would a thief bother with a painting of questionable value?"

The unshakable charm left Galen's features as he took the place beside her. For the first time, Arianne had a glimpse of the man behind the mask of social politeness. He seemed to struggle within himself before deciding on the path of honesty. "The painting was the only thing stolen. This was no ordinary thief. Have you seen Rhys lately?"

Shocked, Arianne clasped her hands and stared out over the greensward where the children romped. They really ought to be in the country, where they could do this every day. Her mother longed for the country again. For her health, it really was a necessity. The painting was a very small step in that direction. A very small step. Its loss really shouldn't matter so much. Someone else must have had a greater need than she.

"Last night. He came by last night. He was in an odd humor, said he was leaving the city for a little while. But he's coming back. I'm certain of it. He couldn't be the thief, my lord. He really couldn't be." Even as Arianne said it, she couldn't know that of a certainty. Rhys had wanted her to stop the sale of the painting. Locke hadn't wanted to comply. How desperate had he been?

Galen's thoughts had apparently taken the same direction. "He asked me to hold up the sale of the painting, but I wouldn't agree without consulting Christie's and yourself. Did he mention the painting at all? Give some clue as to its importance?"

Arianne shook her head and struggled for composure. How could she say that he had hinted he would be returning for her when all was well? That had just been her imagination willing something into words that had never been said. But she hadn't imagined his kiss. She struggled not to touch her lips. He had kissed her, and then he had said good-bye. There was no clue in that.

"He merely said that there were some things he must do outside of the city, something about rectifying a situation that brought shame to those near to him. I know nothing of his circumstances, my lord. You would know more of him than I."

Galen couldn't possibly mention that Rhys had been with him when he entered a brothel but had left before enjoying the selection. He would need to go back and question the girls to see if any knew when he had left. Perhaps he could piece together Llewellyn's activities of the night and thus uncover some clue. But if he had gone to see Arianne . . . That covered the early part of the evening.

"Evan knows more of Rhys than any other, and he's out of town at the moment. Perhaps we are on the wrong path entirely. Perhaps he wanted to remove the painting from sale to protect it, knowing it hides something of importance to someone else. Does that sound like a Minerva novel, Miss Richards?"

"I would rather believe that than the other. I should have known that nothing worth having is gained easily. Perhaps we should forget the whole thing. When Rhys comes back, we'll know the story, even if we do not find the painting."

She managed to sound brave and gallant about the incident, while Galen wanted to rant and rave and throw things. He had taken on the responsibility of her most precious possession, and he had not upheld that responsibility. He didn't like the feeling one bit, and he fretted at his helplessness. "I fully intend to find it, or pay you whatever Christie's considers the actual value. I am the one who persuaded you to place it on public display. I will take full blame for the results. In the meantime, I think I shall find Sir Thomas and see if he can remember the origins of that piece of work. I dislike being taken advantage of."

Arianne turned to him with alarm. "You are not serious? I cannot blame you for what has happened. You asked my permission, and I agreed. That is the risk one takes in life. I could not possibly accept your money. But I will admit to curiosity. If you are to see Sir Thomas, is there some chance that I might accompany you?"

Galen tilted his head as he considered the matter. Since Davie was running full tilt in their direction, it was obvious that their discussion was nearing its end. Reluctantly he nodded. "I will let you know when I gain an appointment. But do not argue with me on the subject of reimbursement. The cost is little to me and much to you. Perhaps Sir Thomas can give us an honest estimate while we are there."

Before Arianne could reply, he stood and captured the nine-year-old before he could propel himself into the bench headfirst. Davie screamed with glee at being put within grasping distance of a sturdy branch overhead, and scrambled up faster than his brothers could run to join him. Arianne watched with equal parts awe and dismay as Galen casually flung both youngsters to his shoulders and bounced them to less dangerous perches. Never in her life had she imagined the fashionable gentleman lowering himself to the rowdy activities of three little boys. Their scrambles succeeded in divesting his cravat of what remained of its elegance and left long streaks of dirt against the blue broadcloth of his coat, but he seemed quite pleased with himself as the boys crowed their delight.

"Devilish little imps, ain't they? Should we leave them there?" Galen inquired imperturbably as he sauntered back toward the bench. The shrieks of protest and laughter behind him rose a degree at his words.

With satisfaction Galen noted the beginnings of a winsome smile upon shy lips as Arianne glanced from him to the boys in the tree. She shook her head in discouragement. "You are quite as hopeless as they, I fear, my lord. You enjoyed that. I hope you are prepared for the result when they are loosed from those branches."

"Ummm, yes, there is that." He gazed solemnly back to the shaking leaves as the boys attempted to find their own way out. "But it would be ungentlemanly to leave you to their rescue, so I shall have to take my punishment like a man."

Arianne nearly laughed out loud at his satisfaction. He really was enjoying himself! All men were children at heart, she decided, and stifled her giggles as Lucinda and Melanie ran up to join them.

Arianne sobered when Locke gave his rumpled attire a sorrowful look upon Melanie's scolding, but that was none of her concern. Holding her arms up, she rescued the youngest cherub from the lowest branch and tried not to think of what might have happened had the painting been sold for an enormous sum. The boys would be fine just as they were.

"Do not let his hauteur disturb you. He is an artist, and they always have eccentricities we must endure if we are to enjoy their genius." Galen handed Arianne out of his carriage before the impressive limestone facade of a London town house.

Straightening the plain rose muslin that matched her hat, Arianne tried to appear unconcerned. They had heard nothing from Rhys these last few days, and no clues had come to light about the disappearance of the painting. Lord Locke had assured her that he had put the word about in all the places he knew to look out for the piece, but neither of them believed the canvas had been stolen to be resold. "I have met Sir Thomas upon occasion. He can be disagreeable when he chooses, but my father's opinion means too much to him for him to be openly rude to me. There is something to be said for having an art critic in the family."

Her wry tone made Galen glance down, but the calm of her oval face reflected nothing more than her words. Offering his arm, he guided her into the apartment to meet the great painter.

When introductions and courtesies were over and

Sir Thomas understood that they were there neither to request a sitting nor to make a purchase, he huffed and puffed for a while before finally condescending to find the time to answer a few questions. Upon discovering that it was the stolen painting that concerned them, he once again became affable.

"Yes, I could not believe that piece came to light again. I had to go see it for myself. Amazing. One of my better early works, I must say, although today's portraits show the benefit of greater experience. I was most dismayed to hear it had been purloined. And you say the piece belonged to you, Miss Richards? However did you persuade your father to part with it?"

Arianne had the grace to blush, and Galen stepped in to avoid the confession. "Miss Richards came upon it personally. We thought perhaps if we knew more of the origins of the piece, we might have a better idea of why it was stolen, and then we would be that much closer to the thief. Could you tell us anything of the subject?"

The artist drew his regal brow down in a frown of thoughtfulness. "It was one of my early works, as I said. I did not do formal sittings then."

Understanding the artist's hesitation as a desire not to reveal his rather plebeian origins, Galen carefully eased his predicament. "We think we have some idea of the background. I would think only the sitters would be of interest. The woman had almost a Gypsy look to her, but she and the boy were gowned so richly that they must have been of good birth."

Sir Thomas nodded affirmatively. "Yes, I quite remember now. Handsome woman. Can't remember the name. Can't remember what happened to the painting after I completed it." He threw Arianne a look of suspicion. "But the man who paid for it did not take it. He sent me a generous sum and said to do with it as I will." He waited for the surprise of his listeners and was amply rewarded.

"He paid you for a portrait he did not keep?" Astonished, Arianne could not keep the words from her mouth.

"Wealthy men are inclined to be eccentric. It had nothing to do with the quality of the painting, I might add, for he never saw the finished work. From gossip I heard afterward, I was inclined to believe that the woman had died. Perhaps, in his grief, he could not bear to see the likeness."

"And you can remember nothing of the name? That would be a most valuable piece of information if you could provide it." Attired in a brown hammer-tailed coat and immaculate buff breeches, impatiently snapping his beaver hat against his leg, Galen appeared every inch the commanding lord as he stared down the artist's reluctant pose.

"It has been a long time, Locke. I would be fortunate to remember my own mother's name after the passing of so many years. Only the circumstances caused me to remember the work at all."

Unsatisfied with this, Galen ungallantly probed further. "The setting is Welsh, is it not? I believe I recognize the mountain in the background."

Stiffly the artist drew himself up and nodded. "One must experience all types of settings before one can develop the expertise to know the best."

"Does the name Llewellyn mean anything to you?" Arianne couldn't bear the suspense any longer. Rhys had known the subject of the painting, of that she was certain. And with a name like his, he had to have a Welsh heritage. The coincidence was too much to be ignored.

Sir Thomas' eyes lit with memory. "Llewellyn! Yes, yes, I believe that does sound familiar. The family name, perhaps. Of course, there are many such of that name, but it does strike a chord."

"The family name?" Galen questioned casually.

"Yes, of course." Sir Thomas gave him a disdainful look. "I only work for the best of families. I cannot remember the title name, but the man who commissioned the portrait was very definitely a wealthy baron."

Galen and Arianne exchanged glances and quickly made their departure. Barons were easily traceable.

6

"HERE IT IS!" Melanie triumphantly pointed her finger at the page of the open tome. "Baron Llewellyn, with properties all along the Welsh border."

Galen lifted the book from her grasp and carried it to the light of the library window to study the details. "This just describes Owen Llewellyn. I've met the man, perfectly harmless old gentleman. He's Rhys's uncle, I believe."

Arianne clasped her hands in her lap and tried to hide her perplexity. The sunshine pouring in the library's west window illuminated the light colors of Lord Locke's hair until he appeared some lordly angel outlined against the panes. If only it were a Bible he was reading . . . She smiled at the image and tried to concentrate on the argument around her. If Rhys truly were of a noble family, then he certainly had not meant anything serious by his words of the other night. But he had seemed in so much pain that she could not believe he was of the same charmed world as Melanie and Galen.

Looking up, Galen caught Arianne's unhappy frown and wondered at it. Passing the book back to Melanie, he leaned against the shelves and studied Melanie's cousin. Arianne was dressed almost severely in a blue frock adorned by nothing more than a frill at the high neck and hem. But the style was becoming to her height and the graceful arch of her long throat. She would do better to wear a softer coiffure, and the purely masculine urge to know what her chestnut tresses would look like upon her shoulders struck him unexpectedly.

Galen pulled his attention back to the woman he intended to make his wife as Melanie searched the shelves for an older volume. Melanie's golden ringlets danced about her throat, and it took no stretch of the imagination to know how they would look spread upon a pillow. He could see her now, all clothed in lace and frills and looking expectantly to him for her initiation into womanhood. It would be a pleasure to teach her, and he had no business considering any other woman in such a way.

But Arianne's unhappy frown itched at the back of Locke's mind even as Melanie produced the volume containing information on the previous holder of the barony. Perhaps it was the fact that as a child he had always longed for brothers and sisters of his own, and he envied Miss Richards her large family. Someday he meant to have a large family, but in the meantime there was no harm in trying to help the Richards youths. If Arianne wouldn't accept his offer for the painting, he would have to track it down.

Melanie gave a purr of satisfaction and held the book from Galen's grasp as she read the details of the prior baron's history out loud. " 'The eldest son of the fifth baron, David Llewellyn, is married to the former Elizabeth Jones, and has one son named after his paternal grandfather, Rhys Llewellyn.' " She slammed the book closed and gave the room in general a victorious look. "I knew it. I knew he came from good family. So why is he not Lord Llewellyn instead of old Owen?"

Galen snatched the book from her and turned the pages to the proper notation. "Why does it say nothing of Elizabeth Jones? These things always give the ancestry of everyone on into infinity." He read the brief paragraph, frowned, and flipped pages in search of noble Joneses.

Melanie gave an insouciant shrug. "What does it matter? She might be a Gypsy for all I care. The mystery is why Rhys is not baron instead of his uncle."

"The mystery is the missing painting," Arianne pointed out wryly. "And the woman in the painting certainly appeared to be more Gypsy than English. What does she have to do with any of this?"

Galen slammed the book shut and heaved it on the table. He could answer Melanie's question, but he was no closer to the truth on Arianne's. "This is getting us nowhere. When is Evan returning? He can probably explain more than we can find in any musty tome."

"There is some question in Parliament for which he means to poll his constituents, or some such faradiddle. It would be faster to write to Gordon than to track down Evan. But neither of my brothers is likely to tell me anything, so you'll have to be the one who questions them." Melanie started for the escritoire as if to provide pen and paper right then and there.

"I'm not writing to your brothers asking for gossip." Irritably Galen removed himself from the wall where he had been leaning. He held his hand out to Arianne. "It is time I returned Miss Richards to her demanding family. I can't see that it is our business to inquire into Llewellyn's antecedents, in any case. We will just have to take a new route in search of the portrait."

Melanie instantly fell into her hostess role, summoning smiles and the butler at the same time, urging Arianne to return quickly, reminding Galen of an affair they were both invited to, and seeing her guests out with all the politeness she had been taught. Only after they were gone did the look of determination return to her features as she gazed up the stairs where her brother's wife rested.

"If you think Melanie has forgotten the question about Rhys and his uncle, you are all about in your head, my lord," Arianne murmured as the carriage rolled down the broad streets of Grosvenor Square. She still felt nervous at being seated in such elegant equipage beside a gentleman of the first stare. Galen Locke had the height and looks that would draw the eye anywhere he went, but she felt particularly conspicuous seated on this high perch. She tried to appear cool and confident as heads swiveled to watch them, but her fingernails would draw blood from her palms did she not wear gloves.

"I think I know enough of the story to know it isn't one that Evan is going to repeat to his sister. I fail to see how old gossip will return the painting. It has been over a week, Miss Richards, and the portrait has not appeared in any of the places where I would expect it to be sold. We must accept that it has been stolen for other reasons than profit and will probably never be seen again. I've spoken to Christie's and to Sir Thomas, and they've agreed that a hundred guineas would be a fair price to replace it. I will deposit that amount wherever you ask, Miss Richards. I will not have your family suffer for my mistake."

Arianne sat rigidly beside him, staring straight ahead and not at the elegant gentleman handling the reins. "I cannot accept, my lord. It would not be at all proper. I took a risk and lost. You are in no way to blame for that."

Determined to win this argument, Galen steered the horses toward Hyde Park rather than in the direction of St. James's. He refused to take her home until he had convinced her to take the money. "My name is Galen. If your cousin can call me that, there is no reason you cannot. And I don't intend to take no for an answer. If you wish to see your home again, you had best acquiesce quickly."

Arianne sent him a swift look, but his genial features had lost none of their affability. If she looked closely, she could see Lord Locke was not precisely handsome. His jaw was too large and his nose slightly crooked. And though his eyebrows were more brown than blond, they were not as dramatic as Byron's, or even Rhys's. Although he possessed all the imperturbable presence of a proper London nobleman, she responded more to his good-natured friendliness. It was that more than looks that made him handsome in her eyes. His obstinacy now was only part of his gentlemanly nature, and she refused to take advantage of it.

"I shall scream and tell everyone I am being abducted," Arianne calmly informed him, lifting her chin and meeting the eyes of the occupants of the first carriage they passed. The occupants stared at her with curiosity, no doubt wondering why such a dowdy pheasant was in the company of the fashionable Lord Locke, but Arianne was engaged in a different battle at the moment, and stares no longer rankled.

Galen fought the amused lift of his lips. "Your father would be forced to call me out, in that case. Or I would have to marry you or be named a rake. Does either alternative appeal to you? And surely by now I should be allowed to call you Arianne, shouldn't I? It's a lovely name, one I've been quite eager to use."

"You are making light of me, my lord." Angrily Arianne fiddled with the strings of her nearly empty reticule. "I have done nothing to deserve the insult."

"I'm not making light of you." Patiently Galen tried to retrieve the wildly departing reins of this conversation. "I am merely pointing out the foolishness of your position. A hundred guineas means nothing to me. I will lose that much at the gaming tables tonight. But my honor is valuable, if only to me. It would impugn my honor not to make good the loss of that painting."

"Balderdash." Arianne refused to succumb to his temptations. Just the thought of accepting such a sum from the gentleman beside her raised heat to her cheeks. What did he think she was?

"It's not balderdash!" Galen spoke so sharply his horses gave nervous whinnies and pulled at their bridles. Galen fought against the sudden rush of temper and returned his attention to his cattle rather than the irritating woman beside him. "I am not offering to buy you. I merely wish to make up my error. I can see no wrong in that."

"That comes of being from two different worlds, my lord. If you will put me down right here, I shall walk home. I see no need to carry this conversation any further."

"I am not putting you down anywhere but the door to your home. You are being unnecessarily obstinate, Miss Richards. And confound it, if you don't stop 'lording' me, I shall throw a proper fit right here in front of everyone."

"It has been my experience that the very wealthy can get away with all types of eccentric behavior. Be my guest, my lord. Throw a fit, then please return me to my home or allow me to climb down from this monstrous conveyance."

"I am likely to strangle you if I have this fit, Miss Richards. And wealth has nothing to do with anything. It is unseemly for a woman of any station to be so damned obstinate. I shall go to your father and offer reparations for the loss. I don't know why I didn't think of that in the first place." Galen shook the reins and steered the carriage toward the far gate.

"You wouldn't!" Arianne turned and stared at him in disbelief. "I trusted you with my confidence. You have no right to betray me now."

"I have every right if you continue on this course of obstinacy. It's for your own good." Too furious now to judge whether he had the right or wrong of it, Galen stuck to his position. The chit would have the money and her family would travel to the country if he had to shove the blunt down her throat to do so.

A tangle of carriages waited at the gate to exit while the contents of a vegetable cart were hastily swept to the side and the owner wrangled with the elderly ladies in the coach causing the accident. Galen was forced to come to a halt, and seeing her opportunity, Arianne gathered up her skirt and her courage, and catching the frame of the phaeton for support, swung herself toward the ground.

"Where in hell do you think you're going!" Locke shouted after her as the carriages began to move and his horses pulled to follow.

Heads turned at the sound of the elegant nobleman screaming like a fishwife after the retreating figure of a rather dowdy female. The female made no effort to answer, and much to their delight, the *ton* was treated to the sight of the notorious whip hauling at his reins and attempting to pull his rakish phaeton from the jam toward the grass in pursuit.

Hurrying as far from the road as she could get, Arianne ignored the commotion behind her. She wanted to scream in return. She wanted to stamp her foot and throw the tantrum Lord Locke had threatened to throw. And she wanted to fling herself to the grass and cry until her heart broke and there was no further reason to cry again. That such an impossible man could bring her to this state was not logical, but logic had nothing to do with the emotions careening through her right now.

She was not normally an emotional person. She had much too much to do to indulge in emotional tirades. Life was meant to be attacked logically and practically if one were to survive in this world. She didn't have time for the fits and starts of the wealthy like Lord Locke. But all the same, she wanted to strangle him for putting her through this scene.

She heard him call her name once more, but she was almost out of range. There would be no room for him to turn his phaeton around and come after her without tearing across the grass and endangering pedestrians. Once into the trees, she slowed and gave herself time to breathe. She could walk home now without being disturbed by any more insults. She should be able to stay safely within the confines of her home for the rest of her life after this incident. She could be certain Lord Galen Locke would no more darken her door.

Melanie would tell her if Rhys returned to London. That was all she needed to know now. The painting was lost, gone forever. Rhys was a nobleman's son, perhaps. She had misunderstood his intentions, but she could still consider herself his friend. She liked Mr. Llewellyn very well, and it would be good to occasionally converse with someone who had other things on his mind than the latest fashions. It had been nice these past weeks to get out of the house and be among other young people for a change, but she couldn't hope for it to continue. Practicality was returning.

When she found the phaeton waiting outside her door, Arianne quickly turned the corner and hurried toward the shops. It had appeared remarkably like

Davie holding the heads of Lord Locke's prized horses. She couldn't imagine any gentleman allowing someone's younger brother to curb the temperamental thoroughbreds. He must have been in a hurry. It didn't matter. Davie would have a treat and Lord Locke would be disappointed. If he told her father about the painting, she would never, ever forgive him.

When next she returned, the phaeton was gone, and she breathed a sigh of relief. Hurrying upstairs, she found the children playing as usual, and no sign of her father about. With any luck at all, he hadn't been home when Lord Locke called. Her mother greeted her with a smile, and Arianne relaxed. Evidently her secret was as yet safe. She would have to get a message to Melanie. Perhaps her cousin could persuade the madman not to reveal her deception with the portrait.

But when Melanie arrived the next day, she held out no such hopes. Throwing off her hat and shaking her curls out, she regarded Arianne with laughter. "I cannot believe that you single handedly placed the imperturbable Lord Locke at point-non-plus. Never in my memory have I seen him up in the boughs, but all the word is that he actually yelled at you! Tell me how you did it, you sly puss, for I have never so much as been able to make him look at me twice."

"He looks at you all the time," Arianne responded irritably. "And being looked at and being yelled at are a world apart. "

"For an intelligent person, you are certainly simple-minded sometimes." Melanie twirled around the front parlor, catching the dusty rays of sunlight through the narrow windows. "I don't mean just *look*; I mean actually *see*. Galen sees me as Evan's younger sister, even though I'm perfectly grown now. He teases me instead of talking to me. Sometimes I think he hasn't a feather for a brain. But *you*"—Melanie swung around to face her cousin—"you he actually fights with! That means you must have had a conversation of some sort."

"I wouldn't call it a conversation. It was more of a

rout. Defy him sometime and see if you can't draw him out as well—as long as your interest in him is merely platonic, that is. If you've fixed your interest on him, then just nod and smile and he'll be certain to offer for you sooner or later." Arianne tried to appear nonchalant, but the scene still rankled. Worse yet, she felt she had come out embarrassingly small in the encounter. Arguing with noblemen in a public park couldn't precisely be called circumspect behavior.

Melanie gave her cousin a sharp look, but Arianne was too good at playing the prim-and-proper. She had taken a chair and picked up her mending while Melanie flitted about the room. "I shouldn't want a husband who must be placated all the time. And I detest being treated like a child. Galen will never be serious. No, I find Rhys much more interesting. I can talk to him, and he takes me seriously. We have the most wonderful conversations. Or we used to have," Melanie added gloomily, or what passed for gloom in her normally sunny voice.

Arianne raised an eyebrow at Melanie's sudden fit of dismals. She had seen no evidence that Rhys singled out her cousin for intellectual converse or any other. The writer had been singularly taciturn in Melanie's presence, in fact, whereas Galen had made every effort to keep Melanie entertained. Even if Rhys ran tame in the Griffin household, Arianne couldn't see Melanie's brothers approving an attachment between the two.

Prosaically she answered, "Mr. Llewellyn is not likely to return your interest in any way but a platonic manner. He is overconscious of his position. He cannot provide you with all the frivolous fashions and entertainments to which you are accustomed, and he is much too practical to try. Although Lord Locke appears quite idle, I suspect there is more to him than he shows the world. You would do better to engage his interest than to seek what you cannot have."

Melanie threw herself down on the parlor sofa with such force that she raised dust from the cushions. "As if I care whether I wear satins and bows! And there is no reason that Rhys should be conscious of his position. He comes of as noble a family as any other. I am quite certain he has been defrauded of his rightful position. I wish I were a gentleman so I could speak to his uncle. There is a mystery there. I wonder if it would have anything to do with your painting?"

"You are not a gentleman and there is very little chance of your discovering anything," Arianne pointed out. "I am quite willing to forget all about that miserable painting. I wish I'd never seen it."

"I think I know where Rhys has gone and why," Melanie announced casually, waiting for her cousin's reaction. She was quite satisfied with the result.

"Where? How could you?" Arianne set aside all pretense of mending, to stare at her wayward cousin with astonishment. She knew better than to expect Melanie to be the flighty package of sunshine she appeared, but this was going further than anyone could expect.

"Daphne and I talk about everything," Melanie replied triumphantly. Her brother's wife was more sister and friend than chaperone. "She said she had overheard Evan and Rhys talking before, and she thinks Rhys has been disowned or worse by his family. She thinks it has something to do with his mother, but she is reluctant to say the worst. I think the lady in the painting was Rhys's mother."

After having cleaned it thoroughly, Arianne knew every inch of that painting, and she studied the idea carefully. At the time she had cleaned it, she hadn't known Rhys, and after meeting Rhys she had had few moments to observe the painting, but putting the two together in her head now, she saw some resemblance. "It is possible," she said slowly, comparing faces mentally. "They both have dark coloring, as does the child in the painting. There is a certain sharpness of features, but the lady was so very feminine and Rhys is so . . ."

"Very masculine," Melanie finished irreverently. "Those deep, dark eyes of his! I feel I could drown in them. It is hard to see the child in the man, but I'm certain I am right. The painting has something to do with Rhys's past, and he has gone to find the truth of it. He must never have seen a picture of his mother before. You said yourself that the woman died soon after the portrait was done."

"You go too fast! We have no certainty that the woman is his mother. There may be no relation at all. Even if there is, where would he go to find the truth? His uncle is here in London."

"To his aunt!" Melanie plumped back against the sofa cushions and waited for Arianne to appreciate her final coup.

Arianne had the vaguest feeling that she didn't want to hear the rest of this. In their younger years, Melanie had managed to get them in and out of all sorts of scrapes with statements similar to this one. She knew they presaged some wild action which she would regret later, but she could not help asking the inevitable. "What aunt?"

"The one is Scotland, of course. Rhys told me of a visit to her when he was young. He did not specify if she was his mother's or father's sister, he merely mentioned the wild mountain streams and the beauty of the hills, but that has to be where he has gone. If she is his only relative besides his uncle, then he has gone to her to hear the details of his past. His uncle came into the title that was rightfully his, so there is little hope of getting truth from him."

"You are spinning Canterbury tales, cousin. There is not one shred of evidence of all this. We will simply have to wait for Rhys's return." There was still the vague hope that Rhys had the painting and would return it to her when he came back. Arianne was certain he wasn't a thief.

As if to destroy that notion, Melanie answered vaguely, "You know, Rhys once lived in the woods and robbed coaches when he was trying to help Evan. If he could do that for our family, surely I can do something much less rash to help him."

Arianne knew she didn't want to hear the rest of this. And just as certainly she knew Melanie was about to tell her.

7

"LOCKE, ISN'T IT?" The slight, elderly gentleman nodded and lit his cigar, drawing deeply on it and exhaling into the cool evening air before speaking again. "What are you doing in these quarters? Deadly dull for the likes of you, I should imagine."

"Family," Galen answered obliquely. "It's not so bad once one grows used to the lack of the usual forms of amusement. I have a fancy for the ladies, myself, but a good game or two would substitute. But the tables appear closed to a fellow like me."

The two men gazed back into the spacious room from which they had just departed. Standing just outside the French doors on a small balcony, they could see clearly the comfortable leather chairs occupied by silent gentlemen perusing their favorite newssheets and the discreet tables in the far corner where others gathered over their brandy and cigars and dealt cards. The club's quiet elegance appealed to an older generation wishing to escape wives and families and find a few moments with the companions of their youth. It did not have the reckless air of White's or some of the other clubs where the younger generation made wild wagers and drank and gambled and gossiped to excess.

"No doubt the stakes would appear meager to you, but I'll see you in a game, if you wish," Owen Llewellyn graciously said to his companion.

Feeling not only out-of-place but also deceitful, Galen shook his head. "I have put in the requested appearance. I need do no more. Have you seen anything of Rhys lately? He seems to have disappeared from his usual haunts." That was invasion enough, and he did it only out of desperation. If the blamed woman had only taken his offer for the painting, he wouldn't be so obligated to locate the deuced thing. Since Rhys was his one and only suspect, it behooved him to find out more of his whereabouts. Did he mistake, or did the old gentleman stiffen slightly at the question?

"Rhys and I have not communicated in years. I cannot blame him for his resentment, I suppose, but it is pure foolishness to deny my offers of help. I hope he has come to no harm."

Having already garnered some of Rhys's story from other sources, Galen nodded knowingly. "He was in the best of health the last I saw of him, but he seemed shocked by a portrait hanging at Christie's. The picture disappeared shortly after, and so did Rhys. It seemed somewhat coincidental. Did you see the painting, by any chance? Lovely woman, but the artwork was a touch dated. Not one of Lawrence's better works, I fear." Galen prayed that his reputation as a collector of art would override his inquisitiveness.

"No, no, I didn't see it." Llewellyn shook his head vaguely, not meeting Galen's eyes. "Rhys saw it, you say? Well, well, I wonder what that could be about."

Someone caught his attention then, and he bade Galen a polite farewell and wandered off to join one of the groups at the tables.

Left frustrated by this lack of solid information and an irking feeling that something was not quite right, Galen departed soon after. Rhys and the blamed painting had become a thorn in his side, one he wished to rip out as swiftly as possible. He had not behaved at all well throughout the whole affair, but he could find no way of compensating for his faults. Miss Richards obviously took him for the sort of idle rake who would carelessly lose her possessions, then offer her *carte blanche* in recompense. He must seem a frivolous fellow for her to take umbrage in that way.

But short of going to her father with the whole

story, Galen could find no way of righting the situation. He could just imagine what Ross Richards would have to say about his losing a valuable painting. The plaster would blister from the ceiling before he was through. But Locke would willingly suffer the consequences if only he thought it would not place Miss Richards in a compromising position. Since there was no way he could imagine her father would forgive her for her presumption, Galen could not bring himself to reveal the story. Without finding the painting, he could see no way of ever returning to the good graces of Arianne Richards.

Not that it should matter. She was a bluestocking of the worst sort, with a ramshackle family to tend to and no time for the likes of him. But it had pleased him when he had been able to make her smile, and he had rather enjoyed her curt assessments of situations and people. Her forthrightness was a disadvantage in the society to which he was accustomed, but it made a pleasant change.

He even found himself wondering if Lucinda would ever enjoy another carriage ride or if Davie had found his way back to the trees in the park yet. It seemed a shame that those youngsters were kept cooped up in a town house when they should be out enjoying the great expanse of the countryside where they belonged. Ross Richards was a poor excuse for a father, to leave them neglected when the sale of a painting would see them comfortable.

Much to his regret, however, Galen understood the man's problem. The art market wasn't such that a family could live off the sale of those paintings for very long. As long as Richards could provide for his family, the paintings were like money in the bank, a financial nest egg against the day when he could no longer bring in income. To sell them now would be to jeopardize the future.

Galen was certain that Arianne didn't see things that way, and if her mother were truly ill, the difficulty increased. And he had ruined her one chance to relieve the situation. Cursing, he swung his walking stick and set out to track down the carriage he had told to come back a half-hour from now.

"Lord Locke to see you, sir." The servant bowed at the study door and stood aside to allow the large gentleman by. Despite the impeccable elegance of his clothes, the visitor was more a force of nature than the idle gentleman he purported to be, and the servant hid a smile as Galen's hat went flying across the room to the couch as his host rose to greet him.

"It's about time you got home, Griffin." Banishing formality, Galen flung himself across the couch to join his hat.

Evan smiled wryly. "Why don't you take a seat, Locke? What have you been about, that my presence was required? I cannot seem to remember my existence being of great pertinence to yours."

"You're beginning to sound like one of those damn awful politicians already. Do you have any idea where your sister is this minute?"

Evan appeared suitably startled. "Melanie? Melanie is the reason you're here?"

That hadn't been what he had intended, but it was time he declared himself anyway. Galen opened his mouth, but the appropriate words didn't come out. "Somebody's got to look after the tyke. You certainly aren't. I suppose I'd better address Gordon, but there's not time to go to Somerset. Meanwhile, she's over at Lady Jersey's trying to pry ancient gossip out of the old biddy." Surprised at the way that sounded, Galen shut up quickly.

Married less than a year, Evan Griffin sat back in his chair with a wicked gleam of laughter in his eye. Shorter and more slender than his friend, he still had the robust good health of a man who spent much time out-of-doors. His hair was of a darker hue than Galen's, his features were more weather-worn, and his clothes, while of expensive cut, were lacking the fashionable elegance of the wealthier man. Despite their differences, they had been friends for some years, and

Evan thought he understood what bothered the other man now.

"Tyke? That doesn't sound the proper terminology for a suitor. If you've set your cap for Melanie, you'd best take another look. She's a flighty little brat who ought to have her neck wrung, but she's far from being a tyke any longer. Even I have noticed that much."

"That's because you were away in the war and missed watching her grow up. It doesn't seem yesterday that I was pulling her on a sled and she was pelting me with snowballs. But young ladies don't go haring off after mysteries. You're going to have to put a stop to it, Griffin. 'Silence' Jersey is quite likely to disclose every tidbit of gossip about Rhys Llewellyn, should Melanie loose her devilish wiles on her."

Evan frowned over this information and pulled his pen idly through his fingers as he watched his friend. He was receiving conflicting messages here. He wished Daphne were listening so she could turn her very perceptive instincts to this conversation, but she was in all likelihood with Melanie at the gossip session Galen was reviling. Why on earth should his old friend be so averse to Melanie hearing a little gossip about Llewellyn? Was it Llewellyn he was objecting to, or gossip?

"I can't think that Llewellyn is a subject for a ladies' conversation, but I suppose she must hear it sometime. My wife has always been curious about Rhys too. They'll pry the news loose one way or another."

Galen glared at him. "And you don't care? Rhys is a damned good fellow and I wouldn't have his name maligned by anyone, but you know as well as I that his parents never married. He has no name and not a feather to fly on. Melanie will be conjuring up romantic dreams of saving his reputation and returning him to society or some other such damn-fool notion, and embarrass Rhys as well as herself if you allow her to go on."

Evan sighed and swung his feet up on the desk, adding more marks to the finish for his wife to bemoan. "I'll be the last one to stop her, Locke. I owe Llewellyn too much to deny him anything. For twenty years we went hand in hand, and then out of the clear blue sky his family declares him illegitimate and he's suddenly a nonentity. I can't accept that. He's still the same fellow who raced Melanie over the moors and danced at our balls, even if he's missing a foot after the war."

Gloomily Galen tossed his hat back and forth. "Women don't need to hear that sordid story. I never listened to it myself. I was just talking to his uncle last night. He doesn't have to live like he does. His uncle is willing to give him some sort of allowance."

Evan made a rude noise. "Owen Llewellyn waited until Rhys's father was dead before telling him that there were no marriage papers and that he could not legally inherit the title or estate. Now, don't you find that just a bit odd? Rhys was raised to be the next baron and to take over his father's estates. Why in hell would a man do that if he knew his son had no legal right to them? Perhaps his father went a little crazy after his mother's death, as they say, but no man is quite that crazy. There is something havey-cavey about Owen Llewellyn, but Rhys won't fight the man, nor will he take his handouts. He has nothing left but his pride, and he's too stiff-necked to let it go."

"Well, once Melanie hears the story, don't be surprised if she launches a campaign to name Owen a fraud or some such folderol. I give you fair warning. You don't happen to know where Rhys is, do you? He disappeared over a week ago and no one's heard from him since."

"Daphne told me about that. You don't really think he stole the fool painting, do you? He knows good and well I'd buy it for him if he wanted it. From what I understand, Arianne would have willingly withheld it from sale. I don't know what the connection is, but I can't believe Rhys stole it."

"Neither do I, but I suspect he knows something. I feel guilty about the loss, since Miss Richards placed it with Christie's at my suggestion, but she won't accept any recompense from me. I don't know how else to make it up to her except to try to locate the missing piece."

Evan grinned and returned his feet to the floor. "I wouldn't argue with Arianne anymore if I were you, my friend. I offered to bring her out with Melanie this Season, and she all but bit my head off. Like Rhys, she has her very own notions of what is proper, and she has more pride than what is good for her. Now, if you told me Arianne was going after Rhys, I'd be worried. Once she takes an idea in her head, she doesn't let it go. When she was little and wore that awful braid, I used to tease her and pull it—until she took to lacing it with hat pins. Stay clear of Arianne, Galen. Find the painting if you must, but don't intrude in my cousin's sheltered world. You might get more than you bargained for."

Galen scowled. "You have been of absolutely no help. Could you not at least invent some flummery to persuade the Richards family to stay at your estate for the summer? Mrs. Richards is not well, and Miss Richards is convinced her health would improve in the country."

Evan leaned back in his chair and tilted his head thoughtfully as he studied his large friend. "For a man who has come courting my sister, you seem to have an inordinate interest in my cousin. If you are attempting to please Melanie by making Arianne happy, you might succeed, but she won't be exceedingly grateful, all the same. Melanie is rather attached to Arianne and would hate to see her gone before the Season is ended."

Defeated, Galen rose to his feet. "Unlike you, I possess no ulterior motives for my actions. I merely meant to help a young lady in distress. Give Gordon my regards and tell him I would speak to him when he has time. If I must, I shall even traipse out to Somerset for an interview. Speaking to you is obviously of little use."

Evan stood and clapped him on the back. "Speaking to either of us will be of little use. Melanie is the one

you will have to convince. But I wish you the best of
luck. She's an expensive little brat. I'll be glad to have
her out of my pockets." He grinned wider at his
friend's annoyance.

Visibly donning his normal affable demeanor, Galen
shook Evan's hand in parting. "Then I expect no complaints when Melanie introduces me as your new
brother-in-law. My pockets can afford her."

For a moment Evan looked serious as he regarded
his friend. Then, seeing the determination in Galen's
eyes, he nodded. "The two of you would suit. I'd be
happy to welcome you to the family."

Satisfied, Galen left the Griffin household and
turned toward the home of Lord Llewellyn. Swinging
his walking stick in the brisk air, he decided if he were
going to become a boring, meddlesome old fool with
age, he might as well practice it now. Perhaps after a
visit to the baron, he might see if the younger Richardses would enjoy a drive in the park. Now that he
had set his sights on one woman, there was no need
to impress any other today or any other day. He was
quite a free man again.

"Daphne says it is wrong to gossip, but you have a
right to know as well as I. I don't believe for a minute
that Rhys's father didn't marry his mother. I know
that painting is of Lady Llewellyn. It has to be. And
there was something in it that proves she was married."

Arianne ran the duster over the porcelain figurines
on the mantel. She had not expected company today
and wore one of her oldest gowns covered by a cum-
bersome apron. It was only because she couldn't find
a cap that she didn't look the lowest of servants. At
the same time, Melanie appeared the most feminine
of angels in her frail white gown with the puff sleeves
and gauzy skirts trimmed with the daintiest of embroi-
dery. A totally useless shawl in matching yards of em-
broidered cotton wrapped gracefully around her arms
and waist in adornment, making Arianne wish for the
kind of idle life that allowed one to be decorated like

a window frame. Laughing inwardly at the idea, she answered Melanie's question without its being asked.

"The wedding ring. The woman in the painting wore a wedding ring. Rhys noticed it at once. For once in your life, cousin, you may well be right."

Gratified at this approval from her older and more sensible cousin, Melanie folded her hands in her lap and waited for the obvious to be stated. When Arianne didn't say more, she demanded, "What are we going to do about it?"

Arianne turned and lifted her dark eyebrows questioningly. "Do about it? What can we do? The painting is gone and so is Rhys. I daresay he knows what he is about."

Melanie's slender fingers clutched in fists of frustration as she glared at Arianne. "Don't you see? Lord Llewellyn has defrauded Rhys of his title and lands. And the only evidence he possesses has been stolen and probably destroyed. We must help him, Rainy. What can we do to help Rhys?"

Arianne stood still, feather duster posed in flight as she contemplated this preposterous assessment. If Rhys were truly the rightful baron, then there was no hope that he would return for her. She might as well expect Lord Locke to come courting as to think that. But her own very tentative emotions had no place in this. It was hard to believe that a man would deliberately deprive a young relative of his rightful place in society, but she knew little about Melanie's world. She supposed if a great amount of wealth were involved, one might be tempted. But what they could do about it, she could not fathom.

"I cannot imagine that badgering the current baron would help his cause to any great effect," Arianne said wryly, lowering her duster and twirling it between her fingers. "It seems if there were anyone to come forward in Mr. Llewellyn's favor he would have done so by now."

Melanie brightened. "That is just it! Lady Jersey says that the present Lord Llewellyn's wife left him right about the time that he came into the title. The disagreement was never made public, but that would explain it. She knew he wasn't the rightful baron. She must have known Rhys's parents were married. If only we could find her . . ."

Alarmed at the intensity of her usually carefree cousin's planning, Arianne attempted to return sense to this conversation. "Rhys Llewellyn is no fool. He was of an age to question something of such great magnitude to his well-being. If his aunt knew anything and meant to reveal it, she would have done so then. There must be any number of other friends and relatives who could have done the same. It is no use trying to change something in which we have no knowledge."

"That sounds just like something Galen would say," Melanie replied huffily. "I thought of all people, you would understand best. But if you have no interest in seeing an old wrong righted, I shall do it myself." Standing, she indignantly retrieved her parasol and started for the door, just as the knocker sounded.

As the only room safe from the disturbance of brothers and sisters was the guest parlor just off the front hallway, Arianne and Melanie had chosen it for their conversation. Now Melanie was trapped into greeting the new arrival as Arianne hurried to answer the door before the noisy horde above could descend to investigate the caller. When Lord Locke entered, Melanie's eyes widened with surprise, but she picked up her skirts and prepared to depart again.

"I thought that might be your carriage. Don't let me interrupt if you are having a private coze." Galen lazily twirled his walking stick and held on to his hat as he observed the guilty expressions on the faces of both ladies. They were obviously up to something, but neither appeared very happy about it.

Struck dumb by his return after being certain that he would never wish to see her again, Arianne recovered enough to see that Melanie was her only protection from what promised to be another embarrassing encounter. She refused to allow Locke's polished elegance to overwhelm her, although the golden blond of his hair in the sunlight put the gloomy parlor to shame.

Not meeting his inquiring eyes as they fastened on her, Arianne hastened to end the impasse. "Melanie has just arrived, my lord, but you are welcome to join us in tea, if you wish. Or if you have come to see Father, he is out at the moment, but I will be happy to give him a message."

Both Melanie and Galen regarded her with suspicion, but Arianne was beyond caring. Her only desire was to escape further embarrassment at the hands of this careless lord. Just as she thought she had succeeded, screams of delight echoed from above, and closing her eyes, Arianne cursed her brothers and their sharp eyes and waited for the avalanche to descend.

8

"SURELY YOU MUST see that if Lord Llewellyn left town as soon as you questioned him about the painting, he must have something to hide! We must *do* something, Galen," Melanie cried plaintively.

"Davie, lad, if you do not climb down from there soon, your brothers will find the muffin man before you do." Locke casually hooked his arm over the back of the bench and gazed up into the canopy of leaves where a barely discernible urchin could be seen in the uppermost branches.

"I vow, I don't know which of you is the most exasperating." Throwing the golden couple on the bench a look of irritation, Arianne left Davie to Galen's casual auspices and went after her two youngest brothers, who had heard the call of the muffin man and had given chase.

Galen continued his tree-gazing as he spoked. "Do you think she includes me in that rash declaration?" he asked laconically, giving no sign of his heart-stomping fear as the boy in the branches began a rather rapid descent.

"Arianne has already cut up stiff with me, so I daresay we are both leveled with her siblings by now. Do you suppose you ought to stop Lucinda from standing between the horses like that?"

Galen attempted to turn one eye on the skinny female patting the noses of his cattle while keeping the other on the harum-scarum lad in the branches. It was a wonder he did not come up cross-eyed from the effort, he reckoned as Davie reached the final branch and appeared ready to jump the remaining ten feet.

"If you break your leg, I'll leave you lying for the pigeons to eat," he warned as he removed himself from the bench to rescue Davie from his perch. To his surprise, Melanie followed after him.

"That's a dreadfully rude thing to say to anybody, but I shall assume you didn't include me in your admonitions." Melanie waited patiently for Galen to extract the child from the tree while keeping her own eye on her younger cousin and the horses.

"If you should be so foolish as to climb a tree and break a limb, you deserve for pigeons to eat you," Galen retorted as he lowered Davie to the ground and let him loose. The boy went careening off across the grass to cut off his brothers at the curve, and he turned his attention next to the carriage horses. It had become more than evident that Melanie had her mind set on other things besides the children, and Galen couldn't help but wonder at the sudden obstinacy of her behavior. Melanie had never been of an obstinate nature. He threw a glance after the sway of Arianne's heavy skirts as she followed her brothers. Now, there was an obstinate miss.

"You have become quite impossible anymore, Galen. You will be as stodgy as Gordon if you keep this up. Once you would have offered to ride out after Rhys, or at least you would have promised me an ice while you think about it. Now you won't even think about it. I thought Rhys was your friend."

After briefly instructing Lucinda on the temperament of high-strung thoroughbreds and promising to allow her the reins briefly on the return home, Galen sent the girl after her sister and began following more sedately in the same direction. He was more than aware of the beauty attached to his elbow, her summer skirts fluttering in the breeze, her fashionable hat perched coquettishly on her head as she berated him. He had known Melanie the better part of her life, watched her grown from willful tyke to lovely woman. He knew her every whim and mood and felt more than capable of dealing with them. But at the moment he felt like turning her over his knee and spanking some sense into her.

"Rhys is my friend, which is why I'm trying to stay out of his business. Not that you make it easy for me," Galen grumbled.

"What if he's in trouble?" Melanie whispered, expressing her worst fears almost to herself.

Galen sent her a curious glance. "Rhys survived a war and a wound that could have killed many another. I shouldn't think he would be in any danger crossing the English countryside in chase of some wild goose."

Melanie sent him a scathing glance, dropped his arm, and gathering up her skirts, went racing after her cousins. Galen had half a mind to return to his carriage and wait for them there, but the sight of a crisp blue skirt swinging toward the gates eliminated that thought. She had escaped from him once like that; he wasn't likely to allow it again.

Striding rapidly after a tall, slender form wearing a less-than-elegant rose-trimmed hat, Galen gave up the pursuit of any rational thought. Soon, he hoped, he would have a wife and children of his own. In the meantime, he could practice by holding tight rein on his intended's heathen cousins.

Melanie tightened the ribbons of her hat, checked to be certain she had her reticule with her quarterly allowance, and nodded briskly at her nervous maid. The girl picked up the one bag Melanie had allowed them and quietly followed her mistress down the front stairs. With the master gone to listen to the speeches in Parliament and the lady of the house upstairs napping—the whole household was expecting an announcement any day now of the future arrival of a bundle from heaven—no one was about to notice their quiet descent. The staff would be about their business elsewhere in the house at this hour. Lady Melanie had chosen the best time for making her escape.

Not that Melanie considered it an escape. Evan and Daphne were more than generous with their time and understanding, but they did not seem to understand the necessity of helping Rhys. Her brother was Rhys's best friend, but even he did not consider it necessary to send anyone searching for him. Rhy's villainous uncle could have had him pushed over a cliff or drowned in a river or any other of a dozen dastardly punishments to keep him from reclaiming his title. And even if Rhys were well and his uncle hadn't found him, he would need help in prying the necessary information out of relatives who had lied too long to be persuaded easily. She was much better at persuading people to talk than Rhys. Rhys was so smart it was almost scary sometimes, but he spent too much time with books and horses to know how to deal well with people. She would help him discover the truth, and then he would have to acknowledge that she was no longer a child but a grown woman.

That thought filled Melanie with satisfaction as she ordered the coach to take the north highway. Lady Jersey had said that Lady Llewellyn now lived in Carlisle. She had family there, any of whom might know the secret of Rhys's birth. It would be better if she knew the family of Rhys's mother, but there seemed to be much confusion over that matter. Perhaps Lady Llewellyn could tell her. If she had left her husband over his deception, then surely she had to be on Rhys's side and would be willing to help in any way she could.

This wasn't the first time Melanie had taken off on her own. She knew Gordon would be furious with her when he found out, but she really could manage quite well. Daphne would understand that and would persuade Evan to come around when she found the note she'd left behind. It was a nuisance having twin brothers who fretted and pretended she was still a child, but her sister-in-law had done much the same when she was the same age, and she would know that no harm could come to a lady traveling safely in her family coach.

Unknown to Melanie, her sister-in-law had social obligations to fulfill that afternoon and was gone when a servant discovered the note pinned to her pillow. It was Evan to whom the note was carried, and it was Galen's arrival that had prompted Evan to send for his sister. When Evan was presented with the note instead, he stared at it in such profound puzzlement that Galen relieved him of it and raised a lofty eyebrow as he read.

"I suppose one of us shall have to bring her back. Does this happen often in your family, Griffin? I can see the Richards brats have a definite tendency for havoc, but I rather thought that was because they were young. Perhaps it is a family trait, after all."

Evan sent his elegantly idle friend a look meant to level. "Stow it, Locke. Melanie is young, but not foolish. Obviously we have been ignoring a problem that is very much on her mind. If I were you, I wouldn't be so confident that it is your suit she wants. She has always idolized Rhys, but I hadn't thought it went this far."

Galen discarded his unconcerned pose to hand the note back to Evan. "You have a meeting with the Regent. I'll go after her. Will your wife be able to accompany me to act as chaperone?"

Evan hesitated. "We have not made the announcement yet, but Daphne is increasing, and the carriage motion makes her ill. Perhaps I'd better go. I could ask Uncle Ross to go with you, but I'm not certain that you would be any better off listening to his eccentricities than to Daphne's upheavals. And to send Ross off on his own would be futile; he would be sidetracked for a visit to some gallery along the way and we wouldn't see him for a week."

Galen picked up his hat and cane and started for the door. "If I am to wed your sister, I might as well learn to deal with her fits and starts as well as your relations. My carriage is already out front and Prinny will be expecting you. Go on. I'll find Richards and have Melanie back by nightfall."

Evan wasn't at all certain that it was wise to unload the burden of his scatter-witted family on his good-natured friend, but Galen wasn't giving him any time to argue. Besides that, Evan's wife and child-to-be depended on him for a living, and he depended on Prinny's good favor to keep that living. It had been easier being a soldier.

Instead of entering the carriage, Galen leapt to the driver's seat and tore the whip from the hand of his startled driver. He knew the way to the Richards home much better than the coachman, and if truth would have it, he could drive it better and faster than his employee. Unprotesting, the driver let him have his way. It didn't make sense to argue with your employer, particularly when your employer was twice the size and angry enough to pop a cork.

The distance from Grosvenor Square to the little house past St. James's wasn't great, but the way was crowded with ladies in carriages out for an afternoon's shopping and gentlemen on horses making calls. Galen ignored their cries of surprise and anger as he sent his team careening down the widest thorough-fares, dodging carts, carriages, horses, and pedestrians alike. Perhaps Evan could be casual about his sister's going off on her own, but Galen had no such frame of reference. His own activities had been strictly limited at that age, and he hadn't been a fashionable female prey to the dangerous denizens of a world outside his own. He didn't even want to imagine the first time Melanie stepped out alone into one of the notorious roadside inns along the way.

Ross Richards was never at home. Galen should have known he wouldn't be. He stalked impatiently up and down the dim parlor as the little maid who answered the door ran to fetch Mrs. Richards. He should have known better than to expect Mrs. Richards to come down alone, also. He looked up to find Arianne's anxious blue eyes fixed on him, and he began to sweat.

"I only meant to inquire where I might find Mr. Richards. It is a matter of some urgency . . ."

Mrs. Richards was a tall woman, nearly as tall as Arianne, but years of bearing children had given her more fullness than her daughter. Were it not for the circles beneath her eyes and the slight cough she tried to hide, she would not appear at all the invalid Galen had expected. He bowed politely over her hand and urged her to a chair, but she refused.

"My husband could be in any of a number of places, my lord. He could appear here at any minute or in hours. I am sorry to be of such little help. Is there anything we might do?"

Arianne studied Locke's harried expression with perplexity. He was not the type inclined to undue emotion. He took most of the acts of mankind in stride, dismissing all but his own concerns as irrelevant. He had been a trifle perturbed by the loss of the painting, but only because it brought his honor into question. Now he was striding up and down the room with an excess of energy much as Melanie would do. Melanie. Arianne choked back a gulp of fear and gently took her mother's arm.

"Perhaps I can give Lord Locke some idea where the best places are to find Papa. Why don't you return upstairs and let us try to sort this out?"

Anne Richards looked mildly annoyed, but noting the relief on Locke's face, she nodded. "I'll have Lucy bring tea. Please have a seat, my lord. Arianne knows my husband's habits better than I do."

When she was gone, Arianne swung around to confront their anxious visitor. "What has Melanie done now? I knew she would not let the matter rest, but usually she gives me some inkling of her plans."

Galen had not come prepared to face the angry miss who had instigated all this turmoil by purloining her father's painting, but pride didn't prevent him from realizing that Arianne would be the best source of knowledge of Melanie's actions. He hesitated only briefly in replying. "Melanie has gone in search of Rhys's aunt. She has some fool notion that she will better persuade knowledge from the woman than Rhys."

Arianne's vague smile didn't reach her eyes as she contemplated the consequences of this statement. The man in the room with her was obviously violently opposed to Melanie's impetuous behavior. Against the gloom of the dusky parlor, his white cravat gleamed with the brilliance of moonlight, but his frown decimated his usual laughing image of a golden god. Hat still in hand, he strode to the draped window and shoved the heavy material aside to stare into the street.

"Melanie is more than likely right in her assumption, but that is no excuse for her behavior. I suppose we must go after her. Do you have some idea where this aunt resides?"

Startled, Galen let the drapery fall and turned to stare at the quiet young woman gracing the room's center. Uncapped, her thick hair was caught up in loose swirls that softened the sharpness of her cheekbones and emphasized the luminosity of her eyes. She looked more than competent to take on the assignment of finding her cousin, but that did not change the fact that it would be highly improper for her to go out in his company. Annoyed at the restrictions that assumed every man was a rake and every woman a man's target for lust, Galen shoved his hat back on his head and started for the door.

"I'll go after her myself. I only sought your father as a representative of the family to save Melanie from idle talk. But since I mean to marry her anyway, it makes no difference. We'll send word when we return."

Arianne disregarded the pain caused by his casual words. Knowing her cousin as she did, she feared there was much to lose if Locke were allowed to act with the same rashness as Melanie. Daringly catching his coat sleeve, she forced him to a halt.

"I don't suppose you have considered whether or not Melanie will be appreciative of your rescue if it means marrying you against her choice?"

Locke halted and stared down into eyes of dark blue. Like the lochs of Scotland, they seemed bottomless, and he gritted his teeth in annoyance for being held by them. "I believe I have made my intentions clear, and she does not seem averse to them. I can see no other choice. She can't be allowed to travel that distance alone."

"She cannot have been gone long. She was here only just this morning. If she took the coach, your phaeton will be swifter. We will catch up to her before nightfall, and none will know the difference."

Locke gave her a look of impatience. "Your father would know the difference when he learns we have traveled together without proper accompaniment. I cannot marry both of you. Do be reasonable, Miss Richards."

"He need never know. I will tell my mother you are taking me to the Griffins'. Evan's coach can return me later. The only obstacle I can see is trying to persuade Melanie to turn her coach around and come home."

Grimly Galen pondered the truth of her words. He had been hasty in telling Evan he could manage this. He had little or no experience at persuading stubborn females from a course they were determined on taking. But Melanie would listen to Arianne if she would listen to anyone. Without really meaning to do so, he nodded.

9

ARIANNE TRIED NOT to clutch nervously at the phaeton's seat as Galen wheeled sharply to pass a farmer and his barrow. With his attention entirely on his horse, her companion took little notice of her discomfort, but she had no notion of complaining. Actually, she was a trifle startled that Lord Locke had allowed her to come with him. She had briefly entertained ideas of abducting one of Evan's vehicles and racing after Melanie herself, but she knew she would never have been able to carry out such a feather-brained scheme. Grateful that she had not been placed in such a position, she held on to her hat and prayed.

Beside her, Galen was more aware of his traveling companion than she knew, but more for her lack of presence than otherwise. She allowed him to concentrate fully on making the best time through busy city streets and over rutted country roads, without a complaint to the damage his recklessness caused to her attire or a whisper of a need to stop for food or drink or any other foolishness. She was so silent, he had to occasionally glance to the side to be certain he had not lost her in the road somewhere. She was not like any female he had ever known, but now wasn't the time to investigate that oddity. He would offer his appreciation when he caught up with her willful cousin.

Thoughts of Melanie kept Galen occupied at any moment when his horses did not. She was little more than a child wandering alone in the wilderness. Even with her brother's most reliable driver and footman, she was little better than unprotected. The stretch of road they had just left behind was notorious for its thieves, and the servants couldn't be trusted to know the right inns when darkness descended. Whatever had possessed her to do such a hare-brained thing as to race after Rhys on her own?

Galen didn't bother contemplating Evan's words. Despite being declared a bastard in the eyes of the world and having to live on what his wits provided, Rhys was a gentleman. He would never risk Melanie's future and happiness by seriously considering her as a wife. There had been no indication that he did so. Sending another quick glance to the woman beside him, Galen wondered if Rhys had not fixed his interest in that quarter. The match would be eminently suitable on both sides. Perhaps that was why Melanie was so concerned: she was worried that something had happened to her cousin's only suitor.

That made about as little sense as anything else that had happened these past weeks. Reaching a straight open stretch before the next town, Galen broke the extended silence between them. "Do you have any notion why Melanie is so set on finding Rhys?"

Arianne tried to hide her alarm at the phaeton's speed and to appear as calm as he as she turned her gaze toward Lord Locke. He had discarded his hat earlier, and now his blond hair blew waywardly in the breeze. Combined with his unfashionably large size straining against the polished superfine of his coat and the cravat loosened by his activity, he lost some of the loftiness that had held them apart. Still, no one could mistake him as anything but a peer of the realm.

"You are the one intending to wed her. I should think you should know more of her mind than I. She had some absurd notion that Lord Llewellyn would do away with Rhys should he uncover the true secret of his birth. Evan really ought to keep those terrible gothics out of her hands."

Galen grunted in agreement and skillfully guided the team around a rather large hole in the road's surface. The sun was sinking rapidly, and they had yet to discover anyone who had seen Melanie's carriage. That was to be expected out here, he supposed, but surely in the next town they would find some evidence that she had traveled this way.

"I am beginning to wonder if she has not had more sense than we. At least she is traveling in a comfortably sprung carriage with servants around her. I should never have allowed you along, Miss Richards. I apologize for my lapse in sense, although it is rather late to do anything about it."

"I would not have allowed you to go without me, so there is no need for apology. Comfortably sprung carriages are as strange to me as this contraption. My only concern is that Melanie come to no harm. We have been cousins and best friends for the better part of our lives. Discomfort does not rank anywhere in my mind under those conditions."

"Your attitude does you credit, but I fear society is not so high-minded. I shall endeavor to keep this part of our little escapade from gossiping tongues. I do not know what there is between you and Llewellyn, but I'll not risk his calling me out over our impropriety. He's a deuced good shot."

Midnight eyes lifted to regard him quizzically from beneath the preposterous bonnet. "If there is any impropriety, I daresay you have more to fear from my shooting you than Mr. Llewellyn. Keep your mind on your horses, my lord."

Not a whisper of a smile crossed her fair lips, but he knew when he was being quizzed, and Galen laughed out loud at the way she had twisted his words. It was better to laugh than to worry. At least laughing made the time pass faster.

They sped along companionably after that, Galen occasionally warning his companion to hold on to her seat when they approached a particularly rough stretch, and offering her his coat when the wind began to grow chilly. But spying the lights of an inn ahead, Arianne refused his offer. Undoubtedly it would have been too early to stop when Melanie reached this place, but perhaps someone within had seen her. She desperately needed the reassurance that they were on the right road.

Galen swung into the stableyard and gave a sharp whistle as he noted the polished carriage tilting precariously on its back axle in front of them. No sign of driver or occupants appeared, and it was obvious that it had been abandoned sometime earlier. It was equally obvious from the discreet crest on the door to whom it belonged.

"Luck is with us, if not with your cousin, Miss Richards. If I do not mistake, that is Shelce's crest. We have found her."

In the twilight, one carriage looked much the same as another, but Arianne agreed it looked like they had discovered their goal. She waited impatiently for Galen to speak with the ostler and come around to help her down. She threw a glance to the bright lights of the inn and prayed it was a decent abode. Surely traveling with maid and footman, Melanie would be safe for these few hours she had been here.

Galen's strength as he lifted her down surprised her. She was not small, but he caught her up with an ease that made her gasp, not giving her time to descend gracefully. Arianne understood Locke's impatient energy had been held in check too long, but she still quivered where his hands had so possessively circled her waist, even after she was on the ground and hurrying beside him.

The inn was so constructed that they had to enter through the main room, where travelers sat and dined and warmed themselves before the fire. Heads turned as they entered, and Arianne wished she had not cut off the long bill of her bonnet. She felt exposed to their stares, and pulled her mother's old shawl more tightly around her. Galen impatiently scanned the crowd, then tugged her along after him in search of the innkeeper.

Arianne was never more grateful for a man's presence. In the sheltered world from which she came, she had never felt fear or had any need to doubt her surroundings. She knew which streets to walk and when, and trusted in the goodness of the people around her, people she had known since childhood. The occasional drunk staggering from a tavern was easily escaped by crossing the street. Here, in this room, escape did not seem so easy, and all the faces were unfamiliar to her. She thought she read hostility in the expressions of some, and even the avid curiosity on the faces of others made her uneasy. She held to Lord Locke's strong arm and concentrated on crossing the room without tripping over her skirt or other people's feet.

Faced with Locke's overwhelming size and intent expression, no one interfered with their progress, and most returned to their eating and drinking as the proprietor appeared to offer accommodations to their noble guest. A shrewd judge of clothing, he instantly classified Locke as a wealthy and aristocratic prospect, but his eyebrows lifted slightly at the sight of the commonly gowned female on his arm. The woman didn't wear the appearance of a painted dolly, nor did she have the lovely wiles of a poor girl about to join their numbers.

Frowning, he halted their progress at the doorway to the hall. "We're all filled up for the night, my lord. This is a respectable place, it is. You'll have to go on to London for your dirty deeds."

Arianne gasped at this rudeness; then realizing what the man thought, sent a startled glance to Lord Locke, who did not seem to see the humor of it. With a curt wave of his hand he dismissed the man's *faux pas*.

"We'll be returning there at once, as soon as you direct us to the room of Lady Melanie Griffin. Her carriage has had a mishap, it appears."

The innkeeper brightened at once. "That is most remarkable that word has traveled so fast. I would not have thought there would have been time for a messenger to reach her family. Do come in, my lord. The lady had hoped to find a blacksmith in the morning, but I'm certain she will be delighted to know that help has arrived so swiftly."

He led them through a dim hall smoking with tallow

lamps, to the door of one of his private parlors. Knocking discreetly, he threw open the door to reveal the firelit chamber beyond.

Melanie sat curled upon a small sofa, reading a tiny volume form the Minerva Press, her maid nowhere in sight. At the abrupt intrusion, she looked up inquisitively, then jumped to her feet with an exclamation at the sight of both Galen and Arianne in the doorway.

"Oh, my goodness, never say the two of you are eloping! That would be the height of foolishness." She grinned as she said it, eyes dancing with devilment at the expression on her visitors' faces. Arianne's humor surfaced faster than Galen's; he continued to stare at her as if she were a peculiar bug on the wall.

"Cousin, you are not just a Feather-Headed Peahen, but a Fowl Goose of the worst sort. I shall recommend that Evan send you to your room with naught but bread and water for this. Do you have any idea what it is like to career along at the not-so-gentle hands of this speed fiend? I shall ache in every bone in my body on the morrow."

Melanie's sympathetic look died quickly with the chastisement from Galen that followed. "Do you have any idea how you have frightened your family? Consider what you have done to your sister-in-law in her delicate condition. She is no doubt fretting the night away, waiting for your return. I had thought you possessed more sense than that."

Instead of looking suitably abject, Melanie turned to Arianne with guileless surprise. "He is angry with me! I never thought to see the day. Do you think he has other humors too? Do you think if I cried it would make him sad?"

Arianne pressed her lips together to keep from chuckling at her irrepressible cousin's good cheer. The same might be said for Melanie's character as for Galen's. She seldom expressed anger or ill humor or sadness. It was as if the two of them led a charmed life outside the world of woe they lived in. Part of their charm was that they were willing to share their happiness with everyone. Unfortunately, Lord Locke's charm had worn distressingly thin these last hours.

Before he could say something biting that would ruin his chances with Melanie, Arianne put a warning hand to his coat sleeve. "I daresay there are other things to worry about besides whether Melanie knows how to cry, my lord. With her carriage incapacitated, our hasty return is out of the question."

Gaining control of his temper, Galen gave a curt nod at Arianne's reminder of their position. It was a good thing one of them had his feet firmly on the ground, although she seemed to take the situation much more lightly than he deemed proper. Bowing, he excused himself. "I'll make inquiries about repairs, and order a supper sent in, Miss Richards."

Melanie drew a prim face and wrinkled her nose after Galen departed. "Now I suppose he'll not speak to me. Men are quite the most irritating creatures." She finally turned her attention fully on her cousin. "I'm sorry that you had to suffer such discomfort on my account, Rainy. You really did not need to come after me, you know."

Arianne didn't feel qualified to speak on the reason she had thought it necessary to cool Lord Locke's rashness. Instead, she removed her shawl and bonnet in the room's warmth and sank gratefully to the comforts of the padded sofa. "And you really do not have to be such a goose, cousin, but you are. Did you really think Evan would let you travel all alone to the north country?"

"Well, he should have thought of that when I tried to persuade him to go after Rhys. It is on his own head. Is Daphne truly expecting? How lovely! I shall be an aunt. That should prove I am no longer a child." Melanie bounced down beside Arianne and extended her hand with a book. "Would you care to read the first volume? It's immensely exciting, even if it is a little silly. Imagine finding villains in every inn. One would think men had naught else to do but wait for hapless heroines to appear on the doorstep."

There were times when it would be much easier to

strangle Melanie than to put sense into her head, but Arianne forwent the urge. "Did you not see any of the villainous characters in that room out there? Even with Lord Locke's company, I felt as if we would be coshed over the head and left for dead. Do you see nothing but happy endings?"

Melanie looked surprised at her cousin's tone. "Well, of course not. There are those poor creatures who live in the streets with scarcely a crust to eat. And I am not so innocent as to think there aren't thieves and rogues who prey on the helpless. But one cannot help everyone. Rhys is my friend. If I can help to write a happy ending for his story, I will have done something useful, won't I?"

There was little argument Arianne could offer to that, and as her supper arrived then, she didn't carry the conversation further.

Galen joined them a little later. The supper he had sent in was more than ample, and he settled in the chair across from Arianne while Melanie remained on the sofa with her novel. At Arianne's questioning look, he shook his head.

"The carriage cannot be repaired until morning. I have sent Evan's servant back on a hired horse to let them know where we are and that all is well, but it appears as if we are stranded here for the night. I hope Evan makes good explanations to your family, Miss Richards."

"My mother thinks the twins can do no wrong. She will accept anything Evan chooses to tell her. I doubt my father will know I'm missing until he wishes to send me on an errand. Do not worry on my account."

Melanie glanced up from her book at their low words. "You needn't whisper, you know. I can hear perfectly well. If you had not been so foolish as to come after me in that ridiculous phaeton, you could be on your way home. Really, you could go on now. The innkeeper assured me the carriage would be fixed in the morning, and I'm quite comfortably settled for the evening. Arianne is needed at home. Although I must say, Galen, it was most improper of you to bring her. There is no telling what such haring about will do to her reputation."

Galen lifted a cool brow in her direction. "What assurance would we have that you would return after us in the morning?"

"Why, none, of course," Melanie agreed in surprise. "I have no intention of going back in the morning. You are welcome to join me, if you like, but I'm going to Carlisle. We visited Keswick one year, and it was quite lovely. I should think Carlisle would be much the same. You really ought to join me. It would be great fun."

Arianne had no compunctions about losing her temper. Turning a sharp look to her thoughtless cousin, she replied, "Fun is for children, Melanie. I don't know why you express such great surprise when everyone treats you like a child. You behave like one. Adults have responsibilities. Obviously you don't. How do you think Mr. Llewellyn would feel should he learn you were harmed in your feckless search for him?"

Both Galen and Melanie looked at her in surprise, but Arianne was tired and politeness escaped her. This time, Locke was the one to intervene.

"I'm certain we will all be more sensible in the morning, when we have had time to sleep on this. Miss Richards, if you have finished your meal, let me escort you and Melanie to your room. Perhaps some solution will occur by the time we wake."

Arianne certainly hoped so. For the moment, the only solution that came to mind was slapping Melanie in chains and hauling her back screaming all the way.

10

WHEN LORD LOCKE entered their private parlor as they breakfasted the next morning, Arianne took one look at the intent expression in his eyes and excused herself, using the door nearest her rather than the one behind him. Melanie seemed no more tractable than the prior night, and his lordship appeared in no mood to brook any nonsense. She had no desire to be caught between two people accustomed to always having their way.

Locke let her go without comment, although Melanie appeared ready to protest. It was highly improper for them to be alone together, but Galen intended to rectify that situation at once. It was time someone took Lady Melanie Griffin in hand, and if her brothers weren't so inclined, then it would have to be him.

"I trust you slept well?" he began innocuously enough.

Melanie shifted uneasily in the hard chair, then indicated the seat across from her. "Fine, thank you. Would you care for some tea? Or shall I ring for something else? My brother prefers coffee. I have never breakfasted with another gentleman before."

"That is a situation that I hope might change before long." Galen took the seat offered and held out his cup. "Tea will be fine. The coffee in these places is never of the best."

Melanie nervously poured the tea and set the pot aside, glancing hastily around the ruins of the breakfast table to see if there were more to offer him. She had thought he was dining in his room, as would have been polite. It was quite unlike Arianne to desert her under these circumstances.

Aware of her sudden shyness and determined to keep the upper hand, Galen located a piece of toast and began to spread it with jam. "You're quiet this morning, my dear. Is this a temporary condition or are you always so in the morning? I find a quiet breakfast rather refreshing, myself."

"I am simply waiting for you to come to the point." Finally understanding that he was baiting her, Melanie clamped her teeth together, tightening her dainty jaw.

Galen lifted an inquisitive eyebrow. "Testy in the mornings, are we? That is good to know. Perhaps I should wait until later in the day to make my proposal."

"Galen, you are being as irritating as my brothers. I like it much better when you are amusing. If you have something to say, say it. The innkeeper has assured me that the carriage is almost ready, and I shall be gone shortly."

"You cannot go traipsing after Llewellyn all alone, my dear. Should word of your departure from London get about, the scandal will be large enough, but an extended absence chasing after a man whom the *ton* does not even recognize as acceptable will destroy your reputation for life. Do you hold some *tendre* for our writer friend, that you find it necessary to harm yourself and break your family's heart?"

Melanie's jaw began to set even more obstinately. "Rhys is my friend, as he is yours and Evan's. If neither of you can take time to help him, I will. I cannot see how visiting an old lady can be termed scandalous."

"Should someone walk in on us right now, you would be ruined. It doesn't take much, as you must certainly be aware. If you are so set on visiting Lady Llewellyn, then we can arrange some respectable retinue with your family's permission and do this without any loss of reputation. But it must be done properly, and not in this havey-cavey manner."

Melanie brightened. "You will persuade Evan, then? Why didn't you say so from the first? Oh, thank you, Galen. I knew you were my friend."

Galen set his bread aside and watched the fairy-child across from him nearly dance with delight. Despite her angelic looks, he now knew her to be as stubborn in character as the rest of her family, a not altogether difficult asset to deal with, but how many other traits had she kept hidden from him? This business of choosing a wife was not so simple as he had originally seen, but he could still fathom no one being more suited to his nature than Melanie. After this night in the inn, Evan would feel much more comfortable should they come back with a proper understanding. There was never a better time than the present, although Galen had some reservations about proposing over a well-used breakfast table.

"I would be more than your friend, my dear." He rose and came around the table to take her hand, gently helping her from her seat.

Melanie appeared momentarily confused by the tone of his voice, but she accepted his hand easily enough. When he continued to hold it instead of releasing her, she tried to wriggle free gracefully. "Well, I am certain that you are, Galen, but it is most improper for you to tell me so in these circumstances. Perhaps we had better find Arianne. I cannot think why she left so abruptly."

Galen could, and he silently thanked the practical cousin, who employed so much understanding in all the right times and places. "There is something we need to discuss before we return to your family, Melanie. Perhaps you would like to take a seat on the sofa."

A small frown of irritation began to cross Melanie's otherwise uncreased brow. "Certainly not. I must see if Arianne is all right and check that the maid has packed everything. Time is running short."

Galen caught her small shoulders in his big hands and held her still. "This is worse than trying to propose to a whirlwind. You could have the grace to stand still for just a few minutes while I do the pretty, at least. Evan didn't say I'd have to shackle you before the vows are said just to pop the question."

That got Melanie's attention, and she froze in place,

staring up to Galen's clear gray eyes to be certain he did not jest. "have you quite taken leave of your senses?" she whispered uncertainly.

"I have not," he said firmly, wondering idly what it would be like to taste those lovely pink lips. Somehow, he had not quite got around to thinking about that. Kissing Evan's sister seemed somehow disrespectful, maybe even incestuous, but that was nonsense. He had her attention now; he must put it to good use. "I am asking you to marry me. I have talked to Evan previously of this, and it seems in our best interests to declare the attachment now. That should lay to rest any hint of rumor that might emerge from your escapade."

Generally sparkling blue eyes widened with horror and dismay, and Melanie hastily backed away. "You've talked to Evan? Without even consulting me? How could you do so? And to use this . . ."—she swung her hand to indicate their surroundings—"to persuade me . . . that is the outside of enough! I thought better of you, Galen, I really did. We would never suit. Surely you must see that. We are much too much alike. I am not certain that it is an honor you do me by proposing in such a manner, but I am grateful for your thought in considering me. Let us leave it at that, Galen. I want to go home."

In the adjoining room, Arianne cringed at the sound of rising voices. Tugging once more at the door swelled shut from recent rains, she cursed at being trapped in here, witness to this entire embarrassing scene. Worse yet, she cursed at Lord Locke for making such a bungle of the thing. Surely he must understand Melanie's romantic nature. To propose out of the expediency of the situation rather than with words of love and caresses was without doubt the silliest thing the man had ever done. She did not think Lord Locke an exceedingly silly man, but when it came to women, most men were impossible. It was a wonder anyone ever married.

The words drifting from the other room were not

angry words, nor were the voices raised done so with
anything more than a slightly louder polite pitch. They
would both bore each other into anger if they did not
cease soon. Arianne wished to scream and kick and
shout herself, and she was not even in the room with
them. She was sincerely grateful for her unusual upbringing. At least she was not required to be polite at
all times and all places. Society did not expect as much
of her as it did one of its own.

Finally she heard the sound of the door being flung
open in the other room. If she waited long enough,
she could be certain they had both gone, and she
could slip out with none being the wiser. At least
Galen had persuaded her wayward cousin into returning home, although after this little altercation it
wouldn't surprise her if Melanie chose to take off on
her own again. She would have to escape here soon
to head her off, just in case.

The sound of Galen's steps crossing the room
brought a sigh of relief. Soon he would be gone, and
she would be relieved from this embarrassing predicament. Scowling and giving another annoyed tug at the
stubborn door, she didn't realize the steps were going
the wrong direction until a hand came out to cover hers
on the knob and a man's strength jerked the door open.

Arianne nearly staggered beneath the abrupt change,
then caught herself in time to gaze helplessly into Lord
Locke's impassive expression. "Th-thank you, my lord."

Now that the door was ajar, Galen didn't move
aside to let her pass. Instead, he stared down into her
fathomless eyes and frowned in perplexity. "Why
won't she marry me? We suit admirably. Anyone can
see that."

Startled that he would mention the subject without
reservation, even though he must know she had heard
every word, Arianne took a minute to recover her
wits. When she did, she allowed some of the irritation
that had been building to escape. "Oh, admirably, no
doubt. Not just any woman would appreciate the fi-
nesse of having her entire family informed of her suit-
or's intentions before she is. And it takes a certain

nature to accept a proposal based on an innocent night's stay in an inn rather than words of love or romance. I daresay you have not even kissed her or given her any token to mark your esteem, either. I'm certain that impressed her mightily. I should think the two of you so well-suited that she must have leapt into your arms with joy after that affectionate demonstration of your feelings."

A bemused look crossed Galen's usually good-natured features as he regarded the dark wren barking at him. Perhaps he had mistaken Miss Richards' nature also. She was certainly no wren to cheep mildly. Running his hand uncertainly through his hair, he stared down at her without an easy quip to relieve the situation. "I made a cake of it, didn't I? Dash it all, how else does one go about proposing to his best friend's little sister? I'd feel a proper cad courting or seducing her like any other female."

"I'm scarcely one to consult, am I? Now, if you'll excuse me, I think I'd better see that Melanie isn't making off with the carriage while we speak."

Since that seemed a definite possibility now that he knew Lady Melanie's impetuousness, Galen allowed Arianne to escape to the upper story while he took strides to command the carriage. He had never proposed to a lady before, and so had never been rejected. He wasn't at all certain that he liked the feeling that someone else did not consider him as good a prospect as he had imagined. Cold water could not have been more dashing, but he wasn't prepared to let the rest of the world know it. Shrugging his shoulders back in his neatly tailored coat, Galen strode out into the inn yard with the assurance of a man in complete control of his world. None of the doubts growing rapidly in his soul could be detected from the outside.

Before any confrontations could occur over the direction of the carriages, a dust-coated rider galloped into the inn yard as the ladies departed the inn. Arianne hesitated on the doorstep, finding something familiar in the rider's form, but Melanie was more intent on having her way and ignored the new arrival in favor of commandeering her own vehicle.

Not having any idea why she felt so irritated with her cousin and Lord Locke, Arianne remained where she was until she had identified the rider, then gave an exclamation of surprise and hurried in his direction as he pulled his mount to a halt and swung down.

"Evan! What is it? Has something happened to bring you here at this hour?" Although she spoke low and only as she approached Melanie's brother, the others noted her direction and finally gave up their war to discover the new arrival.

Galen caught Melanie's arm and they arrived together just in time to hear Evan's greeting. "Everything will be fine once we get you back to town. I'm glad you found her, Locke"—Evan turned to the couple and gave his sister a look that spoke of a lesson to follow—"but I thought you might need some support when it came time to persuade her back to town."

"I'm not a child, Evan. I see no reason why I cannot go visiting without all this pother. Now that Arianne's here, she can accompany me. We will have a lovely time of it."

Evan pulled off his gloves and wiped his gritty brow with the back of his hand while glaring at his sister. "You've become spoiled, brat. Arianne cannot go with you, and that's an end of it. I've come to make certain she goes directly home. Uncle Ross is pacing the floors. Aunt Anne has become ill, and Arianne is needed at home. I do hope you're happy with what your rashness has created."

Melanie paled more at the sight of Arianne's stricken face than at her brother's words. Grabbing her cousin's hand, she urged her toward the waiting carriage. "We will go at once. Evan, you've sent for a physician, have you not?" she asked over her shoulder as they started toward the coach yard.

At her brother's curt nod, she lifted her heavy traveling skirt and hurried after Arianne.

Locke glanced after the two women, then back to Evan. "I should never have brought Miss Richards with me, but she was insistent on saving Melanie's reputation. With reason, apparently, but I am sorry it turned out this way for her. Is there aught I can do?"

"From what I understand, very little, unless you have the power to persuade Richards to send his family to the country. My home is always open to them, but he has already called me an arrogant young pup and informed me in no uncertain terms that he didn't have to take charity from Shelce's get. My uncle holds a grudge well."

Not wanting to inquire into the family argument that had created this division, Locke nodded toward his waiting phaeton. "I will follow them into town and make certain Miss Richards is returned home promptly. You look as if you could use a bit of a rest first."

Evan caught Locke's arm before he could make his escape. "As far as anyone is aware, Arianne has been with Melanie all along. I take it you have not come off on the best of terms with my sister."

"She has refused me. I can only be grateful for Melanie's sake that Miss Richards insisted on lending propriety to our encounter." With a wry grin, Galen placed his hat on his head. "Next time, I think I shall consult your cousin before making a proposal. She seems to see far more clearly than I."

The carriage pulled away with only one farewell wave from the window. Evan lifted his own hand in acknowledgment, then turned toward the inn as the phaeton rattled off after the coach.

Melanie was obviously still angry with him, but even in adversity, Arianne had the presence of mind to recognize his effort on her part. Although she had said not a word, as was her way, that single waving hand spoke for her. She had not forgotten him, as might have been expected under the pressure of the news he had brought; she merely had nothing to say that would make matters better.

A woman like that was worth a diamond mine. Evan sincerely hoped that Rhys appreciated that fact.

11

"THERE YOU ARE! Thank goodness. Your mother has been asking for you. I don't know what made you go gallivanting off like that. It's not like you, Arianne. Hurry on upstairs, now. I'm certain everything will be fine now that you are here. I will see Lord Locke off and thank him for bringing you promptly home."

Ross Richards' dark eyes lacked their natural sparkle as he sent his daughter to the upper regions of the house. He ran a tired hand over the few sparse hairs of his head and turned his gangly frame in the direction of the elegantly tailored young lord waiting quietly in the doorway, hat in hand. Closer inspection revealed the young man seemed somewhat travel-stained and weary, but his expression was only one of concern as he watched Arianne make a hasty curtsy and rush off for the stairs.

"I've heard young Griffin's explanation of this, and I don't believe a word of it. He may think me a doddering fool, but I've not reached my dotage yet. If you have a moment, perhaps you would be so kind as to explain why my daughter was gone all night when she has never done such a thing before."

Galen turned his attention back to the man who had publicly declared his highly prized Rubens a fraud, but again, he saw nothing of the malicious in the man. His appearance was no more than of a doting father worried for his family, and Galen was incapable of holding a grudge, even if Evan was right and Arianne's father held one exceedingly well.

"I believe Miss Richards may explain better than I.

It is a family affair, I believe, but she was only acting in Lady Melanie's best interests." Galen hedged his explanation as well as he was able, unwilling to immerse Arianne in more trouble than there already was. "I understand the two of them are very close."

Richards glared at his guest. "You are the one who came for her and you are the one who brought her back. My daughter is a good girl. Just because she does not travel in your exalted circles does not mean she is to be treated like a lightskirt. You will have to do better than that."

Mildly annoyed by his host's belligerence, Galen retained his cool aplomb. "I am acting on Evan Griffin's behest. You may take the matter up with him. I have all due respect for your daughter, but I question your concern when the one thing you might do to alleviate her fears and repair her mother's health is to accept Griffin's hospitality." Galen knew he was being rude and it was completely out of character for him, but for Arianne's sake he could not hold his tongue. By the time they had returned to London, she had been tense and white-faced, and some of her anguish had rubbed off on him.

"Damme if you aren't as insolent as he is!" Far from appearing angry, the older man turned away, his face gray with worry as he approached the spectacular mythological landscape gracing the place of honor over the rather simple mantel. "You're a collector. What would you give me for this Titian? My grandfather brought it home from his Grand Tour. The theme isn't appreciated much these days, but there is no denying its greatness."

Shocked, Galen stared at the brilliantly colored painting of chariots and gods and briefly wondered if his own poor attempts at collecting would ever contain works of such greatness. The piece belonged in a museum, but no museum could afford its price, even on the current market. But the shock came from Richards' question. Did he truly mean to sell one of the jewels of his collection?

"I would give whatever it takes to own such a piece,

sir," Locke answered evenly, although he was still shaken by the offer. He knew how the question hurt the man, but he also knew what it would mean to Arianne and her family. He could almost feel Richards' pain, and he had no desire to be the cause of such anguish. At the same time, he couldn't help but think what the sale would mean to Arianne and her mother. Of course, he wasn't certain how Miss Richards would feel if she knew it was his money that sent them to Bath. Knowing something of Arianne's pride, Locke wasn't at all certain that the gesture would be appreciated.

As if the question had never been asked or answered, Ross stood staring at the painting. "My sister was the twins' and Melanie's mother, you know. It broke her heart that Shelce never accepted her as a satisfactory wife for his heir. The estrangement between father and son was no doubt caused as much by other factors as by her marriage, but she took it personally. George was a dreamer, much like Melanie, as a matter of fact. The twins take after their grandfather, hard-headed young devils. But George loved my sister, I'll give him that, and they were happy while they lived. I don't know why Shelce couldn't understand that. It's not as if Richards' blood was tainted. We can trace our ancestors back as far as he; there just aren't many titles attached to the name. We're not the type to aspire to power, I suppose."

Galen listened patiently to the rambling monologue. He had vaguely understood the relationship between the two families, but it became clearer now, and the family feud was more obvious. Richards might not aspire to power, but he had all the pride of the Earl of Shelce. Shelce might not consider a Richards good enough to marry into the Griffin family, but Ross obviously thought his sister too good to live with such snobbery. Perhaps the bad feelings might ultimately have been resolved had the two main characters lived to heal the breach, but the death of Melanie's mother at an early age had sealed the argument forever after.

As if following the trail of Locke's thoughts, Richards continued, "Shelce still blames my sister for George's death, as if she, dead and in her grave, would have wished her husband to fall into such a decline that he ended up killing himself with drink. Shelce's an ass. His son would never have been a copy of him; dreamers never are. It's too late to let bygones be bygones. Shelce has his heir in his grandson now, but the past will never be forgotten. My nephews are too much like him to understand, but Melanie, now, Melanie needs someone to look after her, just as George did. My sister ain't there to do it, and I can't, but Arianne does her best. But sometimes a man has to look out for his own first. I'll not have my daughter hurt at the expense of her cousin."

Astounded by this tack, Galen floundered momentarily against the prevailing current, then righted himself with effort. "I beg your pardon, sir, but your nephew has your daughter's protection in mind as well as Melanie's. I do not know the earl well, but I know Evan and Gordon are gentlemen you can trust. If you wish to call me to account for Miss Richards' whereabouts last evening, I wish you would consult with your nephews first."

Ross's expression was bleak as he turned to regard Locke. "I need only consult Arianne. She will tell me the truth. As much as I love my wife, I don't mean to sell my daughter in her behalf. Consult your men of business and make me an offer on the painting. I think perhaps the entire family would benefit from country air."

Thus dismissed, Galen made a polite bow and escaped. Richards was even more eccentric than he had been led to believe. Or else far more intelligent than the usual run of men. The man could not possibly know all that had transpired these last hours. Perhaps he had just been baiting a hook to see what came after it. It very much seemed as if he had been hoping for an offer for Arianne.

The more he thought about it, the more certain Galen became of it. Richards had emphasized the family lineage, made it known that they were firmly connected with the Earl of Shelce—however estranged—and indicated that he knew Arianne might protect Melanie to the extent of harming her own reputation. But he had backed off at the point of forcing the issue. Perhaps Richards had thought there was an attachment between Arianne and himself. Had his calling with Melanie these last few weeks given that impression? Or had Arianne said something to that effect? Surely not. It was deuced odd.

But it made him recognize his behavior as it appeared in the eyes of others. Galen cursed as he reached his chambers and began flinging off his clothing, much to his valet's dismay. He had called on Arianne more than once in these past weeks. His carriage would be noticeable for its frequency in a neighborhood like that. Even though Melanie was almost always with them, he had been seen in public places with Arianne alone at his side. When Rhys had been along, the matter would not have been much remarked upon, but this past week Rhys had not been there, and still he had called. That would have been sufficient to set tongues to wagging. The fact that he was wealthy and titled and Arianne lived modestly, outside of the *ton*, would put the worst possible construction on the matter.

He would have to speak to Evan. He wished Gordon were here. Evan was inclined to act without thinking, and his military training had little patience with the delicacy of social innuendos. Gordon would better understand the situation. But Gordon preferred the country to London, and was more enamored with his position of running his grandfather's estate than the social whirl of the *ton*. Galen envied him his position in the earl's trust, but that did not make it any easier to decide what to do.

Bathed and freshly attired, Galen set out for the Griffin town house. Had his own father seen fit to release some of his duties to his son, perhaps he could have found more challenging things to do than chase after missing portraits and flighty maidens. But the Earl of Deward, his father, considered his charming son to be as useless an ornament as his wife, and Galen did his best to live up to that opinion. Shining his beaver hat on his coat sleeve, Galen arrived at the Griffins' in his more formal landau rather than the rakish phaeton. It wouldn't do to give the appearance of frivolity on this occasion. Idle he might be, but fool he was not.

He twirled his walking stick as he sauntered up the steps, knowing the door would open without knocking should he take his time. As expected, a footman swung the lofty panels back just as he reached the top, and Locke nodded his gratitude. He had been in and out of this house enough to have lavished more than a generous share of the servants' wages in gratuities, and they showed their appreciation with regularity.

"Mr. Griffin is in the study, my lord."

"I'll make my own way, Waits, thank you." Allowing the footman to relieve him of walking stick and hat, Galen sought the small downstairs office that Evan used for business, grateful that he would not have to come face-to-face with the family upstairs just yet. The business of acquiring a wife was becoming more complicated by the minute. He wasn't at all certain that he wasn't better off out of it.

Evan looked up without expression as his friend entered and casually drew up a chair without invitation. He glanced down at a paper in his hand, then back to Locke. "I have a note here from uncle Ross. He wants me to act as intermediary in the sale of one of his paintings to you. I can't believe he is parting with one of his pets. What have you said to him?"

Galen lifted a laconic eyebrow. "What have I said to him? I rather thought the case was reversed. He lectured me on the error of Shelce's ways and aired the family linen. I rather thought it was his way of explaining why he would not accept your hospitality."

Evan scowled. "Why should he have told all this to you? He's never spoken to anyone else about it before. He barely even speaks to me."

Galen had the grace to grimace with guilt. "I may have ripped up at him a trifle. But confound it, did

you see Arianne's face when she heard about her
mother? And I was the one who lost her blamed painting so she could not make the trip to Bath. I had to
do something to make him see sense. I had not
thought that he would rather sell the Titian than accept your offer."

"The Titian? My word, it gets worse and worse."
Evan ran his hand through his hair in a gesture somewhat reminiscent of his uncle's. "The Titian, I cannot
believe it. I take that back, I might believe it. My
father met my mother when he went to see the Titian.
Everyone knew the Richardses were living on nothing
but that the family housed one of the finest collections
known to the area. I don't know the whole of it, but
as I understand it, they used to be fairly wealthy but
they never had much in the way of lands. I suspect
they were all as eccentric as Uncle Ross and spent it
all on acquiring more and more artwork."

He leaned back in his chair and focused his
thoughts. "I digress. Whatever the occasion, my father
went to see the Titian, hoping they might part with it
if their circumstances were as dire as he had heard. I
believe he once said he meant to put it in the new
room under construction at the time. There's a large
paneled wall there that would have been an ideal display for something that large. My father never did talk
Ross out of the painting, but he acquired my mother
instead. It's an old story, repeated frequently throughout my childhood. Ross just might think it a slap in
my grandfather's face to sell the painting outside the
family."

"Or to his daughter's suitor," Galen finished quietly, feeling suddenly rather weak. The whole picture
was becoming all too clear now. He could be wrong,
but he would rather think of Arianne's father as being
too clever for his own good than too eccentric to behave rationally.

Evan's head shot up. "His daughter's suitor? You
and Arianne? Locke, I know you for an idle fop, perhaps, but not a rake. You can't come courting Melanie
and have Arianne on the side; it won't do, my friend."

Galen grimaced, then leaned back in his chair and examined the toes of his highly polished boot. "That's not at all what I'd intended, but it seems I have been enmiring myself deeper than I thought. Rather careless of me, I admit. Have you heard from Rhys lately? He might dig me out of this pit, but the dreadful thing is, I'm not at all certain that I want him to."

Evan threw up his hands and jumped up, dislodging papers and pens everywhere as he restlessly shoved his chair aside and began to pace. "I've heard from him, yes, but he trusts me to keep his secrets. I fail to see the connection. You are talking in circles, Locke. Start at the beginning and explain yourself."

Galen flicked an imaginary dust mote from the leather. "I'd rather not. I'd rather speak with Rhys. You're not exactly in an unbiased position."

Evan swung round to glare at his lordship at his worst. "Stow it, Locke. I've known you since we were lads. When you put on that bored demeanor, it means you're hiding something. We are talking about my sister and my cousin here. I want to know precisely what happened to cause my uncle to offer to sell his painting to you."

Galen gave him a thoughtful look. "Did Melanie explain why she rejected my suit?"

"Melanie never explains anything!" Evan flung himself back into his desk chair. "She said you were much too alike and would never suit, as if that made any sense at all. She's just peeved at being thwarted in her plans. She'll likely come around after a while. Surely you can't be put off by her foolishness that easily? Heaven only knows, if I had taken Daphne's rejection the first hundred times, we would never have been married now. Women are perverse by nature."

"Hundred times?" Galen lifted a languid eyebrow. "I wasn't aware that you knew her long enough to have time for a hundred proposals."

Evan gave a weary grin. "Well, they covered a space of a few minutes. Or hours. I don't remember which. We were rattling the windows at the time."

"Umph," Galen grunted unintelligibly. He had met

Evan's wife on numerous occasions. He had a hard time imagining how a hardheaded military man like Evan had managed to win the delicate and winsome Daphne, but he had a harder time imagining the two of them yelling at each other enough to rattle the panes. The two of them were still a pair of lovebirds after nearly a year of marriage.

"But that is neither here nor there. I must demand to know your intentions toward Melanie."

Galen thought that sounded rather formal for his informal friend. It would really be quite infamous to cry off so easily, particularly when Melanie was all that he had ever imagined a wife to be. Yet he was beginning to get this niggling feeling that fate had more of a hand in this business than he had calculated. And it wasn't just fate that had him wondering if he hadn't been a trifle presumptuous in assuming that he need only mention marriage to have his choice of wives. The more Galen thought about it, the more he doubted that he had made a wise rather than an opportune decision. Perhaps he had better consider duty first.

Locke sighed and returned his boot to the floor. "My intentions have not altered, but you must know it is a little more complicated than that. Melanie isn't going to come around anytime soon, not while she has this notion about Rhys and his imminent demise in her head. And meanwhile, Mrs. Richards is languishing in her sickbed for lack of funds to see her to proper air. I rather thought Rhys had an interest in your cousin, but if he does not deem it necessary to put in an appearance, perhaps the best thing for all is for me to acquiesce to Mr. Richards' wishes."

Evan watched him suspiciously. Whenever Galen put on that innocuous air and began spouting airy phrases, he knew someone was in trouble. He just didn't intend for it to be any of his family. "You'll buy the painting?"

"I'll offer for Arianne."

12

ARIANNE PUT ANOTHER kettle of water over the small fire in the grate. When it started steaming, she would remove the first pot and refill it. She wasn't at all certain that the small amount of steam generated had a beneficent effect on her mother's breathing, but the physician said it might help.

She turned to make certain her mother was still sleeping and allowed a small sigh of relief to escape. After the long night of listening to her patient gasp for air, she thought never to rest again. Her own chest ached from the struggle. Quietly she slipped from the room.

Lucinda was keeping the boys occupied in the far end of the house, but out here in the hall Arianne could hear their impatient cries and knew they would not be silent much longer. Pushing straying strands of hair back from her face, she wished desperately for a few moments to wash and change and perhaps take a brief nap, but she couldn't allow the boys to wake their mother. They were too young to understand the need for silence, although Davie had looked grave enough earlier when he had asked if their mother was going to die.

The physician had said it was not so serious as that yet, but Mrs. Richards needed time to rid her lungs of congestion. He had been quite adamant about the need for fresh air—and not just for a few days. Whatever few pounds Arianne might have realized from the painting would never have been enough for a lengthy stay anywhere. Her father would just have to be made to see that one of his collection would have to be sacrificed.

But right now she needed to get the boys out of the house. Even as she thought it, Arianne could hear hushed whoops of excitement coming down the corridor. There wasn't time to do anything but head them off and get them down the stairs. Ignoring the wisps of hair falling about her face and throat and the fact that she still wore a plain morning gown with only an apron to adorn it, Arianne hurried in the direction of her energetic brothers.

She stopped short at the sight greeting her on the landing. Lucinda was donning her bonnet and talking excitedly to a tall gentleman in high-crowned hat and morning coat while the boys were eagerly striving for his attention by seeing who could whisper the loudest. Arianne's gaze flew to amused gray eyes, and she felt her stomach lurch unexpectedly. Why on earth was Lord Locke here?

Locke whispered something to Lucinda, who immediately shepherded the boys down the stairs while he remained behind, waiting. Arianne approached him slowly, uncertain of the proper greeting for a gentleman wandering loose in this part of the house without any semblance of decorum. One would think he was part of the family.

"How is she?" Now that they were reasonably alone, Galen lost his air of amusement.

"Sleeping." Exhaustion was responsible for the sudden appearance of tears in her eyes at his tone of concern, and Arianne rolled her hands in her apron and looked away before he could see them. "Where are you taking them?" She nodded in the direction of the departing youngsters.

"Out. Anywhere to let them work off their energies so you may have some peace. I had hoped to take you with us, but I can see it would be better if you took this opportunity to get some rest. Your hair is lovely like that, but something tells me you would not wish to be seen in my company in a public park with it down."

Galen smiled as her hand instantly went to the straying strands. She flushed and tried not to meet his eyes, but there was something compelling about them today. Carefully she felt her way around this unprecedented occurrence. "I can be ready in a few minutes. I would not wish the entire tribe on anyone. Is Melanie with you?"

"No, she isn't, so until we have a chance to talk, perhaps it would be best if you stayed here. I have brought along two grooms and my tiger. Surely we will be men enough to keep three little boys on a leash. I think your sister is old enough to help and not be a hindrance. I am quite capable of returning them if they grow too unruly."

He seemed all that was sincere, and Arianne couldn't help but be grateful for the offer. Her mother might wake at any moment, and it really wouldn't do if there was no one here to tend to her. She just didn't know how to graciously accept such an unexpectedly generous offer. "You are very kind. I don't know what to say . . ." She stumbled uncertainly for the proper words.

Galen caught her hand and bowed over it. "Say nothing now. We must talk later, however. Pencil me into your card, if you will."

She didn't know what to say to that either. Her wits were lacking after a night's unease. She nodded briefly, and that seemed answer enough. Locke smiled and took his leave, and she could hear the yells of the children as they went outside to discover his landau waiting. Arianne remained standing near the landing, wondering if the world had turned upside down during the night.

She was better prepared for him when next he returned. Asking the maid to look in on their patient, Arianne had managed to wash and take a brief nap before changing into her best gown of a soft rose wool. The material was a trifle warm for this time of year, but the fine nap was brushed to a polished sheen and felt good against her skin, and she knew she looked as well in it as any other gown she owned. She didn't stop to question why she would wish to look good for her cousin's suitor. She had every right to respond to this distinctly feminine urge. She wasn't entirely on the shelf yet.

Her mother was still sleeping when the carriage returned, but Arianne was prepared. She sent the children back to the kitchen for the luncheon she had already made for them and steered Lord Locke into the front parlor, where she had tea and a few extra finger sandwiches ready with her own meal.

As Locke discarded his hat and cane on the rack near the door, Arianne forced herself to the easy companionship they had enjoyed these last weeks. "Do you see now why those of your set have governesses and nannies?" She gave his tousled appearance a wry look.

Galen gave a boyishly engaging grin and shook a leaf and some bit of grass from his cuff. "I can see why my valet might insist on it. Perhaps I ought to keep an extra set of clothes here, to be used for just such occasions. It's deuced hard to keep a valet who will remove grass stains."

Arianne bit back a smile as she glanced at the knee of his trousers. Thank heaven he had sensibly chosen a loose, casual pair instead of the knit inexpressibles most gentlemen preferred for their trips to the park. She would hate to have seen what a tumble in the grass would have done to them. "At least they spared you Puddles. Your boots show no sign of scratches."

Galen held out a chair for her and settled easily into the one nearest. "I had forgotten my intentions of abducting your dog. Where is she today? If I do not find a solution soon, I will bring mine over here and leave him. He bit the ankle of my man of business yesterday."

"Puddles has been banished to the kitchen temporarily, where her barks won't disturb my mother. And if you bring your wicked animal here, I shall never forgive you. Worse yet, I might even be tempted to take revenge. I'm certain the boys could think of something devilishly suitable."

"No doubt." The irony in Locke's voice was heavy as he watched her pour the tea. He had to admire the way she had so rapidly recovered her equilibrium after his rash appearance this morning. Although he rather preferred seeing her shining tresses down about her shoulders, he appreciated the effort she had made to brush them into proper order for his return. And the gown she wore becomingly emphasized the flush of rose in her cheeks when she became aware of his scrutiny. As much as Galen adored Melanie, he knew she made no more attempt to please him than she did her brothers. The casualness of their acquaintance had been what appealed to him, but Galen found himself intrigued by the idea of a woman dressing just to please him. "But I would not risk your wrath if it can be avoided. I have already botched one proposal this week. I would rather do this properly."

Arianne's head snapped up at this remark. "What has my wrath to do with your proposal? It is Melanie's wrath you must incur if you go to her again so soon."

Galen lounged back in his chair and sipped his tea while he watched the color fade from her cheeks and the irate sparkle dance in her eye. Perhaps Arianne was the practical cousin, but she was also the more volatile one. She would lead some man a pretty dance. He set the cup on his saucer and donned his most casual pose.

"I said we must talk. I suppose doing so over a pleasant cup of tea rather than a dirty breakfast table is some improvement, but I cannot help but feel it would be better if we met over a dinner for two with bouquets of flowers scattered about. Since the irregularity of such a meeting rules it out, I suppose I must settle for what is allowed. Will you listen without getting angry first?"

"I can think of no reason why I should be angry with you, my lord. You have made my day tremendously easier by your timely appearance. I am more than grateful, as a matter of fact."

"Good. Then we can start by calling me Galen, for I fully intend to call you Arianne from now on." He smiled at the sharp look she sent him. "And you're already angry with me. I am beginning to know you, it seems. I think before the summer is over we should know each other a little better."

Arianne gave him a level stare. "I think you had best speak your mind before I think you have lost it. Has Melanie actually accepted your proposal, then?"

"Don't sound so surprised. Am I truly that reprehensible a suitor?"

Arianne felt her shoulders slump as the tension drained out of them. Perhaps there was a twinge of disappointment at the same time, but she could not imagine why. She lifted her cup and eyed him cautiously. "Certainly not, but to Melanie I had rather thought you earned that position. I hadn't thought she was so capricious."

"She isn't. I have had a long talk with your cousin Evan and I mean to have a brief one with your father, but I shan't make the same mistake as I did with Melanie. I will consult your wishes first."

Arianne's hand froze in midair. "My father? What does my father have to say to anything?"

Galen leaned over and gently removed her cup to the table. "He is the one I must consult if you agree to our betrothal."

Shock paralyzed her. Arianne could plainly see the clarity of his gray eyes as they regarded her with some semblance of patience and kindness. She could see the stiff folds of his gentlemanly cravat, somewhat the worse for wear for his tumble with the boys. She recognized the wealth represented by the tailored coat stretching over his broad shoulders and the gold watch fob across his waistcoat. She just could not fully register the words this godlike creature had just spoken.

"I suppose silence is better than instant rejection," Galen admitted wryly as he waited for some response. His first instinct was to lean back in his chair and cross his leg and wait casually as if he hadn't a concern in the world. But as Evan had so succinctly pointed out, that pose was a cover for his anxiety, and it wouldn't serve him well now. He didn't wish to fail in this endeavor, so he exerted himself to the point of rising from his chair and crossing to Arianne's side of the tea table. That placed him awkwardly hovering over her, and Galen was forced to find another alternative. Bended knee was more than he bargained for, but he managed to crouch at her side as he took her hand. "Will you give me time to explain myself?" he asked quietly.

The touch of his hand jarred Arianne's breath loose, and his position was so absurd that she had to submit to her sense of the ridiculous. Despite Lord Locke's casual elegance, he really was a rather large gentleman, and his nearness upset her equilibrium to no small degree. Cautiously, uncertain of her ability to speak, Arianne answered, "I am certain you have a good explanation, but I would prefer you give it from somewhere else other than the floor, if you would."

Galen grinned and removed a cat from beneath her chair before standing up. "The floor gives one a new perspective on life. I think I shall try it more often, but only if you care to join me. I was never allowed to romp about the floors when I was a lad, you know. And I would never have found cats under the furniture if I had."

As the cat in question stretched and butted his head against Galen's chin when he sat down, then curled up and returned to snoring in his lap, it was hard to believe his claim. Lord Locke appeared perfectly at home with the animal. Arianne couldn't imagine another gentleman who would be the same. Guiltily she remembered Rhys, but she knew so little of him that she could not imagine his reaction to a cat in his lap. Or perhaps she could. he would no doubt not notice the creature at all.

"I cannot feature a boy who does not spend at least half his time crawling about the floors. You must have been an exceptional child. But if you feel your childhood has been neglected, you are welcome to crawl about our floors as you like. I will hand you a polishing cloth while you are down there."

Galen scratched the cat behind its ears and felt more than heard the vibrations of its purrs. He was beginning to enjoy this inane conversation, but he didn't think he could keep it at this level for long. He had to make his proposal and he had to make it convincing. He had never made any real attempt at being serious before. Miss Arianne Richards was bringing out any number of new talents in him.

"I did not mean to startle you earlier, but I am still new at this business of proposing. I know you warned me that I should be using roses and kisses, and probably moonlight, but that did not seem quite the thing after what you overheard the other day. Besides, I am well aware that you do not look at me through romantic eyes. I would make a cake of myself in truth if I came to you with bouquets and candy. So, clever person that I am, I thought I would relieve you of the responsibility of your siblings for a few hours to impress you with my dedication."

Arianne could not help but smile at this ingenuous admission. She didn't dare believe a word of it, but he had succeeded in diverting her dismal thoughts for a while. And despite his wealth and elegance, Galen Locke did appear quite at home in their dull little parlor with a cat ensconced comfortably on his lap. "You have successfully impressed me beyond your wildest dreams, my lord. I cannot think of another gentleman willing to shoulder such a burden, including my own father. He tolerates the boys well one at a time, but all at once is more than he can quite deal with."

Thinking of Ross Richards' absentminded view of the world, Galen could very well understand that. He would no doubt misplace the youngest and allow the others to dismantle whatever room they were in before he noticed the destruction. Quite pleased with his success in that direction, he dared continue. "There, you see, I have something to recommend me besides the elegance of my clothes. Would I not make an exceptional husband?"

"Undoubtedly. You need only ask every woman in

London to find yourself a harem. Only Melanie is willful enough to turn down a suit such as yours, and I expect she'll come around soon enough. She's the baby of the family, you know, and she's still a little young to know her mind."

That wasn't the direction he intended, and Galen made a wry face. "You are determined to lead me astray, aren't you? I cannot say I blame you, for I find it deuced awkward to explain myself, but I had better try to make myself clear. I care not a fig for all the other women of London. I have amused myself among them for some years now, and there's not one of them I would care to meet across the breakfast table for the rest of my life. I will admit that Melanie amuses me enormously, and I had thought we should suit, but she does not agree. I am near six-and-twenty and have not been ready to take a wife until now; I can't see why a woman should be any more ready than I at only eighteen. If Melanie is as much like me as I assume, she may not be ready to settle down for years. Perhaps you are not either, but I think you are more mature than Melanie, and you are better able to see the opportunities I can provide. And I have already had a glimpse of you over the breakfast table, and would certainly not object to many more."

"Glimpses?" Arianne raised her eyebrows, still unable to take him seriously. "If we limit ourselves to glimpses over the breakfast table, we should go on famously, I daresay. I could tolerate Satan himself for all that mattered. Do be serious, my lord, and tell me why you really came."

Exasperated, Galen flung the cat to the floor and crossed the room to pull Arianne from her chair. "My name is Galen, and I have come to ask you to marry me. A long betrothal is agreeable, if you will. May I kiss you now to prove my sincerity, or must I wait until you give me your answer?"

The front door thumped as someone entered, and Arianne didn't have time to remove her hands from Galen's before her father ambled into the room. He fumbled for his spectacles as he discovered the two of them together in the dimly lit chamber, and coughed to clear his throat before speaking.

"Thought that was your equipment out there, Locke. Come to speak to my daughter, have you? Have you determined your price for the Titian? I'm willing to be fair with you."

"The Titian?" Arianne tried to tug away, but Galen held her firmly. She looked from her father to the enormous oil filling the far wall of the parlor, then back to Galen. Of all his paintings, the Titian was the last she would expect her father to sell.

Her aghast stare stirred Locke into action. "I have not had Arianne's answer yet. I think, perhaps, it would be best if we all gave ourselves time to think about this. I would suggest a brief sojourn to my father's estate, won't you agree?" This question was addressed to the man in the doorway, for Arianne didn't seem prepared to comprehend the question, much less the answer.

"Couldn't let Arianne go without the proper chaperone, but a small visit might be of advantage," Richards agreed vaguely. "Your parents will no doubt wish to meet the girl you mean to affiance. Yes, I can see that might be best. Don't want any more of these affairs like my sister's. I'll not see my daughter hurt."

"Papa!" Arianne gave a plea for time to think, but she could see the men were involved in some battle of wills that did not concern her. Galen squeezed her fingers reassuringly, but she wasn't reassured. She finally pried herself loose to face her father. He was not a man to talk directly to the point at the best of times, but surely she could not misunderstand what he was saying now.

Galen returned his gaze to her. "My father's estate is not far from Bath. Part of the land includes a spectacular piece of coast. We also have a town house in Bath. Your mother might choose whether she prefers sea air or the waters. I know I am asking an enormous amount from you. My parents are not easy people to know, but I would have them accept you into the family. If you still feel we will not suit, we can call it off before any public announcement is made. Am I not being reasonable this time?"

"Reasonable?" She stared at him with a mixture of rage and astonishment. "I see not one jot of reason in any of this. You have both gone quite mad." Arianne's eyes widened as both men continued to stare at her without comment. It struck her then what they had done, although she could not discover the rhyme or reason behind Locke's part in this. Somehow, they placed her in the same position as her father. If he must sacrifice his painting, could she sacrifice just a small part of her pride to play the part of Locke's intended for a month or so under the most pleasant of conditions? She knew they were asking no more than that. She was not meant to be the wife of a nobleman. But the pretense would give her mother a comfortable rest in the country for a time long enough to recover.

It would be unreasonable of her to refuse. Wondering how she would ever explain this to Melanie and Rhys, Arianne sadly lifted her eyes to her father's and nodded. "I will do as you wish."

13

AT ARIANNE'S INSISTENCE, Melanie was included in the large party traveling by coach, carriage, and wagon on the way toward Bath. Evan contributed his traveling coach for the comfort of Mrs. Richards, Arianne, Melanie, and Lucinda. Galen's landau suffered under the bouncing of three young boys and the Richardses' lone maid, Meg. A hired wagon carried a large quantity of luggage and two small, hairy dogs which alternately snarled and sniffed at one another, and a further, smaller carriage was engaged to carry various other maids, valets, and pets. Galen and Mr. Richards sensibly chose to ride alongside the entourage.

Arianne hid her agitation at her mother's awed acceptance of her daughter's eligible suitor. The invalid's coughing spell had passed after a heavy rain, and she was up and about again, but her pale face had gained a new radiance with every mile they traveled into the country. It was enough to keep Arianne silent, even beyond Melanie's questioning looks.

Melanie's genial acceptance of her cousin's prospective betrothal to her own suitor caused Arianne even more concern. She had tried to explain that Locke and her father were simply upholding their equal prides by this foolish arrangement, but Melanie seemed more interested in returning to an area considerably closer to Rhys's home than London. But whenever Melanie tried to show her concern for Arianne's unusually impetuous decision, Arianne changed the subject. Her own feelings didn't matter if she could return her mother's health.

Arianne's feelings were so confused that she couldn't have explained them to anyone else in any event. In her secret dreams alone at night in her room, she had dared to create marvelous fantasies of a romantic suitor appearing on the doorstep and carrying her away, but her practical nature had known these were no more than dreams. Impoverished gentility did not find places among the *haut ton*, as romantic novels would lead one to believe. Nor was there much likelihood of finding a romantic suitor among the prosaic merchants of London, even if she had any connection among them, which she didn't. The fact that Rhys had taken his time to say farewell to her did not mean anything, and Arianne was wise enough to believe he felt she was in the same position as he, therefore they might suit. There was nothing romantic about two such practical natures agreeing to go through life together, should it come to that.

That she and Rhys might come to some agreement had seemed dream enough to Arianne. She had feared to go through life a lonely spinster, caring for her brothers and living as an outsider in their families as they grew older and married. Rhys had provided food for dreams enough. He was an intelligent, ambitious man, and she would work diligently by his side to help him achieve what he had been denied. Love would undoubtedly follow, if such an emotion existed.

But to suddenly find Lord Locke riding beside the carriage, occasionally leaning in to see how she fared, solicitously leading her into roadside inns and seeing that she had the best tables, the finest rooms—that was a dream she was incapable of comprehending. There had been little time to have a serious discussion with him. Events had moved much too swiftly. But surely he must know the degree to which he was obligating himself in making this incredible proposal. On the face of it, it was incredibly romantic to be swept off her feet by a wealthy, handsome nobleman, but underneath the image they painted for others was the knowledge that neither of them knew anything about the other, and certainly never shared their most intimate emotions.

So Arianne was forced to calmly accept Galen's generous attentions and wait for the moment when she could interrogate him thoroughly on how he planned to extricate them from this delicate situation. Perhaps his parents were so high in the instep that they would forbid the marriage. Perhaps he was hoping to make Melanie jealous enough to declare her love. And barring either of those events, perhaps he thought settling for Melanie's cousin was second best. It was the latter that kept her most worried. She didn't wish to be Melanie's replacement. She didn't wish to spend a lifetime with a husband who wistfully followed her cousin's every movement. But if his offer were genuine, how could she possibly turn down something that would mean so much to her family and give her the chance for a life she would never have otherwise known?

The idea of actually marrying Lord Locke and living in his home and bearing his children was too far beyond the realms of what Arianne knew to even consider. He was charming and handsome, but he was also idle and inclined to boredom. In the world that Arianne knew, there was too much to do to be bored. They had no common ground whatsoever. It would be much better should Rhys return to rescue her from this situation.

When they finally arrived at the immense rambling manor house that Galen called home, Arianne had grown numb to the game they played. She sat in stunned silence as the rows of trees along the splendid drive unfolded to reveal the golden stones and hundreds of sparkling windows of a place so large it could have neatly housed an entire London block. The manor was too unreal to figure any more seriously in her mind than anything else that had occurred these last days.

So when Galen gallantly tucked her arm inside his and led her up the wide stone steps to the towering front doors, Arianne merely tried to picture which character in Shakespeare's plays she most resembled. She favored the farces, but the situation did not quite suit any of the plays she knew. They were creating a new one, writing it as they acted it out. None of this had anything to do with reality.

They were obviously expected, much to Arianne's relief. The butler and head housekeeper appeared like royalty to preside over the dissemination of passengers and luggage, directing an army of maids and footmen to the upper portions of the house, and in the case of the dogs and cats, to the stables. Arianne found herself separated from the remainder of her family and ensconced in a room—a virtual palace—of her own, which she vehemently rejected in favor of sharing a more modest boudoir with Melanie. The housekeeper looked suitably enraged, but Arianne had no intention of succumbing to awe. Let them call her common, for she was. She simply did not intend to spend her time isolated in grandeur.

Melanie welcomed the suggestion gladly, but earned the housekeeper's disfavor even more when she insisted that she would share her maid with her cousin rather than introducing one of the earl's servants to the position. Since Melanie was granddaughter of an earl and sister to a viscount, the housekeeper couldn't make mutterings that "ladies certainly knew better," and, frustrated, the servant carried her indignation out of the room with her. Melanie and Arianne broke into elated laughter behind her as the door closed.

The laughter helped. Surrounded by a room larger than half the first floor of the Richards' house, expected to lie in a bed with opulent draperies that might have graced the beds of queens, talking in hushed whispers for fear the foolishness of her conversation would be overheard by silent servants swooping in and out with baths and water and luggage, Arianne needed to cling to some sense of the humor of the situation. She had all of four decent gowns to wear interchangeably over the coming weeks. She really could not pretend she was anything but what she was.

After changing and resting from the journey, Galen sent a message asking if they would care to walk through the gardens before it was time to prepare for dinner. Perhaps with the intention of leaving the love-birds alone, Melanie declared she wanted nothing more strenuous than a trip to the library, but she gaily accompanied Arianne downstairs to hand her over to Galen. Glaring darkly after her cousin for this defection, Arianne reluctantly accepted Locke's hand and allowed him to escort her toward the terrace.

"Does your room suit?" he inquired politely as he held open the glass door opening out onto the terrace, and from there, the gardens.

"Were I Princess Charlotte, perhaps. I would not dare sleep in such a bed myself. Rather than sleep on the floor, I asked to be put in with Melanie."

Galen gave her a sharp look from beneath lifted eyebrows. "Do I detect a hint of irony?" She turned her calm gaze to him, and he found the hidden laughter in her eyes. "You can be quite impossible, you realize. How am I to know when you are laughing and when you are being critical?"

"You seem to do very well," Arianne admitted, not at all certain that she liked the idea of him knowing her so well. "I had thought I would be at my most annoying, to put you off this ridiculous betrothal forever."

Galen gave a bark of laughter and pulled her around to face him. His hands held her elbows firmly so she could not break away. He could read consternation on her wide brow, but dancing lights of mischief hid somewhere in the depth of her indigo eyes. There would be time to discover what made them dance openly. "I had chosen that suite just for you. It seems there is much I have to learn. Should I have chosen the monk's cell?"

No wonder the housekeeper had sniffed with disapproval. An intended bride should not reject her suitor's offering so openly. A small smile slipped unwillingly across Arianne's lips as she imagined the woman's consternation. "My first day here, and I have already offended you and the estimable staff. My apologies, sir. And no, a monk's cell is not necessary. I am quite content as I am."

"Why do I have the lowering feeling there is more behind those words than your satisfaction with your room?" Galen released her so they might continue walking more sedately down the path. It would not do to rush things at this point.

"Perhaps because you are finally listening to the voice of reason I know you must conceal in your head. I don't know why you have manipulated this mad affair, but surely you must be beginning to realize how it must look to the rest of the world."

Galen dipped his head to gaze upon her with amusement. "And how must it look? That I have been far beyond impetuous and rash this time? Is that how it appears to you?"

"Quite frankly, yes. You are a baron in your own right. You are heir to all this." Arianne swung her hand to encompass the magnificent house and grounds. "You are handsome and witty and all that any lady might wish. You could have your choice of wives. There is no sane reason to declare yourself to someone who cannot offer you anything in return, other than your apparent determination to have your own way in the matter of my mother's health."

Galen caught his lips from turning upward and forced himself to look away from her stern expression. "Handsome? Surely not. I do not have the dark good looks that make the ladies swoon. All I have is this deuced amusing face no one takes seriously. And you must admit that I am awkwardly large. I am forever dancing on the ladies' dresses, although why they insist on wearing them to dust the floor is beyond my comprehension."

Arianne gave him a look of frustration. "That is not to the point. They say looks are in the eye of the beholder, anyway. If the matter worries you, then let us say no one will call you hard to look upon. The point is that you can do far better than a penniless spinster. So this elaborate charade is merely a devious and very dangerous scheme to bring my mother here. I could very well hold you to your offer; then what would you do?"

He shrugged nonchalantly. "Marry you, of course. Is that not what I asked you to do? If I have all to offer that you say, it cannot be a horrible fate, can it?"

Clenching her fists with exasperation, Arianne swung around to stop him where he stood. "Will you stop that? I am trying to be practical. You must know how this looks. I cannot even come down to dinner without shaming you for my lack of wardrobe. Your parents will think you are being blackmailed or worse to lower yourself to such an unsuitable choice. Do you have some mad notion that they will attempt to buy me off? That's it, isn't it? You mean to make up the loss of my painting by having your parents pay to rid you of me. Perhaps there will be some folderol with the Titian too, bringing twice its worth or some such nonsense. I cannot like it, Galen. We are not some amusing charity to be played with like cards."

Irritation twitched briefly across Locke's face, then was gone as he offered the languid smile for which he was famous. "Ahh, I have persuaded you at last that I have a name. We are making progress. What will it take to convince you that my offer is serious? Do you really think me so low in character as to play with your feelings?"

"That is just the point," Arianne replied triumphantly. "I do not know you well enough to know what you would do. How can one make a decision so enormous as the one to marry when we do not even know each other?"

"But that is why we are here, my dear, to learn to know each other. I have become certain you are the part of me that has been missing, and I mean to convince you of the same. You will temper my rashness, balance my lack of responsibility, and be the anchor to keep me from dashing myself on the rocks. I have thought on what Melanie said, and she is quite right. We are much too alike to suit."

Arianne surrendered the senseless argument. He was not about to admit his true reason for creating this elaborate charade. "Melanie is a romantic. She is looking for true love. I am surprised, if you are so much alike, that you do not do the same."

Galen frowned thoughtfully as he turned her to continue their walk. "I rather thought respect and friendship would lead to what the world calls love."

"Perhaps so, but I cannot help but look on what my mother and father have and wonder if there is not some deeper binding. They cannot be more unalike, yet they understand each other very well, and the affection between them is so deep that the other can do no wrong, no matter how wrong they might be in truth."

"That sounds more like an affliction than a blessing," Galen answered crossly. "Should I be so blind as to think your stubbornness is charming, you have my permission to kick me back to my senses."

Arianne's peal of laughter startled him, and Galen began to grin at the infectiousness of the sound. Before it occurred to him that this would be the perfect time to steal that kiss he had promised himself, a screech from down the path interrupted, and a hairy body hurtling between their legs prevented further pursuit of romantic notions.

"Puddles!" Arianne identified the culprit at once, then swung to watch Davie flying down the path toward them. "What on earth is going on?" she cried as her brother attempted to cross the rose garden to intercept the dog.

Galen gave a sharp whistle, bringing the racing animal to a halt to investigate the sound. While Arianne extricated her brother from the roses, the mischievous dog sniffed the air and came trotting to better examine the shiny black boots with the interesting scent. Before the animal could leap to leave scratchy reminders of her exuberance on the leather, Galen caught her leash and picked her up.

"Thank you, m'lord," Davie breathed in relief as he shook off his sister's restraining hand and reached for the unrepentant animal. "She ain't never been in the country before."

"And neither have you, I would say." Galen eyed

the boy's crumpled coat, calculating it was his best one. "I don't recommend coats in the rose garden. Mothers tend to faint at the thought. Deliver Puddles back to the stables and run up to your room. I'll meet you there shortly and we'll see if we can't find something more suitable for you to wear. I'm quite certain nothing in this house has ever been thrown out, so there's bound to be some of my old togs hereabouts."

Davie grinned in understanding and ran off with the dog in tow. Arianne shook her head, but whether in exasperation with little brothers or in wonder at the idle lord's instant reparation of the situation, she couldn't say. When she lifted her gaze to his, Galen grinned unabashedly.

"I've already located the key to your heart. You don't stand a chance, my lady. Shall we return and prepare ourselves for dinner? My noble parents have agreed to meet all of you in the first salon beforehand. It seemed simpler to wait until then, if you don't mind."

"As if anything I thought had aught to do with anything," Arianne sighed, taking his offered arm. "I really do believe I am superfluous to whatever is going on, so I shall just follow your lead, if you don't mind."

Her mockery kept him grinning the rest of the way into the house.

14

ARIANNE TOOK ONE last look in the mirror, stuck out her tongue at the image, and swung back to face the room. Even sporting a lovely Kasmir shawl from Melanie's wardrobe, with her hair dressed becomingly by Melanie's maid, Arianne could not disguise the fact that she was wearing a dinner gown whose age was revealed by its design if not by the well-worn hem. Only the puffed sleeves and the low décolletage gave evidence that the gown was any different from her others.

Melanie nodded approvingly at the result. The gown's deep blue almost exactly matched the color of her cousin's eyes. Never having seen Arianne in anything but her high-necked muslins and wools before, she had to admire the effect of the blue against skin the hue of rich cream. Arianne's height gave natural grace to the classic lines of the gown, and although her build was not of the fragile delicacy fashion preferred, Melanie didn't think Galen would object. She smiled as Arianne attempted to adjust the neckline of her gown upward.

"Don't you dare! Galen will not be able to tear his eyes away. All it requires is a small rope of pearls. Elsie, fetch my pearls, please."

Arianne started to protest, but the militant gleam in Melanie's eyes deterred her. Whatever was going on here, it was becoming obvious that she was to be the innocent lamb led to slaughter. She allowed the pearls to be placed around her throat and adjusted her elbow-length gloves nervously. She had never been introduced to an earl before. Even Melanie's grandfather was some invisible spider living in the hidden depths of Somerset, never to be seen but whose edicts were always obeyed.

"There, you shall be all that you ought. Even Deward cannot complain of your noble grace. We can only hope that Uncle Ross won't begin pricing the artwork until after dinner."

Melanie's casual sprinkling of the earl's title into the conversation didn't ease Arianne's tension. It was all very well to gad about town with a gentleman who had nothing better to do than visit Christie's and artists, but it was quite another to act his intended before the Earl and Countess of Deward, his parents. Closing her eyes, she swayed slightly and wondered if she ought to make her excuses. Arianne couldn't think of any enormous enough to free her from weeks of this.

"Off we go. It won't do to keep them waiting. Can you not imagine what the topic of conversation must be with Uncle Ross and Galen in the same room? I'm certain the earl will be thoroughly relieved to have someone sensible to talk to."

Arianne doubted that very much, almost as much as she doubted that she would be able to produce a single intelligible word. Gathering the shawl around her as a shield, she obediently trailed in her cousin's exuberant path.

Galen instantly came forward upon their entrance, taking Arianne's hand and drawing it through the crook of his arm, offering his other arm to Melanie. Arianne drew strength from this contact, clenching her fingers to his coat sleeve as she was led toward the far end of the room, where the earl and countess awaited.

They were older than she had expected. Galen was not so very much older than she, but his parents were considerably older than hers. The earl's autocratic posture as he stood behind his wife's chair was straight and strong, but his hair was white and the lines on his face were enhanced by his stern frown. The countess was of a more petite stature, her expression slightly more welcoming despite the frosty coolness of eyes the color of Galen's. The diamonds about her throat sparkled in the lamplight, creating a regal setting for the simple coif of her graying hair.

"Miss Richards, how pleasant to meet you at last," she murmured after Galen's introductions. "You must tell us all about yourself at dinner. We have despaired of our son ever settling down to his responsibilities."

"So have I," Arianne murmured wickedly under her breath as Galen led her away. She knew he had heard her from the quick look he bestowed upon her, but they were already in the presence of her parents, and he could not make a suitable reply.

Her mother looked immensely restored by her nap, and Arianne was forced to regret her waspish words. Whatever Galen was doing, he had her mother's best interests at heart. She shouldn't discount his actions so rapidly.

"There you are, Arianne. I was just telling Locke that his father's collection is in need of immediate repairs. Some of those oils must have hung there a hundred years without being touched. Won't do at all, you know."

Arianne sent Galen a despairing look, but it was Melanie who laughed and took her uncle's arm. "Uncle Ross, you cannot talk business so early in the evening. We must be gay and carefree, is that not so, Lord Deward?"

The older man had relaxed his military bearing enough to pour himself another drink, but he regarded this inanity with a loud "humph" and a look of irritation for Melanie's forwardness. "Don't see why we should if we don't want."

Galen chuckled. No one had ever responded to Melanie's cheerful forthrightness with such dampening effect. "I believe, Father, you have found the cold water that dashes Lady Melanie's effervescence. Would you care to seek the fire that defrosts Miss Richards' icy practicality?"

The earl gave his outrageous son a glare from beneath one bushy eyebrow as he swirled his brandy. "I daresay you've done that already. I prefer the lady as she is, thank you. Never was one for dithering females."

Arianne nearly swallowed her tongue at this remark, but the countess neatly interfered before a reply was necessary. "I'm certain Miss Richards is all that she should be, dear. I believe I hear Dodson approaching to call us for dinner. Must you drink hard liquor before your meal, Ogden?"

By the end of that nerve-racking dinner, Arianne felt she must either have a collapse of the nerves or a bout of hysteria. Lord Deward griped or made pointed remarks when he was not silent. Lady Deward deftly shielded his targets and turned the conversation to more general topics. Ross Richards turned general conversation to art. Anne Richards wrenched art from his grip and praised the flourishing countryside. Galen adroitly embellished whichever topic came into the open, drawing Arianne along with him. Melanie limited herself to watching with amusement and speaking only when spoken to. Arianne had a wild desire for Rhys to complete this eccentric table, and wondered at her ability to think at all.

Not until the ladies withdrew to the salon, leaving the gentlemen to their drinks and cigars, did any sense come from the meeting at all. Lady Deward immediately set about the inquisition she had promised earlier, although with such polite delicacy that Arianne felt she was being picked apart with tiny tweezers and placed in bits of cotton to be studied at leisure.

"Galen never showed a partiality for any one lady before," the countess announced toward the end of this interrogation. "I have wondered that he has not done so. We are well-acquainted with Lady Melanie and her brothers"—she nodded in her subject's direction—"and thought for a time there might be some interest in that direction. But she is of much too lively a spirit for this household, I can see now, my dear."

Melanie pulled an irreverent face. "You mean I am much too young, my lady. That is not so, but I shan't argue over Arianne's superior qualities. I daresay she is wholly responsible for my brothers not having hanged me yet."

Arianne had to smile at the mild shock on the countess's face, but her mother stepped in to alleviate her niece's rashness.

"Melanie has a blithe spirit that lights even the dimmest of rooms. She is a pleasure to have around. But even knowing I sound immodest in praising my own daughter, Arianne is a treasure I will have difficulty doing without. It is not surprising that Lord Locke has the presence of mind to recognize her quality. I understand he is much like my husband in his appreciation for the finer things of life."

"Indeed." The countess would undoubtedly have said more, but the men chose that moment to return, and her attention at once turned to her irascible husband, who seemed to be berating their son for some imagined transgression.

"Ogden, you do go on. We will not see Galen for another year if you continue so."

Galen made a formal bow over his mother's hand. "Do not fret, *ma mère*, we only argue to show our affection. Would you have us otherwise?"

"Yes, I would," she replied tartly, indicating he take the chair nearest her. "I am perfectly aware that you behave like a simpleton just to annoy your father. And he puts on his worst cross-bear pride when you are around." She threw her frowning husband an apologetic look. "You know I am right, Ogden. I have watched the two of you behave like sapwits long enough, and I am grown too old to watch it silently any longer. Our son is about to take a bride and have a family of his own. Unless you wish to lose him entirely, it is time to mend the bridges."

"Can't lose what ain't there," the earl growled. "Not seen the pup since this time last year."

"I say, my lord, is this not a Reynolds?" Ross Richards turned at the silence greeting his question. Absently noting the tight expression of his host, he shrugged. "Pardon me, but your son is quite an expert on these things. His collection is becoming well-known."

Smiling fondly at the eccentric but effective tactics of Arianne's father, Galen addressed his elders. "I thank you for your recommendation, sir. Mr. Richards is known for his discerning eye, Father. I know you have occasionally wondered about that landscape over the sideboard. Perhaps we should allow him to examine it."

Since the only times the earl had wondered about the landscape were when he was cursing its deplorable existence, the countess winced inwardly, but the men drifted into a discussion of the difficulty of pricing artwork, and that particular argument was diverted. From the sounds of the discussion under way, a new one would undoubtedly come along. Shaking her head, Lady Deward turned to her son's betrothed.

"I shall have it on your shoulders, Miss Richards, to see that my son spends more time here in his home. It is time he began taking responsibility for what he will someday inherit."

Dismay merged with dread as Arianne looked from the countess's lined and sincere face to Galen's absorbed discussion in the far corner of the room and around to the grandeur of this enormous hall. This wasn't real, she reminded herself, but it felt very much like a trap closing around her.

"The Llewellyn estate is not far north of here. You must persuade Galen to take us there." Melanie excitedly bounced upon the bed when they were alone later that night. "I found a map and the directions in the library. It would make a lovely day trip. You can tell him you have an urge to see the mountains of Wales. He won't say no to you."

Arianne groaned and buried her head in the pillow. "He most certainly will say no to me. He's very good at ignoring anything I say. And what do you intend to do, waltz up to the gates and smile at the gate-keeper and ask if he knows who is the true heir to the title?"

Melanie flung a pillow at her. "I am not so simple-minded. There must be a village there. People love to gossip. Perhaps Rhys's mother's family lives near there. They are bound to have opinions on the subject."

"Melanie, you are a goose! If anyone knew anything at all, they would have said so by now. And don't you think Rhys has already questioned everyone extensively? How can you think you will do better with strangers than he does with his own family?"

"Perhaps he is overlooking the obvious," Melanie replied stubbornly. "Sometimes someone from outside can see much more clearly than those directly involved. We have to do something."

"If I could do anything at all, I wouldn't be here," Arianne muttered into the feathers of her pillow, but her cousin was busily describing how she would go about winning Rhys's fortune and didn't hear a word.

Surprisingly, Galen agreed to the expedition when approached the next day. "I will send for Gordon. He works too hard and deserves a day of rest. We can take Lucinda too, and make a party of it. If I remember correctly, there is an excellent tearoom there, and some ruins nearby we can explore. We need only keep Melanie bound and gagged, and it should be an excellent outing."

Arianne laughed at Melanie's strangled look, but Galen was quite correct. With her brother along, Melanie could not be too outrageous. They might not discover anything, but it would serve to ease some of the tensions that seemed to be pulling at them. Although everyone was pleasant to each other, there were too many undercurrents tugging away at the foundations of the friendships they had formed. Arianne didn't dare confess she had been coerced into this betrothal, nor did she wish to refine upon Rhy's last visit to her. Galen was being closemouthed about his reasons for constructing this betrothal so soon after his proposal to Melanie. Melanie was saying nothing about her feelings toward either gentleman or why she was so determined to discover Rhys's origins. Talking around these topics had a decided wearing effect.

The party set out merrily the day after Gordon, Viscount Griffin, arrived. Arianne thought Gordon the more dignified of Melanie's twin brothers, but on this outing he had obviously abandoned the daily concerns of his estates in favor of enjoying himself. Since Arianne and Lucinda could not ride, an open landau had been provided for their convenience, and Melanie chose to ride with them. Galen and Gordon tested the mettle of each other's mounts by racing far ahead of the carriage, then returning in a swirl of dust, to the protests of their ladies.

The spectacular countryside begged to be explored, but Melanie was insistent on not stopping until they reached their destination. Lucinda cried out in joy at the sighting of each new bird and flower, until she had the men searching the hedgerows for new forms of wildlife with which to surprise her as the carriage sedately traveled the narrow back roads. All but Lucinda erupted in laughter when Gordon located a toad and carried it back in his closed fist for Lucinda's approval, only to have the creature leap for her new straw hat. Her shrieks and the wild scramble to locate the terrified toad kept everyone laughing well into the village at the base of the mountain that was Rhys's home.

They were not yet in Wales, but the backdrop of the mountains in the distance provided as Welsh a setting as the ladies could desire. Arianne stayed seated, staring up into the distant hills with enchantment until Galen came to take her down.

"Should I be jealous of your fascination with Llewellyn's home?" he murmured as he indecorously lifted her from the landau by the simple expedient of wrapping his large hands around her waist.

Arianne rested her hands on his shoulders as he swung her to the ground. Slightly breathless from the encounter, she stood like that a moment longer once her feet touched ground, the mountains forgotten as she gazed up into Galen's silvered eyes. Then, remembering his question, she tried to extricate herself gracefully as she sought some sensible answer.

"I cannot envision you as a jealous man, my lord, but if you are often jealous of landscapes, then you have much to fear, for I have a passion for nature."

Galen allowed his hands to linger a moment longer on her slim waist, liking the way her head came up above his shoulder, liking the way she met his eyes. Actually, he liked the hint of a smile playing at her lips as she spoke, the sound of her voice as the words wrapped around him, and the tinge of humor hiding behind her perfectly correct phrases. Anyone not listening closely might miss the slight challenge in her voice, but Galen was beginning to understand that behind Miss Arianne Richards' serene exterior lurked a rich and exciting mind. He was beginning to wonder just how much more was hidden behind her dowdy plumage as he watched the color rise to her cheeks.

"A passion for nature, you say?" Reluctantly he removed his hands from their dangerous position, but his gaze never left her face. "We might have more than a few interests in common, then, Miss Richards. Shall we explore them together?"

From the low timbre of his voice, Arianne surmised he was not precisely talking about flowers and trees. Birds and bees were much more likely, and she flushed an even deeper rose at the thought. Carefully taking his arm and stepping in the direction of the others, she attempted to steer the conversation into more neutral waters. "It seems we will have some weeks in which to entertain ourselves. I'm certain we will discover all manner of interests in common. But then, the same can be said for Melanie and Lucinda."

"Melanie and Lucinda may discover all the common interests they like; it is your interests that interest me. I would explore your passion for nature more fully. Shall we let the others take tea while we walk toward the mountains?"

Arianne understood that Galen was playing the part of London rake for her benefit. His voice had just the right seductive tenor to send shivers down her spine,

making her entirely too aware of his masculine size
and strength. Her gaze dipped to the leather of his
high riding boots and attempted to stay there rather
than wander back to the disturbing gold of his hair or
the dancing silver of his eyes. But it was impossible
to keep looking down when his very nearness demanded that she face him. With a sigh of exasperation
at her inability to meet this man on the simplest of
terms, she looked up again.

"I would suggest it would be better to let the others
walk to the mountains while we take tea." She nodded
toward Lucinda and Melanie, who were unabashedly
darting from sight to sight, exclaiming over a rose-
trellised wall, chattering over the age of an old stone
church with its Gothic steeple, and debating the relative merits of the various tea-shop signs seen up the
steep hill into town.

"Gordon has them well in hand; they may do as
they like. I would rather spend these few minutes with
you. Courting is deuced awkward when constantly surrounded by friends and family."

"Is that what we are doing? Courting? I had fancied
that was what you and Melanie were doing when you
were going about to the park and meeting each other
at dinners and dances. Have you decided that routine
was not highly successful?"

"I have decided that I will most likely have to wring
your neck before I can make you forget that damnable
proposal." Galen looked up in time to note that Gordon had stopped at a shop window with Lucinda, leaving Melanie momentarily free to interrogate one of
the villagers coming down the street. He grimaced and
began walking quickly in that direction, thankful that
he did not need to adjust his stride greatly to Arianne's as she hurried to keep up with him.

Melanie saw them coming. Waving a farewell to the
woman, she turned to greet them excitedly. "Lord
Llewellyn is in residence. Did you not say you know
the man, Galen? Should we not call and give our respects before we leave?"

"We most certainly should not. I barely know the

man, and I certainly wouldn't saddle him with a wigeon like you. Come along, then, and I will show you the tea shop. Perhaps, if there is time, we can go further up the mountain to those ruins I spoke of."

"Galen, you are in danger of becoming toplofty. I never would have thought it of you." Huffily Melanie disengaged her hand from his arm and sauntered toward her brother.

Gordon sent Galen a sympathetic grin and captured his sister's arm. "After an insult like that, I should call her out myself. Shall I arrange seconds?"

"Oh, do be sensible." Lifting her skirts from the dust of the street, Melanie hurried up the step of the shop Galen had indicated, ungallantly leaving the others behind.

Melanie's shriek of joy once inside brought Arianne's suspicious gaze back to her escort and her cousin. The exchange of glances between the two men confirmed her suspicions, and giving them both a fulminating look, she lifted her own skirts and ran after Melanie.

15

"RHYS! RHYS, IT IS YOU! I cannot believe it." Melanie would have thrown herself into his arms, but the man coming to his feet in the small tearoom caught her by the shoulders and held her, looking to the others entering through the door.

Arianne thought he looked somewhat dazed by his reception. He sent a nervous glance toward Gordon, nodded a greeting at Galen, and gently released Melanie into her brother's care as he turned to acknowledge Arianne. Lucinda immediately stepped to her sister's side, and the introduction eased the awkwardness momentarily.

"You knew where he was all along, didn't you?" Melanie turned accusing eyes from her brother to Galen, both of whom made little attempt to deny her. "You should be ashamed of yourselves, letting me fret and worry like that."

Rhys's dark gaze returned to Melanie's soft, blond, and very irate figure. Shorter and stockier than the other men, he still stood a head taller than Melanie, and his look was stern as he pulled out a chair and pushed her into it. "Behave yourself." He spoke softly, but his words were curt and decisive.

Melanie instantly obeyed, though she sent Rhys a flashing look that warned him explanations had better be forthcoming.

"It is good to see you again, Mr. Llewellyn," Arianne murmured as he pulled out a chair for her. The last night they had seen each other came between them, and she quickly looked away from his questioning gaze. She felt rather than saw Galen's brief frown as he noted this interchange, but he merely drew out the chair beside her and claimed his place.

"I do not know whether to be honored or peeved with this reception." Rhys cautiously took a chair beside Lucinda while Gordon ordered tea and sandwiches. "I had not expected so much interest in my activities."

"That is because you are a fool, Rhys Llewellyn," Melanie glared at her brother as Gordon lowered himself to the seat she had left vacant beside her, venting her ill humor on him as well as on Rhys.

This was not at all like Melanie, and Arianne raised her eyebrows slightly, turning to see how Rhys took this slander. Rhys had a thunderous expression upon his face as he glared back at Melanie, and Arianne had the astonishing feeling that these two scarely knew the rest of them were present. She glanced at Galen for confirmation of these feelings, but he had a thoughtful frown upon his brow and did not notice. She didn't know why she had turned to him in the first place. It struck her as an odd thing to do when she had both Melanie and Lucinda near. They were both much closer to her than Lord Locke.

"The ladies had some foolish fear for your safety, Llewellyn. They could not believe any man capable of looking after himself without their help. Perhaps they will rest easier now that they see you have survived their absence these past weeks." Gordon's mockery held a hint of challenge, but Rhys avoided his gaze.

"Your concern overwhelms me, ladies." Rhys nodded to Melanie and Arianne, then winked at Lucinda, sending her into a fit of giggles. "You are quite right. You see a man before you starved for the company of loveliness and broken by the trials and tribulations of fending for himself. Give a poor starving man a smile and a cup of tea, will you?"

"You'll not have a smile, and the tea shall be over your head if you don't be sensible. Where have you been? What have you found out? Do you know where Arianne's painting is?"

Arianne could have kicked her cousin, but Rhys seemed more than adequately prepared to do it. She felt Lucinda perk up her ears beside her, but blessedly, her sister knew when to stay silent. Leaving the stage to Rhys, Arianne found herself again turning to Galen. This time he caught her look and reached for her hand beneath the table, giving it a gentle squeeze. Embarrassment once again flared in her cheeks, but she controlled it. He was merely being perverse, insisting on playing the part he had assigned himself. She returned her attention to the battle raging between Melanie and Rhys.

"I have been visiting relatives, Lady Melanie. I have discovered I have a great many of them. And if you insist on asking personal questions, then you are not the well-brought-up lady your brother thought you were."

"Then you have discovered something!" Not to be conquered by Rhys's reminder, Melanie triumphantly engaged him on other grounds. "Then we are here to help you. You must admit, Gordon and Galen have excellent connections."

Arianne couldn't hide a smile at Melanie's irrepressible advance. She had truly cornered the unfortunate man now, and since no one else seemed inclined to come to his rescue, she stepped into the breach. "Then, Melanie, I suggest you leave Gordon and Galen to deal with the matter, which is undoubtedly not a public one. I would suggest you try the watercress sandwiches. They are quite delicious."

The hand covering hers squeezed a little tighter, then reluctantly departed as Galen reached to pass the tray. Arianne rather missed the warmth once it was gone, but she felt a little relief at the release also. She wasn't ready to admit that Galen's courtship was beginning to affect her.

The tea went on more normally from there, with Lucinda unconsciously monopolizing the conversation with her description of all the sights and wonders she had encountered since leaving London. The adults seemed content to let her have the floor rather than return to their earlier disputes. Galen had a fit of coughing when the fifteen-year-old went into raptures over the elegance of his stables, totally ignoring the historical and architectural attributes of his home. Rhys grinned and encouraged a description of the occupants of the stable, until Gordon pointed out the necessity of supplying his young cousin with a riding habit upon their immediate return.

From that moment on, Lucinda was walking on clouds, and she gazed upon her noble cousin with eyes of worship as they completed their meal and returned to the street. Resting uneasily under such open adoration, Gordon turned to Arianne for rescue. "You don't think your father will mind, do you? I know we're not always on the best of terms, but the chit ought to ride, and I don't mind the cost. We could call it an early birthday present, perhaps."

"You may call it what you like, but even my father would be hard pressed to refuse her after this. Do not let her cozen you into more than that, though. You will have her quite spoiled."

"I doubt that either of you could ever be spoiled," Galen intruded into the familial argument, "but there will be time enough to find out. You do realize that my mother has been busily enjoying herself choosing a large quantity of cloth with which to enhance your wardrobe? She has it in mind to show you off to the neighbors and has thus convinced herself that it is her civic duty to see you suitably dressed for the occasion."

Arianne stared at Galen in alarm. "You are jesting, surely? It will not do at all."

"Why should it not?" Gordon intervened. "If Locke wishes to make a settlement on you before your marriage, I cannot see why it shouldn't be in the form of clothes. You know perfectly well that I would have seen you gowned and brought out with Melanie had Uncle Ross let me. He cannot keep you in aprons forever."

With Melanie on his arm, Rhys stopped in time to hear Gordon's declaration, and his gaze swiftly lifted

to meet Arianne's. She felt the question there and
knew that whatever his communication was with Gordon and Galen, neither man had informed him of the
impending betrothal. She wished to sink beneath the
cobblestones, but there was naught to do but follow
the party back to the carriage as if nothing had
happened.

Melanie's insistence that Rhys must accompany
them back to Deward was joined by invitations from
Galen and approval by Gordon, until he was given no
other choice but to agree. Joining the women in the
landau and giving directions, he guided them down
the steep hill and around a cottage lane to a small
stone house, where he leapt down and promised to
return shortly.

When Rhys returned with his satchel of belongings,
he was followed by an elderly lady of diminutive
height but eyes as dark and flashing as his own, who
came to wave him off. He introduced the woman as
his grandmother, and she nodded approvingly at the
young ladies in the carriage, offering greetings and
admonitions in a heavily accented voice as they prepared to leave.

Rhys brought his own mount around, kissed his
grandmother's cheek, and swung into place beside the
carriage as the driver cautiously maneuvered the team
though the narrow lane and back toward the main
road.

Melanie's questions began the instant they were out
of sight of the cottage. "Your grandmother? You
never told us about a grandmother. Is she foreign?
How did she come to live here in the middle of nowhere?" She would have asked more, but Arianne
caught her arm and pinched her into silence.

Not completely caught off-guard by this barrage,
Rhys only hesitated long enough to formulate the replies. Riding beside the carriage, he didn't look at the
occupants, but spoke with his gaze on the road ahead.
"My grandmother is a Romany. She has only come to
live here these last years, when she decided she was
too old to wander any longer, and had no people of

her own to travel with. My mother had the house built for her long ago, for those few times when she came here. It is as close to a home as she has ever known. My grandfather was English, but a younger son with no land of his own. He died when my mother was quite little, without having time to acquire any."

His words cut off quite abruptly, as if, having answered all the questions, he need say no more. Arianne was afraid the explanation would only lead to a dozen more questions, but for once Melanie had the sense to keep quiet. She gave Rhys's straight back a thoughtful look before speaking.

"I liked her. I wish we could have had time to talk longer."

Rhys gave her a startled glance, then looked away again. "Perhaps some other day. She enjoys company."

Arianne glanced back up the hill to where Galen had indicated the Llewellyn estates were located. Had Rhys been allowed to keep his home, his grandmother would undoubtedly be living in the splendor of the manor house instead of that cold stone cottage. She wasn't certain the old lady would be any happier there, but it seemed criminal to allow a relative of the family to live in such poverty just outside the gates of wealth. How could the present Baron Llewellyn live with the knowledge of what he had done?

Provided he had had any hand in it, which she couldn't prove at all. Knowing that Rhys was part Romany made what had happened a little clearer. The marriage may have been irregular, a ceremony of the Gypsies rather than in the Church of England. The family would have been horrified at the thought of a Gypsy heir. They could have conspired to keep quiet once the legality of the marriage was questioned. It all made some kind of mad sense. But that didn't make it any more fair.

As much as Arianne would like to, it wasn't her place to question Rhys further. The topic quietly dropped and turned to the subject of hunting when a hare burst out of the hedges in front of them. A quiet harmony bound them through the return journey, though Melanie's determined look caused Arianne occasional uneasiness. She would have to question her cousin more thoroughly when they returned to the house.

But when they returned to the house, it was to the chaos that three unsupervised little boys could create, and there was no immediate chance to corner her cousin for a private discussion. Rounding up the youngest, who was cheerfully playing with flowerpots in the gardener's compost pile, Arianne tracked down the other two from their screams of glee. Wondering how she had ever thought that her father might watch the trio for a few hours while her mother napped, she shook her head at her foolishness and nearly walked into Galen as he came around the corner of the greenhouse.

Catching her elbow to steady her, he grabbed the youngest, who seemed prepared to toddle off as soon as his hand was released. Arianne kept a firm hold on the next youngest and gave a warning frown to Davie before he could launch into excited explanations of their adventure into the apple orchard. Galen decided she very much resembled a mother hen at this moment, but he wisely refrained from stating this aloud. As fond as he might be of this reference, he was quite certain that Arianne would prefer to be thought of in other terms.

"They apparently had no notion they were supposed to obey the maid with whom they were placed. I can see we must fetch a dragon from the dungeons to supervise their activities." Galen sent the eldest lad a stern look, but rather than appear nervous at this threat, Davie grinned and produced a small green apple from his coat pocket for inspection. Obviously, Locke decided, he had not yet perfected an authoritarian image.

"Unless the dragon is prepared to romp about the countryside, I see little hope of success, my lord. Lucinda and I shall have to stay near at hand from henceforth; it is the only solution." Inwardly Arianne bewailed that fate, but she kept her rebellion hidden.

It would be very pleasant to lead her own life for just a little while, but she was aware of the earl's generosity in allowing this visit, and she would not impose on that generosity any further.

This time Galen's frown reached his eyes, and the boys looked up at him with some semblance of awe when he turned it on them. "Did you hear that lads? Your sister says you cannot be trusted out of her sight. I should be ashamed to think that is so. Would you be tied to her petticoats forever? Can you not show you are men enough to behave as you ought when she is not around? I shall be very disappointed if I cannot have your sister to myself upon occasion, and when I am disappointed, I do not help selfish little boys find ponies or climb trees."

Immediate protests pierced the air, resulting in the two older lads dragging the youngest back to the house in a great hurry in search of the maid who was to look after them. Arianne shifted her astonished gaze from her brothers to the man who had sent them on their way, then looked away in embarrassment at the gleam she found in his eyes.

"I think I deserve some reward for that act of deliverance," Galen noted with satisfaction.

"I think you are more boy than they are," Arianne responded tartly, unable to conquer the strange feelings of warmth he produced in her. She should be offering gratitude, but she had a decided notion that was what he expected, and that he fully intended to take advantage of it. She didn't know in what way he would take advantage, but she couldn't allow any. She was much too confused by her situation to allow any outside interference.

"That is possible, I suppose. There are some who might say I was never allowed to be a child and so must make up for it now. But I see nothing wrong in keeping the child alive inside all of us. The innocence of a child is infinitely preferable to the cynicism of the adult world."

"Not to mention the responsibilities. I would prefer to play, if I could, but I am old enough to know I must meet my obligations first. I must see that the boys go back where they belong."

Arianne's attempt to brush past him was unsuccessful. Galen caught her arm and held her, forcing her to look back at him. The dancing lights in midnight eyes were clear now, but they weren't playful lights. He suspected a combination of anger and tears produced them, but he wasn't certain how to resurrect the laughter. Without another thought, he bent to soothe the wounds she kept hidden in the only way he knew how.

The shock of Arianne's generous lips against his drove all thought of reparations from Galen's mind.

16

THE SUN HEATED her uncovered hair, but in no way could that warmth compare with the heat of Lord Locke's lips as they touched, then closed more forcefully over hers. Arianne gasped, then grasped his strong arms for support as the moment slipped away from them, becoming a natural force over which they had no control. She doubted that she would have stopped him even if she could have had they not been interrupted by a rather loud cough.

Galen regretfully lifted his head, searching her eyes briefly before placing her carefully behind him, away from the intruder, so she might have time to recover herself. He then turned a less-than-pleasant expression upon the man coming around the greenhouse in search of them.

Rhys kept his features aligned in pleasant neutrality as he approached, but a hint of concern darkened his eyes as they strayed in Arianne's direction. His limp brought him to stand before Locke's imposing figure, and he showed no apparent regret at intruding. "I believe the earl is looking for you, Locke. And there is a trio of little heathens raising the nursery roof in their insistence that you promised them a pony ride. I think your mother has threatened to join them shortly in search of you. Perhaps you might make haste back to the house to avert any further turmoil."

Galen contemplated nodding curtly and appropriating Arianne to accompany him, but he could tell by the look of guilt and anguish in her eyes that he had placed her in a compromising position from which he could not immediately extricate her by pretending it did not exist. He did not regret his rashness in persuading her to his wishes, but he would not hurt her if it could be avoided.

Releasing Arianne's arm, Galen stepped back out of the way. "I will bring the heathens to heel if you will escort Miss Richards back to the house. This holiday is meant for everyone, but she will insist on worrying herself if someone does not take her firmly in hand."

Rhys was the one to nod curtly and watch as Locke departed, leaving Arianne in his care. He turned a thoughtful gaze to hollowed cheeks brushed with rose and met her confused eyes with a question.

"Shall I wish you well on the excellence of your match with Locke?" he inquired gently.

Arianne crushed her skirt between her fists and fought down the bewilderment threatening to engulf her. The man standing before her was more than she had ever hoped for in a suitor. His intelligence and gentle concern appealed to her better instincts. She knew he had a strength of character as well as mind and body that she could rely on. But despite all that, he was a stranger, much as Lord Locke was a stranger, and neither man had the right to make these demands on her. Forcing her head upward, she met his eyes without hesitation.

"You might consult Galen about that. This is all his idea. Have you mended your fences with Melanie yet?"

Ignoring the reference to Melanie, Rhys replied, "I believe it takes two to make a betrothal. These are not feudal times. There were no promises between us, and I would not stand in your way when the match is so obviously an excellent one for you, but I will admit that my curiosity requires some explanation. I thought Locke and Lady Melanie were to make a match of it. How have things changed so abruptly in a few short weeks?"

Arianne found herself taking Mr. Llewellyn's arm and pacing slowly at his side through the darkening gardens. He was so easy to talk to. She felt none of the nervous starts and anxieties she knew around Lord Locke. The pressure of Galen's lips upon her own still stirred her blood to unreasonable lengths. It was a relief to speak logically. "Melanie rejected Galen's suit. I do not believe it is as simple as that, but that is the essence of it."

"So he turned to you in anger? That does not sound like Locke. His regard for you is very obvious."

"His regard for Melanie is very obvious." Arianne wished her tone did not sound quite so petulant. To make up for it, she launched into her own theory. "I think Galen wished to make up for the loss of the painting by bringing my mother out here, and this was the only way he could think to do it. If he makes Melanie a tiny bit jealous in the process, then it is all to the point, is it not?"

Rhys regarded the thoughtful oval of her face with fondness. She really was quite handsome with her hair curling softly about her face like that, and her eyes were sufficient to send men to the outer reaches of the earth to please her, were they intelligent enough to look past the fault of poverty and not be intimidated by her strong mind and character. He shook his head with a smile at her innocence. "No, my dear, it is not. By bringing you here, Locke has irrevocably declared his intentions. You may call if off, if you wish, but as a gentleman, he cannot. That is a little more than is required of a man wishing to make up for the loss of a painting."

"Oh." Arianne looked away, uncertain of the rush of feelings his words produced. Looked at from a logical point of view, she could see that Mr. Llewellyn might be right. Still, it only meant that Galen was settling for her instead of the cousin he could not have. That thought was not any more pleasing than being used to replace a painting. "I suppose I shall have to break it off, then. but I don't know that I can do so immediately. This may be the only chance my mother has to recover her strength. Is that so very terrible of me?"

"That depends on how deeply everyone's feelings are involved. I know I have been accused of being unfeeling, but I do not think I am so cold as to not see that you are in danger of falling under Locke's spell. And for all his worldliness, Locke is not a rake. He is a man looking for a wife. Lady Melanie is a wayward chit who undoubtedly dealt a blow to his self-esteem, but whether it was a blow to the heart as well, I cannot say. You tread dangerous waters when you play with people's hearts."

That did not sound as if his own heart was involved in any way. Arianne sighed and pulled Melanie's shawl more tightly around her. "Then I suppose I must call this whole thing off until there has been time for everyone to examine his feelings. I never realized this courtship business could be so dreadfully confusing. I'm not a romantic, like Melanie. I just thought I would one day meet a gentleman whose tastes mirrored mine and we would amicably agree to go through life together."

"Like you and me?" Rhys asked wryly, against his better judgment.

Arianne threw him a rueful look. "I suppose. We do suit, do we not?"

Rhys halted in the towering shadow of a clipped yew. Catching both her elbows, he turned her to face him. In the twilight her face gleamed with the hues of polished ivory, and he had the mad urge to press his kisses there, upon her cheek. But she was searching for truth and not passion, and he wasn't certain he could offer her either. "I suspect we would suit very well. You are accustomed to dealing with a man whose head is not always in the same room as his body. I am as selfish as your father. You would be a great deal of help to me if I am to make my own way in this world. Your name would add prestige to my tarnished one. In return, I can provide for you as well as your father, if not better. I have friends among the aristocracy and relatives who will not disdain me despite my fall from grace, so you will not be lowering yourself in any way. Unfortunately, I cannot bring to you an untarnished name or title, nor even a body perfect in limb and stature, but I am of sound mind and character. I think the match would balance on all points as a fair one. is this how you would choose a husband?"

"It is the sensible way, is it not? Neither one of us would feel lowered by the other. Should I take Galen seriously, he would overwhelm me with all he has that I have not."

"It would be as unequal as if I offered for Lady Melanie," Rhys agreed. "We simply must make them understand our position. Melanie was made for the kind of life that Locke can offer her. What do we need to do to bring them together?"

Arianne felt a rush of relief that someone finally viewed this situation as sensibly as she, though she felt a small bite of disappointment at the loss of even a glimpse of the fantasy Lord Locke offered. It was all very well and good to dream of rich confections, but it didn't put nourishment in the stomach. She would enjoy this brief interlude as she would a particularly delicious box of chocolates, but she would not fool herself into thinking she could live on it.

Grateful for the sturdy hand at her back as they continued to traverse the garden, Arianne turned her thoughts to the straight-and-narrow path she must walk to produce the proper results. Someday she and Rhys would look back at this with laughter, but right now she felt only a glimmer of sorrow. Determinedly she lifted her chin. "We must start with Melanie. I shall speak to her tonight."

Speaking with Melanie wasn't so easily done when she was squealing with delight over a package addressed to her cousin. Arianne gazed at the opened box with a shake of her head, wishing she could show the rapture that Melanie so easily gave in to. The ivory silk lying in folds of tissue paper begged to be touched, and the arrangement of blue ribbons to match the overskirt appealed to her artistic senses, but Eve had surrendered to temptation, and everyone knew where that had landed her.

"I cannot possibly accept it," she announced firmly.

Melanie stared at her cousin as if she had finally taken leave of her senses. "You cannot possibly refuse. The countess must have gone to a great deal of trouble to have this made. I cannot imagine how she managed to have it done without a great number of fittings." Seizing that idea, she carried it further. "Perhaps it won't fit. You must try it on, then you can honestly tell her some adjustments need be made before you can wear it. That will settle the matter to everyone's satisfaction."

"Until she sends a seamstress to adjust it," Arianne answered pessimistically, staring at the tempting fabric with all the hunger of years of deprivation. She knew it would fit. She knew if she tried it on, she wouldn't take it off should it hang to her knees. But then, she couldn't insult her hostess by refusing it outright.

Sighing, she touched the delicious fabric with one finger, stroking the ephemeral silk with longing. She would have to at least try it on. Just this once, it would be pleasant to know how she would look dressed in something fashionable. Then she could go back to the plain cottons and wools that suited her station.

Delighted at this decision, Melanie took charge, ordering maids and baths and producing exotic bath salts and dancing happily about at this chance to transform her attractive cousin into a princess worthy of the highest houses. Immersed in bubbles, then surrounded by hands pulling at her hair or adjusting her clothes, Arianne was left with no time to confront her cousin with the topic of Lord Locke. Instead, she found herself startled speechless by the results of Melanie's tampering.

Shoved in front of a full-length mirror, Arianne could only stare at the image reflected there. She had always felt gracelessly tall in her shapeless frocks, but the woman in the mirror stood proudly regal in a gown that clung fashionably to curves she had never considered worth showing. Although a blue ribbon held the high waistline beneath her breasts, the rippling silk shifted with her every movement, revealing more than Arianne thought quite decent. She was grateful for the minuscule protection of the gauzy blue overskirt that draped from her waist into a small train at her sides and back, but it did nothing to conceal the revealing neckline or cover her nearly bare arms. The woman in the mirror almost looked seductive, with curls dangling about her throat and ears, emphasizing eyes wider than seemed natural. It was as if Melanie had created another person in her place, and Arianne gave in to a giggle at the thought.

"You laugh! What is there to laugh about? You look positively resplendent. I shall demand that Gordon increase your wardrobe at once. I will not have you go back to those shapeless rags again." Melanie looked peeved that her cousin took her transformation so lightly.

Arianne turned and hugged her younger cousin, unconscious of the crushing of her new gown. "Don't be a peagoose. You have worked miracles, and I am properly grateful, if somewhat disbelieving. I don't think the boys would obey that woman in the mirror, but it will be fun to play the part for just one evening. But if you should speak to Gordon, I'll never forgive you. Papa will not like it if I should accept charity."

Melanie pouted, but laughter filled her eyes. "But I am so very good at choosing fashions! I shall speak to Uncle Ross, then. How can he deny me the fun of dressing you to the nines? Come along, then, and let us see how the multitudes applaud."

Laughing, they hurried down the echoing hallways of the stately manor as if it were the rabbit warren of Arianne's home. the echoes preceded them into the salon, where all attention turned on the doorway as they entered. Laughter still dancing in their eyes as they brought themselves to a decorous entrance, they painted more than a pretty picture for their audience as they came in, arm in arm.

The ladies nodded approval and the men rose from their chairs, at least two of them with dazed looks upon their faces as they came forward to lead their ladies into the room. A moment's awkwardness occurred when both men seemed ready to offer their arms to the same lady, but Rhys bowed to his host's greater claim and protectively took Melanie's arm into his, ignoring her scathing glance. When next he looked down on her, she was all smiles again, but laughter no longer lit her eyes.

Arianne felt the heady warmth of Galen's gaze go straight to her head and send her senses reeling, but she managed to balance superbly on his arm without revealing a portion of her giddiness. Just for a little while she would enjoy playing the part of a member of these heightened circles, and she would enjoy the attentions of a man accustomed to such heights. Tomorrow, perhaps, she would return to the ground, but for right now she was enjoying her flight of fancy.

"I now know what the phrase 'divine beauty' means, Arianne. I should have known you would be the one to teach me," Galen murmured in tones that did not quite carry to their elders.

Arianne colored, but before she could make a suitable reply, Lady Deward reprimanded her son. "If you cannot say things aloud, Galen, then they should not be said at all. I wonder that Miss Richards does not slap you for your forwardness. Come here, my dear, and let me admire your gown. The local seamstress is not all that she should be, but she could not fail with someone of your proportions. I knew you would appear favorably in that style."

The countess's blunt comments brought more color to Arianne's cheeks, but she came forward as bidden, making a polite curtsy before taking a seat near her hostess. Lady Deward nodded approvingly, then turned to her son.

"You would do well to take lessons in obedience and respect from your intended, Galen, but the fact that you have chosen someone with those qualities shows that you have more sense than I gave you credit for. When do you propose to set the wedding? June is but a few weeks away, you realize."

Not taking his gaze from Arianne, Galen noted the alarm briefly flaring in midnight eyes, and felt a moment's discomfort, but smoothly he gave a reply to settle all question momentarily. "We have not yet made a public announcement, Mother. There is no need for us to join the flock of end-of-Season weddings." He gave Arianne a small grin. "Besides, I am not at all certain that Arianne finds me suitable. If you continue to point out my failings, she will almost certainly flee back to the city in horror."

Polite laughter accompanied that jest, as it was meant to do, but Arianne felt sudden shifts in the currents around her. She looked up to find Rhys's gaze fastened intently upon her. Melanie's smile seemed fixed to her face as she released Rhys's arm to take a seat near her aunt and chatter lightly. Even Arianne's father was looking at her with curiosity, but there was nothing she could do or say to relieve the situation. Should she protest Galen's words, she would not only make a liar of herself but also earn the disapproval of Rhys and possibly Melanie. Should she agree with him, she would alienate everyone else. It was an impossible situation, and she could only ride it out by smiling and turning the conversation to other channels.

"Llewellyn? Of course! How could I have forgotten?" At a question from Arianne, her father's face lit with remembrance as he turned to the young gentleman who had so recently joined the party. "David's son, are you not?"

Rhys warily nodded. "You knew my father?"

"The few years I managed to attend classes, we went to school together. And then, of course, we shared an ale or two, or otherwise, while we were both young men. He had the best of me by a few years, but he was one of those rare ones who find friends wherever they go. A fine man. I'm sorry I did not recognize the connection earlier."

Harmed too many times by accidental forays into his past, Rhys remained stiff in his reply. "It is of no moment. My father passed away some years ago."

Frowning, drifting off into his own thoughts, Ross suddenly returned to the present with a more precise question than Arianne thought him capable of, and she flinched when she discovered its direction.

"David's son, that does bring back memories. I remember you as a lad. Quite the lordly manner you had then, scamp that you were." Before any knew where his reminiscences had carried him, Ross asked, "Why'd my daughter address you as 'mister'? You've not been playing light with her, have you?"

The innocent question exploded with the force of a bombshell, leaving a great hole in the tapestry of conversation as all talk died and everyone stared blankly at each other and away.

17

GUILT PARALYZED Arianne into speechlessness. She should have known that despite his absentminded eccentricities, her father was sharp enough to have noticed both men calling upon her. That he would have chosen the innocent Rhys as the one who would play with her feelings and not Galen came as a surprise, but she was too immured in her own feelings to come to Rhys's rescue. She glanced helplessly to Galen.

Galen caught her look, but he knew better than to interfere in a matter of a man's pride. He nodded encouragement to his guest, and left the floor to Llewellyn.

"I believe Miss Richards is aware of my status, sir. I have not deceived her in any way. I can understand your position if you would prefer I not be in the company of your daughter and niece. If you will accept my excuses, I will be on my way shortly." Rhys started toward the door, his back held straight despite his limp, his dark eyes opaque as they stared straight ahead.

"Don't be a sapwit, Rhys." Melanie leapt from her chair to run after him, catching his arm and hanging on despite his effort to disengage her.

"What's the lad gadding on about?" Ross looked with confusion to his daughter, then to Locke. "Did I misunderstand something?"

Before Galen could murmur something polite, the cantankerous earl snorted rudely. "Obvious the man don't hang about the clubs much. Even I've heard that old story. Your rare gentleman friend never married his son's mother. He's a mister, right enough, though it's questionable if he can claim the name Llewellyn."

He turned his glare to Rhys. "Sit down, boy. I never liked your uncle and I don't give a damn who your mother was. And if you've got eyes to see, you can see no one else gives a pin for it either."

Rhys's military bearing didn't unbend an inch as he turned to face the room, but this time he didn't try to remove Melanie's fingers as they wrapped around his arm. His searing gaze swept from the countess's haughty nod past Ross's puzzled expression and his wife's warm smile to fasten on his friends. Arianne's eyes reflected the pain in his, and Galen held out his hand in welcome. With a wry twist of his lips, he nodded acceptance.

"Pride goeth before a fall," he murmured to the room at large as he turned toward his seat, stopping before Ross Richards first. Meeting his gaze directly, he attempted to answer the man's questions. "My father was as rare a gentleman as you claim, sir. There is no doubt in my mind that he married my mother, but there seems to be doubt in the minds of others. Forgive me if I misunderstood your questions."

"Not married your mother? Bigad, sir, that's a lie! Would a man have a portrait made of his leman and his bastard for all the world to see? Your mother's death nearly destroyed him. Who's telling these tales? I'd like to meet him face-to-face." Sublimely unaware that his words had caught the full attention of everyone in the room, Richards shook his fist as if prepared to take the malefactor to task right then and there.

"You're familiar with the painting?" Arianne came to life under this new line of attack. She should have known that her father would be familiar with any aspect of artwork connected to his friend's life, and that the artwork would be the first thing that came to his mind when confronted with memory. She just hadn't known that her father knew Rhys's father.

Distracted from his tirade, her father turned his gaze to her and visibly diverted his thoughts from Rhys to this new question. His eyes lit as he dredged up the memory with a clarity for details that eluded him in everyday life. "Of course. I arranged it for him. Lawrence was begging for work and Llewellyn wanted to show off his wife and heir. Best piece of work he'd done by far at the time. Let them sit natural, he did. All that black hair filling the foreground and the mountains in the back. Excellent piece." He turned back to Rhys. "Whatever became of that portrait? It should bring you a pretty price in the market, if you're interested."

Rhys glanced helplessly to Arianne, who diverted her father again with another question. "You saw the finished work, then? Do you remember the details? Are you certain that it was Rhys and his mother?"

Ross gave his daughter a look of irritation. "Do you remember a time when I have forgotten such details? Of course it was Lady Llewellyn and her son. I was there once when Lawrence was painting it. Had a devil of a time getting the two to sit still, he did. What details do you want? She wore a gown of the most lustrous ruby I've ever seen. Only Lawrence could have created the palette to show it. The mountains were a damnable piece of business, but he never was a landscape man."

Gently Rhys intruded. "Do you remember if the portrait showed her wedding ring, sir?"

A light began to dawn on Richards' face. "Is that how it is, then? Of course there was a wedding ring. A family heirloom, if I remember rightly. Shows it right there in the portrait. I always thought Gypsies liked lots of gaudy jewelry, but Lady Llewellyn never wore any other but that one ring. Distinctive, it was, with roses and leaves all twined about it. I told you they were married, boy. Just look at the portrait."

"The portrait disappeared, Papa." Arianne took a deep breath and felt the bands of her stays constrict beneath her breasts as she tried to make the explanation that was needed. "Lord Llewellyn sent the portrait away before seeing it, and Sir Thomas used it for the backing of another painting. When the painting was found and displayed at Christie's, it was stolen. The painting is the only evidence Rhys has that his parents were married."

Ross gave her a sharp look, then ran his hand over his balding head. "Balderdash. David was delighted with that painting. He even gave me other commissions because of it." He hesitated, then searched his memory a moment. "Lawrence offered to paint Anne's portrait right after he completed that work. He should have given me part of the proceeds from Llewellyn, but I agreed to the oil instead. Not one of his better works, I'm afraid, but he was practicing for society then." He dragged his wandering thoughts back to the point. "The thing is, I remember David's wife died suddenly soon after that. Anne was with child and we couldn't attend the funeral. It was a tragic affair. I suppose it is possible he never saw the finished painting. But I cannot imagine him sending it away, even in his grief."

Rhys seemed about to speak, but the call came for dinner, and those present shook themselves out of their various reveries to conform to protocol. If they were a more silent group going into dinner than the night before, no one commented upon the fact.

Arianne found herself seated with Galen at her side and Rhys across the table, but she could not dispel the mood her father's story had laid upon the company. Occasionally she sent Rhys's dark face a quick glance, but his expression was impassive as he engaged in polite conversation with the earl on politics. At his side, Melanie looked distraught, and Arianne tried to remind herself to have the discussion with her cousin soon. Galen was the one who squeezed her hand in understanding, who studiously signaled the servants when her glass was empty or her plate lacked a particular delicacy. He kept the conversation flowing around her, including Arianne when she could make general replies that required little thought, and leaving her to her own thoughts elsewhere.

She was grateful for Galen's perceptiveness. Perhaps she had judged him unfairly in the past. She had thought him just one of the idle fops of the nobility, with nothing else to do but look pretty for the ladies and play games with the men. Perhaps Locke was that, but he was something a little more too. Was she judging him wrongly again when she thought his feelings of little account in this matter of their betrothal? As she left the dinner table with the other ladies, she could not help but revert to her original belief. She could not think of a single reason why Lord Locke would look on her with any more affection than he showed any other woman.

Yet he was the first to return to the salon afterward, leaving Rhys behind to continue his discussion of politics. While Melanie attempted a plaintive melody on the piano, Galen crossed the room directly to Arianne, offering his arm and suggesting a walk in the garden. It was exactly what she would have liked most of all, but the memory of their last walk heightened her color and caused her to hesitate.

"I cannot think that would be wise," she murmured under her breath, so only he could hear.

Amusement danced briefly in Galen's eyes as he gazed upon her bent head. "Do you cry craven, then? Perhaps you're right. There have been enough surprises for one day. Let us ask Melanie to walk with us, just tonight. There are days ahead when I mean to teach you what you are too stubborn to admit freely."

Arianne glanced upward and was captured by the sincerity of his crystal-clear gaze. She had not thought Locke the practiced charmer who could speak lies and innuendos with such expertise, but were he not, she would have to believe that he actually harbored a true affection for her. The tone of his voice and the look in his eye were that transparent. Not knowing what to believe, Arianne accepted his hand and agreed.

Melanie was on the point of refusing to accompany them when Rhys finally joined the ladies. He pointedly ignored her in preference to continuing his conversation with the earl, and taking a sharp breath, Melanie closed the music and took Galen's arm.

"You will become known as a ladies' man if you continue so, dear Galen," she admonished in mincing notes that could be heard across the room. "Arianne, I think I shall steal him back from you. He has become much more flattering since he met you."

Flirting her fan, sweeping up the slight train of her

dinner gown, and ignoring the black scowl forming on
Rhys's face, Melanie focused her attention firmly on
Galen's grinning visage. She would have preferred to
stamp on his foot to wipe the laughing look from his
eyes, but that would not serve her purpose. Instead,
she simpered and smiled and hurried him from the
room, with Arianne lingering uncertainly as she threw
a last gaze back to the company.

Rhys caught her look and quickly disengaged himself from the conversation. Her relief at his accompaniment made his tread firmer as he strode after them.
Arianne's tug on Galen's arm brought the other couple to a halt, and Rhys joined them easily, appropriating Arianne's other arm as he caught up to them.

"A stroll after such an excellent dinner is just the
thing," he agreed, as if he had been asked.

"One might think so," Galen replied wryly, looking
down the chain of linked arms and up to the single
doorway through which they must pass to reach the
gardens. "But perhaps a healthy conversation might
aid in the digestion also. Lady Melanie, if you
would?" He emphasized her title as a brother might
use a full name in admonishment, taking Melanie's
arm and leading her through the door, leaving Arianne to Rhys, for the moment.

Rhys's fingers closed comfortingly around Arianne's
elbow, but she didn't feel comforted as Galen led Melanie into the gardens and she was forced to follow.
This was the way it was meant to be, she knew, but
she couldn't rid herself of the confusing feelings generated by Galen's warm gaze and voice as he looked on
her. He undoubtedly used his charms on every lady
he met, and she was just unaccustomed to such attentions, but it would take her a little while to convince
her heart of that.

They strolled in silence until Galen stopped abruptly
before the fountain in the courtyard and turned to the
couple behind him. "All right, Llewellyn, there's just
the four of us now, and I think it's time we heard
what you're planning to do. Had you been a kettle of
water, there would be steam coming out your ears by

now. I'll not be responsible for riding herd on these females any longer while you gallivant the countryside again." The water in the fountain pattered in a steady stream in the surrounding placid pond, adequately drowning out the other night sounds of the gardens beyond as he waited for a reply.

Tall lamps in the corners of the small yard illuminated the fountain, casting Galen into large silhouette as he stood against it. Beside him, Melanie appeared daintily frail and almost ephemeral with her light muslin gown blowing around her in the breeze. She had released Locke's arm to wrap her arms around herself, and Arianne came forward to offer her own shawl. She didn't think any amount of night air could cool her off quite yet.

Galen captured Arianne's waist before she could escape, pulling her close to him as he faced Rhys. She meant to protest, but Rhys's scorching reply prevented any thought other than of his pain.

"I'm going to confront him. What else can I do?" Fury propelled the words, but pain and betrayal edged the silence that followed. Hearing what wasn't said, Rhys hurried to fill the gap. "There is nothing I can use as proof. My aunt was not married to Uncle Owen at the time, but she says she remembers my father bringing home his new wife after an extended journey. It was all the talk of the town, especially since no one knew of anyone who had attended the wedding. My mother never denied her Romany heritage. There were always rumors, but I cannot believe my father would not have married her legally. Neither can any others with whom I've talked. yet there is no proof. I've even searched the records at Gretna, but there is nothing. I am convinced my uncle knows the whole. He has no heir. He must admit the truth sometime."

Melanie drifted forward, coming between the two men. "We will go with you, but you must know the truth does not matter. Your friends know who you are, and they believe you. We will spread the word about the wedding ring in the portrait, and before long your uncle will be the subject of gossip, not your parents. You have no reason not to hold your head up in the best of society."

Rhys talked over her head, as if she were not there. "I want no one involved in this, Locke. It's a family matter. For myself, I would leave it alone. My uncle is not a well man. But I'll not have my parents' names besmirched, and should I have a family of my own, I would not have them bear the burden of scandal. I'll not be gone long. We can settle our differences when I come back."

Galen caught Arianne and prevented her from going to Melanie or Rhys, whichever was her goal. Melanie's small shoulders literally drooped as she twisted away, and Rhys's voice had gone cold and distant, as if coming from some lonely valley. Locke heard the tones of anger in his own voice as he spoke.

"You don't have to do this alone. If nothing else, let us have signed affidavits you might present, confirming the knowledge of the wedding ring. You cannot simply go to the man and call him a liar."

"But you see, that's what he is, and he knows it." Softly Rhys made the condemnation and turned away. His limping stride could not take him away swiftly enough, but no one made any effort to follow him.

"He's not just a liar, but a thief." The words were said so low as to be a part of the night air and the fountain's waters, but Melanie's quick steps back toward the house gave evidence of their reality.

This time, Galen did not stop Arianne from running after her cousin. It was not how he had meant for the night to end, he thought, watching the slender figures of the women disappear into the brightly lit house. But he should have known not to count out a man as formidable with pride and courage as Rhys Llewellyn.

Cursing the man and his tale, Locke stood bleakly waiting for the upper-story lamps to flicker on. He had always known life to be unfair, but until now he had been the one to benefit from the disparity.

He wasn't at all certain that he liked being on the wrong end of the ladder.

18

"WHAT DO YOU THINK you are doing?"

Arianne whispered into the gray shadows of early dawn as the figure beside her rose form the bed and slipped into the darkness of the far corners of the room.

"I'm going with him." The whispered words were adamant, leaving no room for argument. The rustle of clothing followed.

Even though she had suspected this was coming, Arianne was still horrified. She pulled back the covers and brought her feet to the cool carpet, not even lingering over the pleasures of soft wool over cold planks. "You can't! You'll be ruined. And he doesn't want you. Melanie, please be reasonable."

"What has reason to do with it?" The question was muffled behind the layers of cotton being pulled over her head. With the chemise settled, Melanie pulled on the shirt of her riding habit. "I have waited all my life to be old enough to marry Rhys. He didn't discourage me when he showed up with one foot and posing as my brother's stableboy. He'll not discourage me now."

"But, Melanie . . ." Arianne scrambled for her own clothing, knowing she would be handicapped without it if Melanie persisted in this madness. "Has he given you any encouragement? How do you know he returns your feelings?"

"I just know." Stubbornly she jerked on the long, heavy skirt of her habit. She gave an anxious glance to the gray oblong of the window at a sound from below, then hurried even faster.

Arianne hesitated, not knowing if she ought to reveal the gross betrayal Galen had perpetrated on them all, or Rhys's wishes in the matter. She was too confused to be certain if her interpretation was correct, but she had to say something, if only to return Melanie to her senses. "Melanie, you can't just know. Rhys and I . . ." How could she say it?

Melanie's attention jerked toward her as if she had. "Rhys and you have what? You're betrothed to Galen. It is an excellent match. He's quite mad about you, you know. I've seen that ever since the incident when he chased after you and yelled at you in the park. That was most unlike Galen, and I've watched him ever since. He's thrown his cap over the windmill this time. What can there be between you and Rhys? You've never even met him until recently."

Despair swathed her in helplessness. Arianne pulled the dull folds of her morning gown down around her shoulders before answering, and then she used her most blunt and practical tones. "Galen is merely circumventing Papa's pride in order to bring Mama to the country. I thought surely you understood that. I cannot ever move in the same circles as you and Lord Locke, no more than Rhys can aspire to those same circles, not while his name and title are questioned. I suppose, should he be able to clear his birth, he might seek higher than the likes of me, but as it currently stands, we are suited. Those are Rhys's words, not mine, Melanie."

Melanie pulled on her jacket without bothering to smooth the heavy fabric into the proper lines or button it up to the ties of her shirt. "No doubt they are. You and he are the most practical, perverse, blind-headed people I've ever met. If that's what he means by being well-suited, he is entirely correct. But in any other way, he is wrong. Names and titles are nothing. He loves me, as Galen loves you. If the two of you cannot return our feelings, it is a sorry state, but I cannot deny what I feel or fail to act on it. Apologize to Aunt Anne and Uncle Ross for my behavior, but I have to go with him. It is simply not in me to do otherwise."

Arianne had the sense to recognize the difference between the voice of a woman in love and that of a giddy child. This was no child speaking now, and there was naught she could do to stop her. But she could be there to help her, whatever came of it. While Melanie pulled on her half-boots, Arianne slipped into her kid shoes and hurried toward the bedroom door.

She knew Melanie would be on the way to the stables before she could follow, but since Arianne couldn't ride, there was only one other solution. Her brothers had shown her the door to one room where Galen had taken them to properly outfit them for the country; it was undoubtedly his own room. Her heart beat heavily against her ribs as she raised her hand to knock on the paneled door.

It swung open before she could make a sound. Galen caught her wrist, dropped a brief kiss to her cheek, and pulled her after him as he hurried down the hall.

"I'd hoped you would be ready. Hurry, the horses should be almost harnessed."

Arianne flew after him down the stairs and through the back hall to the entrance leading into the stableyard. A cock crowed somewhere in the distance as they stepped out into the cool morning air. Pink gleamed through the clouds on the horizon, but a fine mist coated her hair as they hurried across the yard to the stable.

"I knew Rhys would do it this way, so I had the grooms up early. I heard them ride out just a few minutes ago; we'll not be far behind them. I hope Melanie was discreet about following, or we'll likely find her trussed up in one of the stalls."

Arianne would have giggled at the accuracy of Galen's assessment of the situation had the matter not been so urgent. Rhys would be furious to know he was followed. Melanie's reputation would be in tatters should it be discovered. Perhaps the damage could be recovered if Rhys were made to marry Melanie, but that wasn't how either of them would want it. She gasped in relief as a lightweight phaeton appeared at Galen's signal.

"I'm sorry to have to submit you to another ride like this, but at least it's not my reckless high-perch this time. I'm thinking of getting rid of that rig. It's not at all appropriate for a married man, is it?"

He threw her up in the seat without waiting for a reply, stopping to check the harness and pat the horses before coming around to the driver's seat. He swung up with the agility of an athlete, and with a whistle to the groom at the distant gate, set the horses into motion.

Once on the road, Galen steadied the horses to a gentle canter, and Arianne had time to realize the thoroughness of her disarray. Her hand flew to the long braid with which she had bound her hair the night before, then discreetly attempted to restore it to order.

Nervously she inquired, "Do you think Rhys has any chance of persuading his uncle to tell the truth?"

Galen caught the reins in one hand and used the other to stop her from twisting at the thick lengths of loosened hair. "Melanie will no doubt beat him into it, if he does not. We can stop somewhere along the way for you to arrange yourself. Leave it be, for now. Your hair is too beautiful to disguise, the way ladies insist on doing. I want to have your portrait done in dishabille, with your hair spilling over your shoulder like that."

Arianne clutched her hands in her lap, not daring to lift her gaze to his. "I would feel better should I think Melanie looked the disaster I must for our hurried dressing this morning, but I know she will not. She could look smartly turned out in sackcloth, I'm certain."

Galen grinned and clucked the horses to a greater speed. "Melanie would look a hoyden in ostrich feathers and court dress. Since I've never had a little sister, she suits the part admirably. But you were never the little-sister type even when you were in pigtails and giving me a much deserved set-down. For your information, I am not going to stop down the road to allow you to arrange yourself because you look a disaster, but because I fear I will be forced to fight off every man who sees you. I don't mind a good fight, mind you, but we really must catch up with Melanie and Rhys sometime this day, and it's not likely to happen should I be at fisticuffs with your admirers."

"You have learned to play the part of rake well, my lord," Arianne said coldly. "I had not cast that disparagement upon you before, but you have done your best to convince me of it these last days. I may not be accustomed to traveling in more enlightened circles, but I know Spanish coin when I see it."

"Were I not so thoroughly enjoying this morning, I would call you to account for that, Miss Richards, but I have decided not to be downcast by anything you say this day. You realize you could be thoroughly compromised did I decide not to follow Melanie, but to take another path instead?"

"That would be extremely foolish of you. What would you have to gain? I am not an heiress and you are not a fortune hunter. If we can catch up with Melanie, we can save her from disgrace, and her family will shower you with gratitude. You might even persuade Melanie to reason when she finally sees Rhys does not mean to marry her."

"I shudder at the thought of a reasonable Melanie. No, I much prefer her as she is, or even better, as Rhys's wife. The poor fellow deserves her. No, the only reason I do not compromise you right now is that I want to show you what a good fellow I am before I propose to you properly. I think you are almost beginning to believe it. Why else would you come to me this morning instead of to anyone else?"

That silenced her, and Arianne glared at a wren warbling throatily in the hedgerow as they rattled across a narrow bridge. Why, indeed? He was making her life much too complicated. There wasn't an honest response she could make, and she held her tongue as the horses began the climb to the village Rhys called home.

As promised, Galen stopped at a small roadside inn when the sun was well above the horizon, burning off the last of the morning mist. While Arianne borrowed a small chamber to perfect her toilette to the best of her limited ability, Galen secured a small breakfast of rolls and cheese for them to eat along the way. When she returned to find him holding the large parcel of provisions and a yellow cotton bonnet to match her round gown, she had to laugh aloud at his boyish eagerness for approval.

"How could you know I was regretting my haste in leaving without a hat?" she demanded as they returned to the phaeton. "And how could you possibly find one to match so superbly?"

With an inordinately self-satisfied smirk at her pleasure, Galen shrugged his large shoulders. "You look stunning in yellow, and when I saw the hat hanging idle, I was unable to resist inquiring. Some guest left it behind, so you may have it snatched from your head if the original owner should see it, but I would not have you burn your lovely nose because of my neglect."

Arianne sent him a sidelong glance, hearing the pleased tones of his voice at her approval and wondering at them. She knew him to be a strong, capable man who moved with confidence through the highest society as well as the rarefied atmosphere of London's art world, yet his delight in achieving her approval seemed to be as great as if he had just purchased the *Mona Lisa*. She had seldom been in a position where her approval was sought, and she was left with a rather tingling sensation of anticipation that Galen might consider her wishes after all.

They eagerly consumed their breakfast as the horses carried them ever upward. The phaeton was of necessity slower than the single mounts ridden by such expert equestrians as Rhys and Melanie, but knowing their destination, there was no reason for concern. Without speaking the words aloud, they both knew they would be of no use until after the confrontation, when all they could do was pick up the pieces and sort them into respectable order before returning home. Rhys would not appreciate their presence in his private argument with his uncle, but someone had to protect Melanie from her rashness, and Rhys would not be in a position to do so.

So they laughed over the antics of the birds as they threw crumbs into the wind, sang songs without heed to the niceties of melody, and avoided the mention of what was to be done when they arrived. Despite her protests, Arianne bloomed under the attention of Galen's compliments and concern, and his delight at achieving this reaction made for a merry journey.

Arianne thought she could very well travel like this into eternity were it not for her concern for her cousin. It had been so long since she had felt the wind in her face and smelled the earthy scents of cut grass and plowed fields that she had failed to remember their heady perfumes. She longed to sit in the long grass under the May sun and braid wildflowers into fairy crowns. She feared the longing had much to do with the attentive and handsome gentleman at her side, but that was another subject she tried not to think about. Infatuation was no sound basis for the future.

As they drew closer to the village nestled into the side of the hill, their voices grew silent. Galen stopped to ask directions of a hay-wagon driver, then urged the horses upward. He turned to check Arianne's nose for sunburn, pulling the loose bonnet forward proprietarily to better shield her face. She didn't remonstrate, but gazed up at him with big worried eyes that made him feel ten feet tall. Somehow, he had to bring this day to a happy conclusion just to see the joy return to her eyes.

They drove on through the sleepy village without any sight of Melanie or Rhys. They could have stopped to make inquiries, but they had mutually decided it would only stir talk, and for no reason. Rhys was going to his father's estate, and Melanie was fol-

lowing. They didn't need anyone to confirm their conclusion.

Galen turned the light gig from the main road onto
a narrow lane shaded occasionally by overhanging
trees. Arianne tightened her hands in her lap. She had
come away without gloves, and she felt a veritable
country bumpkin traveling to a manorial estate like
this. Galen shifted the reins to one hand to reach over
and squeeze her bare hands as if he knew her
thoughts, and when she looked up, his smile was reassuring. She shouldn't let the warmth from his smile
affect her so, but she needed his confidence to get
through these next hours. It was one thing to visit the
estates of an earl in the company of family and
friends, quite another to appear unknown and un-
wanted on the doorstep of a haughty baron who had
every reason to look at her with contempt. She would
feel much better had she Melanie's claim to aristocracy and the garments to go with it. Galen's presence
was scarcely protection enough from these insecurities.

"Llewellyn is only a man, not a tiger or bear,"
Galen admonished, looking down at her worried
frown. "We have only come to lend propriety to Melanie's presence, not to beg a handout. And if you are
worrying about your appearance, I shall shake you
until your teeth rattle. You would look majestic in
your nightrail—a sight which I am much looking forward to, I might add."

Shocked, but also finding an unexpected heat in the
image his words conjured, Arianne stared up at Lord
Locke. The laughing mischief was no longer in his
eyes. His glance seemed frightfully serious, and she
gulped at the brief glimpse of something else in his
gaze before he returned it to the horses. If they continued so, she would find herself married to this man
in truth, and the thought frightened as well as excited
her. No romantic like Melanie, Arianne had no illu-
sions about marriage. It wasn't just singing through
sunshine, but struggling to live with another's beliefs
and demands, trying to please someone besides your-

self as well as yourself, hearing complaints about cold meals and extravagance, crying over illnesses.

But the same could be said if she were to marry Rhys. Marriage was a frightening enough step without this tremendous uncertainty nagging at the back of her mind. She wished she could be the kind of woman whom Galen admired, but she felt she fell far short of the ideal. She wasn't at all certain why he had entangled her in this way, but his heart couldn't possibly be in it. And she was beginning to have dire doubts about her theory that respect and friendship were all that were required for marriage.

And on top of all that, she was experiencing the lowering feeling that Lord Locke was beginning to stir those emotions whose existence she had denied, seriously undermining her determined attempts to regard this affair logically.

19

THE BOXLIKE TWO-STORY stone walls of the Llewellyn estate suddenly rose before them as they rounded a bend in the lane. The grounds were elegantly manicured, but they lacked the life Arianne had discovered in the painting. She could see where the portrait had been done, with the mountain towering in the background, but the oil seemed more alive than the reality.

The rambling roses covered with buds that should be climbing the walls were pruned as severely as the yews. The ivy had been scythed to a level with the grass. The riotous rhododendrons were now clipped to a neat hedge. The childish toys Arianne had sensed would be strewn upon the ground in the landscape in the portrait were nowhere in evidence. Not even a servant appeared as the phaeton rattled up the drive.

Galen took the carriage into the stableyard, searching for some sign of Rhys's and Melanie's horses. Finding them grazing contentedly at the edge of the cobbled yard, he drew his grays to a halt. Someone should have come running from the stable to tend them, but lacking any evidence of such a personage, Galen leapt down and came around to lift Arianne from her seat, then turned to tending his animals himself.

Arianne nervously paced the cobbled area, glancing up at the cold stone walls with trepidation as Galen watered his horses and released their harness so they could join the others at the edge of the yard. She didn't like the atmosphere of this place. She had been worried about making an impression among haughty strangers, but now she was more concerned for Melanie's safety. There was an emptiness here that did not bode well.

Galen came up beside her and caught her hands, rubbing them between his to warm them as he gazed into the upturned oval of her face. He read the worry in her eyes well enough, but there was little he could do to assuage it. "I am beginning to think it was a mistake to bring you. This isn't at all as I expected."

"Nor I. Do you think anyone will answer if we knock?" Arianne found herself clinging to the strength of his hands, and gently she tried to pull away.

"There is only one way to find out." Releasing only one of her hands, Galen pressed the other to his coat sleeve as he led her toward the main door. Beside him, the bright yellow of her bonnet and gown made a splash of joyous color against the dismal gray of the stone walls. Surely, naught could go wrong in the presence of such color.

The knocker sounded loud and hollow as Galen brought it down with great force against the high door. If footsteps responded to the call, they were given no chance to discern them. A scream of terror echoed through an open window somewhere above, and Galen no longer considered politeness as he tested the door and threw it open without waiting for permission to enter.

Arianne picked up her skirts and ran after him despite his admonitions to wait outside. That was Melanie's scream, and Arianne had no intention of waiting anywhere. She paid scant heed to the fading tapestries on the old walls or the worn carpets underfoot. Like Galen, her attention focused on the loud voices carrying down the spiral stairs from the hall above.

They raced up the steps, Galen taking them two at a time, Arianne lifting her narrow skirt and petticoat to follow as swiftly as she was able. Noting a suit of armor complete with battleax on the landing, she briefly contemplated securing the weapon for her own use, but caution warned that she would be bested in any struggle with decades of rust. She raced upward in Galen's trail.

The sharp, curt tones of Rhys's voice suddenly lowered to angry reassurances, and Melanie's screams fell abruptly silent as Arianne and Galen raced down a cavernous hallway toward the only open door visible. Situated at the front of the building, the doorway spilled a block of sunlight into the corridor, apparently from a bank of windows within the room. A shadow passed across the squares of light, and another voice spoke in answer to Rhys's.

"What is it you want me to do? Name you my heir before I die? Will that repair the damage that has been done?"

Galen caught Arianne's arm, and they stepped silently to the room's entrance. The morning sun spilling through the windows temporarily blinded Arianne to the room's occupants, but she could discern the silhouette of a short, rotund man striding behind a massive desk in the center of the room. She gasped, and Galen covered her mouth with his hand as the silhouette carelessly raised a long-barreled pistol and gestured with it.

"I want my parents' name cleared. What could they ever have done to you to deserve the dirt you threw on them after they were dead?"

Vision beginning to clear, Arianne turned in the direction the baron faced, and had to hold back another cry as she recognized the portrait hanging in splendor over the wide mantel at the far end of the room. Streaming black hair seemed to fill the canvas, and dark eyes gazed down with love and sympathy and just a hint of laughter from her high position upon the wall.

Quickly Arianne scanned the room, finding Melanie hovering helplessly near the doorway where they stood, her gaze fastened in horror on the gun that the baron swung so casually in his hand. Rhys stood firmly between her and his uncle, his stocky figure seeming to swell to twice its size as he waited with arms akimbo for his reply.

"I loved her first." The man's face was gray as it turned toward his only nephew. If he saw the new arrivals lingering in the doorway, he gave no evidence of it, but his gaze shifted upward to the portrait. "I should never have sent that away. I thought those years would go away with it, but they didn't. David missed her so terribly, he never even questioned me when I told him the painting had been destroyed. Stealing it back hasn't made this place any happier either."

Galen pushed Arianne back against the hall wall and stepped into the room, reaching for Melanie's arm. But she resisted, digging her feet firmly into the carpet and clinging to the paneled wall as the baron continued speaking.

"I was the one who found her, you know," he said to Rhys as if the others weren't there. "I met her at a country fair when she was staying with her father's relatives in Keswick. I was up there hunting with some friends. They called her a Gypsy and said insulting things and we had a falling-out. One of them must have written to David. He came flying to the rescue of his foolish younger brother. I was barely out of school at the time, and perhaps he had some right for concern, but he had no right to steal her from me."

Arianne stole up behind Galen, unable to remain hiding in the hall while all she knew and loved stood bravely in the face of danger. Melanie grasped her hand gratefully, but they said nothing, understanding there was nothing to be said while the baron unburdened his guilty conscience.

"After David arrived, she never looked at me again. I cursed her for a fortune hunter, but the truth was, she had never looked at me as anything more than a distracting amusement. It was David who cast his spell to bring the Gypsy to her knees. But she returned the favor, and he proposed marriage before even a month was out."

The baron stared up at the laughing Gypsy of the painting, the pistol hanging loosely in his fist. Arianne watched as Rhys gauged the distance between himself and the weapon, could almost see his calculations as he judged his ability to disarm the older man without harm, and felt his torment when he realized it could not be done without risk to others. Galen's hand came down on her shoulder and squeezed, and she knew he had followed her thoughts precisely.

"I stood up for David after he obtained the special license. An aunt stood up for your mother. The woman is long since dead. I was the only witness left to that ceremony. It seemed such a simple thing. The marriage was brief. Six years was nothing. Why should six short years destroy everything?"

"My father had to go to the bishop for a special license. How could you deny what took place in the church, within the records of the church? Why can't anyone find those records, if what you say is true?"

The baron swung around, his ashen face marred by the sardonic line of his mouth. "I thought God favored my position. I'd lost my love to David, and my inheritance to David's son. When the cathedral burned, taking with it all the records, I thought God had answered my prayers. He had, you know, but just as you can't bargain with the devil, you can't get the best of God. I gained the title and the wealth, just as I asked. At the time, I had no idea of the cost."

He lifted the heavy pistol and caressed the barrel thoughtfully. Melanie stifled another scream and cringed against Arianne, but her arm went out to Rhys, beckoning him to retreat to safety. He seemed to have no recognition of the gesture, but strode forward instead.

"You cannot correct one wrong with another. Put down the pistol, Uncle Owen. It serves no purpose. You can keep the title and estate if it makes you happy. All I want is my father's honor returned. Surely you can invent some lie to explain why the marriage was hidden all these years."

"Does one lie right another?" the baron asked wryly, facing his nephew, but this time giving a nod of acknowledgment to the man behind him.

Galen returned the nod and caught Melanie's arm firmly in his grasp when she seemed prepared to fly to Rhys's side. If tragedy were to be averted here, it would be by caution and not emotional theatrics. But he judged the presence of others besides Rhys would lessen the chances of unpleasantness. Whatever Owen Llewellyn might be, he was too much the gentleman to subject the ladies to violence.

"What is one lie in a whole list of lies? Tell them you have recently uncovered evidence of the marriage. I'll denounce the title in your favor. I've lived without it all these years, it means nothing to me now. I just wish to be able to offer an honest name to the woman I wish to marry."

Arianne jerked involuntarily in Galen's grasp, then turned quickly to give Melanie a warning glance. He was throwing away any chance of a future with Melanie with these words. It was a reckless, mad thing to do, but if it would ease the situation . . .

The baron glanced briefly to the two women behind his nephew, as if seeing them for the first time. He nodded in recognition at Melanie, then studied Arianne before returning his gaze to his challenger.

"I don't think either of them is much concerned with your name, but you have a right to it, as you have a right to your estate and title. Six years might be a small part of a lifetime, but it was enough to give you what I had always wanted. Or thought I wanted. You've seen Sarah. How is she? She never answered my letters, and I haven't heard anything from anyone going in that direction lately."

"My aunt is well and doing comfortably. She thought I might be coming here and sends her respects. She's a lovely lady."

"Yes, she always was, but she wasn't your mother. I married her because I didn't know what else to do. Your mother was dead, you had the inheritance, it seemed the thing to do. We had some good years together, before your father died. I regret that I didn't understand happiness wasn't in possessing what I didn't have, but in enjoying what I already possessed. She wanted to give me sons, but I longed for stone walls. Foolish, the things we think are important when we're young. You'll have the lot shortly. Tell Sarah I'm sorry I gave up the best thing in my life when I let her go. I want her to know that."

Tears streamed down Arianne's face as she heard the finality in his words. She found herself clutching Galen's handkerchief and huddling against his side. The baron's words came so close to hitting topics she had debated with Melanie for so long, but she didn't have the clarity of mind to examine them now. She feared for Rhys, and for his uncle, and wished there were some way to stop them. Galen's arm was reassuring, and when he hugged her briefly, she looked up to him with expectation.

He pressed a kiss to her forehead, then released her into Melanie's desperate grasp before striding forward between the two men.

"Tell her yourself, Llewellyn. She deserves that much. Now, give me the gun before you frighten the ladies witless. I don't know about you, but I could use a good glass of brandy right now, and if there's any canary, I think the ladies would benefit from it." Galen calmly appropriated the weapon, carrying it with him to the wine cabinet as he searched for glasses and the appropriate spirits, as if they had just come in from an evening at the club.

Arianne sagged with relief as Rhys grabbed his uncle and pushed him down into the desk chair, then reached for the large snifter of brandy Galen handed to him, passing it to his uncle. Melanie ran to take the next glass poured and to deliver it to Rhys. For the first time, he gazed into her pale face, and his fingers closed around her hand as he took her offering.

"I'm going to put a harness and bridle on you one of these days, my lady," he said without inflection.

"Well, perhaps if you think of me as one of your horses, you will understand me better," Melanie replied tartly. The tearstains on her face belied the tone of her voice, however.

Rhys waited until Galen had handed Melanie a small glass of wine before sipping his own drink, and then his reply wasn't directed at Melanie but at the man behind her. "Locke, I'm certain her brothers will be properly appreciative that you have managed to keep her in sight, but I think you'd better take her home now. My uncle and I have a few things we need to discuss." He sent a quick look to Arianne. "Miss Richards, I apologize for inflicting you with this unpleasantness. Will you reserve a few minutes for me when I return this evening?"

The wine in her glass shook as Arianne absorbed the tableau playing before her. The baron stared out the window, numb to the happenings around him. Rhys stood cold and unresponsive near him, his dark eyes filled with wells of pain as he gazed over Melanie's head to Arianne and Galen. It was Melanie's stricken face that shattered all of Arianne's firmly held beliefs. Melanie had discovered the anguish of love. Why hadn't she seen it before?

Arianne glanced back to Rhys, noting how tightly he held his glass, how carefully he avoided looking at the distraught female before him. He was being sensible, of course. Even if by some miracle his estates could be restored to him, Rhys would still be only a baron of a small west-country property, with a scandal for the *ton* to whisper about for years to come. He no doubt would prefer to keep to his writing and his horses rather than indulge in the social whirl of London. The granddaughter of an earl could do much better than that, particularly one as lovely and wealthy as Melanie. She would be much better off with Galen.

Or would she? Melanie's tearstained face was turned to Arianne now, and Arianne couldn't deny the love and hope and plea burning in her cousin's eyes at her hesitation in replying. After the tale told here today, Arianne could no longer pretend that love wasn't an emotion to reckon with. She didn't love Rhys; she had known that from the start. They might respect each other and live their lives as friends, but they would never know the passion shining in Melanie's eyes, nor the one Rhys struggled to conceal. Who was she to destroy their happiness because of a few weak promises and a vague understanding that she wasn't good enough for love?

Arianne met Rhys's gaze with sympathy, and shook her head. "I think it is time that you quit pretending you aren't good enough to have what you want, Rhys. After what you have suffered all these years, you deserve the best of everything. It's not my time you seek." She glanced hesitantly to Locke. "Galen, should we leave now? It wouldn't be proper to leave Melanie . . ."

Galen shook his head slowly, meeting Rhys's tormented gaze. "We'll not leave yet. We'll make ourselves comfortable in one of the rooms below until Rhys is ready to leave with us." He turned a thoughtful gaze to Arianne. "Perhaps we could spend the time more wisely than we have in the past."

Hope warred with fear as Melanie watched the battle of wills between her cousin and Locke. Turning to Rhys, she daringly reached out to touch his rumpled cravat, smoothing it awkwardly with her fingers. He seemed frozen beneath her touch, but she thought she could feel the erratic pounding of his heart, and she looked up to find his gaze fixed hungrily on her.

"I think perhaps Galen has a few things to say to my cousin that he wouldn't appreciate my hearing. Shall I stay with you just a little while? I promise not to interfere."

Rhys had enough to deal with in his uncle and the threat of suicide that his current state implied. To add his concern for Melanie to his list of chores seemed too much to bear. But as her gentle fingers closed around his cravat, Rhys closed his eyes and surrendered to the floodwaters of emotion released by the broken dam of today's discoveries. If he could just float along on the water for a little while instead of climbing onto the banks of reality . . .

When he opened his eyes, Galen and Arianne were gone, and the misty blue of Melanie's gaze pulled him deeper.

20

"I DON'T THINK we should have left her there. She's distraught. She cannot be helpful in such a painful situation." Arianne paced the floor of the library to which Galen had directed her. Her own emotions weren't much better than Melanie's. They galloped riotously through her breast, flinging sense and logic aside.

Galen placed the pistol inside a high bookcase and closed the glass door before turning to watch her pace. She still wore the silly bonnet he had found for her, and the yellows splashed like sunshine against the dusky gloom of the draped room. "I would have had to carry her out. And then we would have had to rope and tie her to keep her. I've known Melanie as long as you have. Let Rhys deal with her. He has enough sense for both of them."

"But his uncle is in a very dangerous state," Arianne protested, swinging to glare at him. It was much simpler to be angry with him than to confront her other feelings. "Where are the servants? Shouldn't we send for someone in authority?"

Galen's smile didn't reach his eyes as he stalked toward her. "There is no need for servants to spread the sordid story. I daresay Llewellyn dismissed them shortly after he returned, knowing Rhys would follow soon enough. And the baron is the authority around here. Shall we flee back to my father and seek his help?"

"There must be something we can do!" Arianne retreated to the nearest shelves, searching their titles

as if the answer could be found there rather than face
Galen. "I don't think he is quite sane. We ought to
get both of them out of here and leave someone else
to deal with him."

Galen stood behind her, leaving her with nowhere
else to run. "I don't doubt that love is reason enough
to surrender sanity. We are not all mechanical creatures, you know. Emotions drive us to do exceedingly
irrational things at times."

She couldn't continue standing with her back to
him. Reluctantly Arianne turned in the small space
left to her. She couldn't quite catch her breath. Her
eyes came level with the squareness of Locke's chin,
and she realized he hadn't had time to shave this
morning. She squirmed uneasily at the intimacy of this
discovery. Gentlemen were supposed to keep their
distance. She shouldn't know about such indelicate
things as whiskers. She shouldn't be able to notice
that it was actually his shoulder muscles straining at
his coat, and not the usual buckram padding. And she
certainly shouldn't notice that Lord Locke possessed
a heady scent of his own, not one combined of co-
lognes and snuff, but the fresh scents of soap and skin
and healthy flesh. Her cheeks pinkened under his
close perusal, and she answered defensively.

"Then perhaps we should beware of emotions, particularly when important decisions must be made. We
claim to be a civilized society. We cannot behave as
barbarians and do as we please because we feel like
it."

"I suppose not, or I would have most likely strangled you by now," Galen replied calmly. "Or made
violent love to you. I'm not at all certain which. Look
at me, Arianne. Am I such an ogre?"

Clenching her fingers into fists against the wall of
books, Arianne slowly raised her gaze to meet
Locke's. Despite his strength and size and words, he
did not threaten her in any way. He merely stood
there waiting for her to see what she wouldn't believe.

He was no ogre. She shook her head, unable to
express her feelings. "I don't think this is at all proper,

my lord. Perhaps we should seek some servants to prepare tea. Surely there must be someone in the kitchen."

"I don't think strangling would be enough," Galen mused aloud. "It's too final. I would want to strangle you every night for a lifetime before I'd be satisfied. The other alternative makes much more sense. Don't you agree?"

His smile was wicked as he leaned one hand on the shelf behind her head. If Arianne had thought him too close before, his proximity was suffocating now. She edged away before he could trap her entirely. "I don't know what you're talking about. I'm certain I have done nothing to earn your wrath. I only meant to see that propriety is observed. Is that so wrong?"

"Have you never done anything improper, Arianne? Of course you have. You stole your father's painting. And see where it has led us. Everyone is in an uproar. But your mother is enjoying the country, is she not? And it looks as if Rhys might have his inheritance returned. And perhaps even old Llewellyn might be reconciled with his wife, if the fates are kind. And maybe Melanie will persuade Rhys of her affections. All because you did something improper. So maybe it is time I encouraged you to more impropriety."

Arianne stared at him as if he had gone mad. "You blame me for all this? I fail to see—"

Galen continued as if she had not interrupted. "I am beginning to fancy the idea of Scotland. Gretna Green is but a few days' journey from here. The scenery should be magnificent this time of year. What do you think, Arianne? Let us do something impetuous. While everyone else is happily occupied, let us run for it. We can come back and do all the sensible things later. For just this once, let us do something for ourselves."

Arianne was too aware of Galen's lips so close to hers. They stopped her ability to think. She knew what he was suggesting was quite insane, but she couldn't quite remember why. Pressing her hands against the bookshelves, she tried to force herself into flight, but it was too late. His head lowered, and his mouth closed over hers, and all chance at sense or logic fled.

There had to be madness in the magic just the touch of their mouths created. Arianne quivered beneath the gentle softness of his lips stroking hers, and she reached for more when Galen began to move away. She knew it was a mistake the moment she did it. Instead of brushing his kiss lightly across her cheek as he had intended, he returned to eagerly pursue her reaction, and she lost all sense of what was right and wrong beneath his expert onslaught. Her hands even went so far as to betray her by stealing up his coat and clinging there when she could no longer stand on her own. Eyes closed, she let his hand steady her head and drifted into some dream world where only Galen's kisses existed.

It couldn't last, of course. A door slammed somewhere above. Angry voices rang out. Heavy boots pounded against wooden floors in pursuit of the light drum of feminine feet. Galen stepped back, releasing Arianne's head, although his hand remained protectively resting on the shelf behind her. Arianne disentangled her fingers from his cravat where they had so amazingly strayed.

"Galen! I want to go home. Right now. Where are you? I shall go by myself if you do not appear at once."

There was no mistaking Melanie's voice, or the rage in it. Arianne glanced briefly to Galen's face, seeing his struggle for composure as a reflection of her own. But he was much more experienced at it than she. With a wry look he pressed a kiss to her forehead and righted himself.

"Perhaps we could take her with us as a bridesmaid?" At the dazed look of incomprehension in Arianne's face, he managed a small chuckle. "Perhaps not. Come along, then. I do not wish to engage your family's fury just yet, and certainly not over the matter of a willful brat."

He pulled her along after him, leaving the gloom of

the library for the brightness of a hallway illuminated
by a gaping front door. Rhys had just maneuvered his
wooden foot down the last of the stairs when they
appeared, and the anger and pain in his expression
left little room for question.

"Go after her, Locke. I cannot leave my uncle alone
like this." The unspoken plea in his voice said all that
he could not.

"Melanie's wayward, but she's not a fool; she'll be
waiting out in the courtyard. Bring your uncle back
to my father's if you will. It would be better to settle
these matters in the company of others."

Rhys looked relieved at Galen's reassurances. The
men shook hands, and Rhys spared Arianne a brief
look as Galen reached to pull her after him again.
"Miss Richards, I don't know what to say. Melanie . . ."

"Say nothing. I understand. Please hurry after us,
or we shall worry." Arianne felt Galen's eager tug on
her arm, but she felt some empathy for the worried
man casting glances after her departed cousin. Rhys
seemed to be caught up in the same gale-force winds
that buffeted her about. With a rueful smile she waved
and ran after Galen.

They entered the stableyard just as Melanie gained
her seat on the horse. Galen left Arianne standing on
the lawn as he swiftly crossed the drive to head her
off. "I'll turn you over my knee and beat some sense
into you if you ride out of here without us, Melanie
Elizabeth!" He grabbed the horse's bridle before she
could whip it into motion.

Sighing, Arianne lifted her skirt and hurried to
come between these two. It was rather like watching
her two youngest brothers scuffle over some toy. Perhaps they were too much alike. Melanie appeared
ready to use the crop on Galen, and he seemed quite
prepared to carry out his threat. Neither one of them
cared a fig that the other might have equal right for
being upset.

"Melanie, I wish you would ride with me in the gig.
Galen has a passion for speed and I'm not certain
I'm prepared to go down the mountain in full flight."

Arianne pressed her hand to Galen's arm, forcing him into a less threatening position, while she looked up to Melanie with her request for aid.

Melanie blinked back tears and attempted to focus on her cousin. It took a moment for her to realize that Arianne was requesting her help, a practice that was almost unheard-of in all their years. She wasn't even certain what the request was, but she nodded blankly, not caring what was asked of her. She threw a hopeless look back to the house, wishing for the magical appearance of a dark-coated masculine figure, but the house loomed as cold as his heart. Without protest, she allowed Galen to help her down.

Arianne sent Galen a concerned glance over Melanie's shoulder, but he could only shake his head in reply. They could not know the argument until Melanie told them. All they could do was get her home.

Clouds pushed across the sun as they made the journey back down the hillside. What had begun as a beautiful promise of a day now became overcast and their silence reflected the same mood. Galen rode Melanie's horse beside the phaeton and made occasional attempts at wit, but Melanie had lost her usual cheerfulness, and Arianne's concern didn't allow for much laughter. She thrust aside all memory of those minutes in the library. They hadn't been themselves, that was obvious. That house back there had cast some pall of madness upon them all. She could only hope Rhys could pull himself away.

"Do you think Gordon will take me back to Somerset with him? I don't wish to finish the Season. It's quite boring, actually." Being more experienced with carriages and horses, Melanie handled the reins, not realizing she left her cousin with nothing to do to choke back her thoughts.

Arianne grasped this topic eagerly. "I'm certain Gordon will be happy to do whatever you request, knowing Gordon, but are you certain that is the best thing to do? There will be questions. Daphne and Evan will be concerned that their hospitality was not as it should be. Are you not taking the coward's way out?"

Melanie's delicately lovely face somehow adopted a mulish expression. "I am merely being sensible for a change. Such frivolity is meaningless. I can be of help to Gordon, I know I can. He really ought to marry, but until he does, I can be useful. Perhaps I can even look about to find him a wife." She brightened slightly at that thought.

"I'm certain he will be appreciative," Arianne responded dryly, looking to Galen as he approached the carriage now that the road had widened slightly. His buckskins strained tightly over muscled legs as he maneuvered his horse around in the road, and she had to force her gaze upward in the direction of his cravat before she could recover her train of thought. She seemed to be quite rapidly losing her mind. The brilliance of his smile as he walked the horse back to them made her cheeks hot with guilt.

"Have I missed something?" The question was directed at Melanie's rebellious expression, but Galen's gaze was arrested by the interesting flush on Arianne's cheeks.

"I have decided to return to Somerset with Gordon," Melanie replied defiantly, clicking the horses to a faster gait.

"And to help Gordon find a wife," Arianne added, certain Galen would appreciate the irony.

His look of amusement told her he did, and she felt some satisfaction in that. Perhaps he was not playing a part when he said he thought of Melanie as a sister. She just wished he hadn't proposed to her cousin first. Perhaps under the circumstances he had felt obligated to do so, but the memory still rankled. He didn't have to look so smug.

Galen continued in the same strain, ignoring the tempest beginning to form in Arianne's eyes. "But don't you think you should see me married off to Arianne before you start on poor Gordon? She's quite likely to stray without someone helping her stay in line."

Melanie gave his cheerfulness a suspicious glance. "I'm not at all certain I would be doing her a favor to see her married off to the likes of you, Galen Locke. I cannot imagine why she agreed to marry you in the first place. She is usually much more sensible than I."

"Will the two of you quit talking about me as if I'm not here?" Irritably Arianne shook back her bonnet and tried to arrange a tickling hair back into her braid. "If our wayward attachments are open for discussion, we would do better to discuss why Rhys is not here with you now. I'd thought the two of you would finally come to some understanding."

"Whatever gave you such a thought?" Melanie asked sharply. "He is naught but a friend, a very annoying friend, at the moment. I think he has been too much around Evan, if you must know. He is most . . ." She struggled for an appropriate phrase.

"Annoying," Galen supplied with a smile. "Brothers are like that. But it is good to know that you think of us all as brothers and that you will come flying to all our rescues when the need demands. Which brings us back to the topic at hand. I need your help in securing a wife. The one I want is sitting next to you, but she is being most . . . annoying."

Arianne couldn't help the quick upward twist of her mouth at Galen's suggestive tone. She knew if she caught his eye she would start laughing, and he needed no further encouragement. So she gazed resolutely out over the fields ahead, denying his plea.

Melanie gave her cousin a quick look, finding nothing in her countenance to explain or protest Galen's complaint. Deciding she was being the brunt of one of his jests again, she donned an aggrieved expression. "You make light of everything, Galen. It is most unfair of you. Wouldn't you be much happier back there with Rhys, dealing with men's problems? We are quite old enough not to need a nanny to see us home."

"A nanny! Now I am not only a brother, but a nanny. I truly ought to leave you to yourself for that. You have incalculably damaged my male pride, you ungrateful little hoyden. I can only hope you have not irretrievably ruined my position in your fair cousin's eyes. I shall hold you solely responsible if she calls off our betrothal."

Arianne heard full well the laughter in Galen's voice, but the banter seemed singularly inappropriate after this morning's events. When Melanie came after him with another gibe, she intruded sharply. "Will the two of you stop it? You may tear each other apart tooth and claw when I am not here, but I would be most appreciative of a little sensible conversation right now."

That silenced them briefly, until Melanie inquired softly, "Would you rather I sat and cried?"

21

By THE TIME they returned to the Deward estate, Arianne had taken over the reins and Melanie had dissolved into teary oblivion after spilling out the whole argument that had taken place that morning.

The confession had even managed to take the laughter out of Galen's eyes, Arianne decided as she cautiously followed his instructions in bringing the phaeton up the drive. Only a fool in love would send a rich prize like Melanie away because he could not offer her all the advantages which her position demanded. Arianne was quite glad she had been out of range of that argument. Rhys was undoubtedly right and acting sensibly, but Melanie's heartbroken sobs did not seem to make being right a thing to be desired.

But now that it was perfectly obvious that Melanie and Rhys were madly, however wrongly, in love, the relationship between Galen and Arianne changed, and they both sensed it. They had gone into this betrothal on the basis of pleasing Arianne's father and helping her mother, but they had both been aware that there were other alternatives. Those alternatives had suddenly evaporated, and they were left with each other or nothing.

Galen's hand closed tightly around Arianne's as he helped her from the carriage, and his look was searching as she came to stand beside him. There was nothing she could say to relieve the strain. It no longer seemed sensible to marry a man out of respect and friendship, particularly if that man was in love with her cousin and best friend. And she could no longer throw Melanie up to Lord Locke as the preferable woman for his wife. Even she could see that Melanie would be miserably unhappy with any man other than Rhys.

The world wasn't a simple place, and life did not always go as one planned. Sadly Arianne pressed Galen's palm and let it go. She had to smuggle Melanie up to their bedroom without being condemned to an interrogation by everyone waiting in the house. There wasn't time to determine where they stood in relation to each other right now.

Gordon was already striding steadily toward them, and two of Arianne's brothers were emerging from the shrubbery with Indian war whoops. Any moment now, chaos would ensue. Arianne offered what she hoped was a reassuring smile and turned to guide Melanie quickly past the shoals of disaster.

Diverting Gordon with a tale of cinders in his sister's eye and sending her brothers chasing off in search of Puddles, Arianne deliberately steered Melanie to the safety of their shared chamber. Galen remained behind to catch Gordon's questioning demands.

"I take it this was not a pleasure outing. Where has Rhys got to? It is near time for tea and no one seems to know where the lot of you have been."

"Arianne and I seem to be at odds," Galen responded lightly, "and Melanie was lending us countenance. Rhys struck off to visit the baron. The earth may shake and the mountains crumble ere this day ends. Come along and help me find some nourishment before my mother presses little tea cakes on me. And while you're at it, tell me the key to your cousin's cold heart. She cannot be as obstinate as she seems."

Distracted by this tissue of evasions, Gordon fell into step with Locke as they returned to the house. "I thought you had already discovered the key to her heart, her family. By bringing them here, you have surely endeared yourself to her for all time. Everyone seems to assume you have all but set the date. What argument can she possibly have against you?"

"I rather believe your practical cousin has suc-

cumbed to Melanie's romantic tales. She thinks I do
not love her. I don't understand what women want us
to do to prove ourselves. Shall I slay a dragon for
her?" Galen's tone was almost wistful as he contemplated this part of his problem.

"Evan would be a better person to ask than I. Perhaps if you found that infernal painting they were rav-
ing about . . ."

At the approach of Arianne's father, Galen threw
back his head and laughed at Gordon's innocent suggestion. "The painting has been found, and that is
even a sorrier tale yet. Mr. Richards, how do you do?
I trust you have been adequately entertained this
day?" He slipped into his role of host without effort,
leaving Gordon to give him a worried look but effectively ending the topic.

"My baby is so well-behaved; you have trained him
wonderfully, Galen." The countess lifted the newly
washed and brushed animal into her lap, petting and
crooning over the contented dog as if it truly were a
child.

"Obviously he had needs that weren't being answered, Mother. I think I can vouch for his behavior
in the future." Galen's eyes gleamed as they fell on
Arianne's irate expression. She was holding back a
smile, he could sense it, but she would have great
difficulty explaining her laughter in present company.
Maliciously he egged her on. "If only Arianne would
vouch for mine."

He watched her furious blush with delight. She was
doing her very best to cling to the obedient behavior
expected of her, but Galen had tasted the passion in
her kiss, and he was beginning to learn the rebellious
byways of her mind. He could easily spend a lifetime
delving into the fascinating nature of one Miss Arianne Richards. If only he could pry her away from
her sense of duty and her confounded logic.

His mother gave him a sharp look, not entirely deceived by her son's innocent expression. "I should
think you old enough to be responsible for your own

behavior. A lady is in no position to correct her husband."

Wild joy swept through Galen as the laughter erupted in Arianne's eyes and she had to turn away to keep from smiling. He wanted to see her laughing all the time. He wanted to dance with her. He wanted to pick flowers and cover her with rose petals. It was insane what she was doing to him, this modest little wren he had plucked from her nest. But he could not call her a wren anymore. The plumage his mother was providing for her proved she was an elegant swan after all. He had scarcely been able to take his gaze from her all through dinner. How could the foolish creature think she was not the most desirable woman in all of England? How was he going to prove to her that she was everything she should be, and more?

"Let us have music, Mother. Do you know, I have not once had the opportunity to dance with my intended? Gordon, you must lead Melanie out on the floor, and Arianne and I shall complete the set." He strode forward to firmly grasp Arianne's fingers before she could wriggle away.

"I cannot," she whispered, horrified, as the countess agreeably sat down at the piano. "I have not danced since Melanie put a spider down the back of that odious dancing instructor. Do not do this to me, Galen, I beg of you."

"I'll hear more of that tale at some other time. There is nothing you can do to persuade me out of this, my love. I have the strongest urge to dance with you."

The husky murmur of Galen's voice against her ear spoke of more sensuous urges than that, and Arianne clung to his coat sleeve out of desperation as the music started and he led her out onto the carpet. It was much better that he amuse himself in here, in full view of both families, than to give in to those other urges they had both displayed earlier this day. Or she thought it was better. As the music progressed and she found herself more and more frequently in Galen's arms, the innocent dance seemed to take on hidden meanings. The possessive hold on her waist, the warm grasp of his hand, the occasional caress of his coat against her skin as they maneuvered through the figures in this limited space, all served to undermine her feeling of security.

Arianne wasn't certain whether to be relieved or sorry when the rapid knock on the distant door below distracted the attention of several of the room's occupants. The music continued playing, but Melanie no longer seemed to be attending. She had been on edge all evening, and she stumbled now in Gordon's arms, stopping without explanation as the sound of voices carried up the stairs. Gordon looked at her with curiosity, then followed the sounds of the voices too. Even Arianne's mother appeared enticed by the intrusion, although her father and the earl were too engrossed in some esoteric discussion of their own to pay attention to their surroundings.

Galen didn't appear to be the least bit interested in the newcomers. As long as the music continued, he was prepared to hold Arianne in his arms, but it became a trifle difficult to complete the set without the participation of their partners. He gave Gordon a look of annoyance and would have turned to his mother to demand a waltz had not Melanie suddenly given a small cry of recognition and run for the door.

That effectively ended the interlude. With a wry twist of his lips, Galen gazed down at Arianne. "Do we follow or let her tear into our guests alone?"

"She is too well-brought-up to be rude. But I daresay since you have invited them, you must welcome them. Have you ordered their rooms prepared?"

"What a wifely thing for you to say, my love. I do think I could get the hang of this business quite easily. Speak to my mother, will you? And I shall lead the prodigals to safety."

Arianne seriously considered punching him, but their audience was too great. She didn't know at what point they had become intimate enough to exchange such gibes with this ease; she only knew she no longer felt the discomfort of strangeness when Galen was about. It was an odd sensation, this give-and-take between man and woman. She had never experienced it before and wondered if it were not a natural development of being in company. Even as she thought it, Rhys and Gordon rose to mind, and she knew that was not so. Even though Gordon was her cousin, she could not jest and laugh with him as she did with Galen. And although she had once thought Rhys suitable for her husband, she knew instinctively she would not find the same rightness in his arms as she did in Galen's. There was a difference, but she could not put her finger on it.

She went to inform the countess of Galen's impromptu invitation to the Llewellyns, and a maid was summoned to air and freshen a room for the baron. Gordon had joined Galen in going down to greet the guests, but the remainder of the room's occupants turned to Arianne for explanations.

Nothing she could say seemed right, so she diverted their questions with a description of the baron's imposing home. The earl obviously thought she had lost her wits, but the women seemed to understand, and they turned impatiently to satisfy their curiosity in the appearance of the guests.

Some of the baron's coloring had returned after his ride down the mountainside, but he still appeared old and tired and rather confused. Arianne glanced anxiously to Rhys, but despite his weariness, his whole being seemed focused on Melanie, who was busily flirting broadly with Galen and ignoring him. Arianne gave her betrothed a scathing look, but he merely winked in return and introduced the baron to his company.

The earl and Owen Llewellyn greeted each other gruffly, with the restraint of two men who knew each other well but didn't get along. Arianne's father greeted the baron with the same amiability that he met everyone, but with none of the enthusiasm with which a long-lost friend would be met. Llewellyn shook their hands, then turned to find Rhys.

His nephew stepped forward with the same pride

he had carried with him when garbed in frayed coats
and stained with the ink of his trade. Tonight, though,
he wore a navy long-tailed coat with fabric so stiff it
could never have been washed before. The fit was not
precise and the style was not that of London, and
Arianne very much suspected it had been lovingly constructed by his grandmother, but it hid the worn spots
on his linen and added veracity to the declaration that
followed. Topped by a starched white cravat from his
uncle's wardrobe, his attire told the tale before the
baron's words.

"Deward, I want you to be the first to know that
we've found evidence that should restore Rhys's estate
and title. I'm surrendering all claim in his favor, as I
told the boy I would do whenever he was ready.
We've had words between us, I'll admit, but he's always been David's heir to me. But now we have proof
for a court of law."

Owen's declaration was a little shaky, his carriage
not what it should have been as he leaned weakly
against a chair back, but the words were out and could
not be taken back. He straightened sufficiently to pat
Rhys's back and propel him into the room.

Rhys was ignoring Melanie with some difficulty and
blindly accepted the hand of Ross Richards before
that of the earl. In the confusion, no one seemed to
notice. The men made appropriate exclamations,
pounded each other on the back, and poured drinks.
Arianne joined Galen in congratulating him. The
countess sent for refreshments. Anne Richards smiled
from her invalid's chair and beamed with delight when
Rhys came forward to bow over her hand as a friend
of his mother's. The room quickly filled with the noise
of congratulations and questions. Only Melanie ab-
stained from the general confusion.

Arianne watched with concern as her cousin slipped
quietly from the room. She turned to Galen, who
managed to stay by her side throughout the celebra-
tion, but he only nodded his head to a far corner.
Rhys was already making his excuses and hurriedly
pushing through the crowd.

Abruptly Galen deserted Arianne to corner Gordon, who seemed prepared to follow the fleeing couple. He launched into a witty and prolonged story he had heard at his club, ignoring Melanie's brother's restless impatience. A maid was called to show the now sagging Owen Llewellyn to his room. Anne and Ross Richards made their excuses shortly after. Arianne conversed nervously with the earl and countess, and still Galen rambled on, following one story with a related one, all well told and charmingly done.

Gordon was obsessively polite, but even his patience had its limits. When Galen's monologue threatened to continue into still another anecdote, he caught his friend by the lapels and steered him to the right, not an easy task, since Galen's size outmatched him by several stone and inches.

"They've been gone long enough, Locke. I'm going to find them." With that simple statement Gordon proceeded around Galen and stalked from the room.

Hastily making her excuses, Arianne ran after her cousin. Perhaps she had no right to interfere, but if Melanie needed her, she meant to be there. The question was, where might "there" be? She nearly bumped into Gordon when he stopped to contemplate this same puzzle.

Galen came up behind them, simplifying the problem with a wave of his hand. "You check the library, Griffin. Arianne will check their chamber, and I'll go this way. One of us is bound to discover at least one of them."

Without a better plan of action, Gordon nodded stiffly and set out for the distant library. Instead of sending Arianne off down the hall to the chamber she shared with Melanie, Galen caught her arm and led her downstairs in the direction of the conservatory.

"If they had any sense at all, this is where they would be. Have you seen the orchids blooming yet? It's the most romantic place in the house. If I know Melanie, this is where she would lead him."

That seemed reasonable, certainly more so than expecting her cousin to have retired to bed. Arianne raced after Galen's long strides as they hurried down dark corridors devoid of servants. She was just beginning to realize how late it was when they entered the moist warmth of the darkened conservatory.

The lamp in Galen's hand merely flickered against the leaves of budding trees, enclosing them in shadowy walls of vegetation. Arianne had not realized the room was so overgrown with plants as Galen guided her down a narrow walkway arched over in brilliant blooms and heavy greens. She heard no sound that might be Melanie and Rhys, but she was uncertain whether that was good or bad.

At last they came to a low divan surrounded by pots of normal-size plants, although their heady blooms gave off perfumes that scented the night. The flickering light of the lamp revealed no sign of the truants, but Galen didn't seem much concerned. He set the lamp on a low stone wall and turned to reach for Arianne.

"Well, if Melanie didn't have enough sense to come here, I am not so foolish. I believe we were interrupted before we could conclude our earlier conversation, my love." Without any other warning than that, Galen bent to capture her lips.

22

"GO AWAY, YOU BEAST. I never wish to speak with you again. Never!"

Swift, small footsteps hurried down the terrace stairs to the unlit gardens, but the brief flash of a white gown revealed the direction, and the man in the doorway never hesitated. His halting stride carried him down the stairs and onto the graveled walks with assurance.

His soft calls after the fleeing figure went unheeded, however, and he began to curse under his breath as his artificial limb stumbled over a misplaced flowerpot and he was brought to his knees. Within seconds he was barreled over by a furry body leaping at him from the side, and a raspy tongue proceeded to wash his face despite his vehement protests.

"I've got him, Lucy!" a small voice cried from the shrubbery before branches began crashing outward, creating an access to the walk that shouldn't be there.

"But I have him over here!" A feminine voice carried across the length of the garden, followed by a loud "Ouch!" and a mild epithet as further struggling in the shrubbery ensued.

"Lucy! Davie! What are you two scamps doing out here?" the ephemeral white figure retraced her steps, only to give a small scream and fall to her knees before the newly acclaimed baron. "Rhys! Oh, Rhys, are you all right? Whatever happened? Here, let me . . ."

Rhys removed the furry body from his face and held it up to the disheveled tyke in his nightshirt hovering over him. "I believe I found Puddles. I suspect the

gardens are a popular trysting place hereabouts.
Hands off, Melanie, I can do it myself." Coming to a
sitting position, Rhys ruefully dusted off his new coat
while gazing around at his attackers, trying not to look
too closely into the lovely face nearest him. "I suppose
that is Lucy destroying the rest of the shrubbery with
Locke's wretched animal." He nodded toward the
other white-shrouded figure coming through the access
Davie had created.

As Rhys maneuvered his leg into a working position, Melanie stood and with hands on hips regarded
her contrite young cousins. "I don't even want to hear
what the two of you are doing out here at this hour.
Let me have those dogs, and I want the both of you
to go straight up to your beds before I tell Uncle Ross
about this."

Regardless of the fact that Lucy already stood several inches taller than her older cousin, both young
people nodded and began to hand over the wriggling
animals. A muffled groan from behind them caused
the cousins to hesitate, but not soon enough.

"Not the dogs! For pity's sake, Melanie . . ."

Before he could finish, the dogs had taken advantage of the moment and leapt from the loose grips of
their young masters, scrambling off into the darkness
with triumphant barks as they resumed their pursuit.
The children ran screeching after them, leaving Rhys
to pull himself to a stance in front of a bewildered
Melanie, who wasn't certain whether to run after the
children or stay to help the injured Rhys.

"I think you and your cousin Arianne were mixed
up at birth and placed with the wrong families," Rhys
remonstrated as he caught Melanie's arm and made
the decision for her. "You have more in common with
yon heathens than their sister."

"Well, if you are so fond of Arianne, why don't you
go propose to her? I am certain she will agree that you
suit." Melanie attempted to shake off his imprisoning
hand, but his grip was firm.

"Yes, we agreed that we suit, but that doesn't seem
to be the basis for these things, now, does it? Hold

still, Melanie, or I shall be forced to do something quite desperate. My leg is still wobbling."

Startled, Melanie looked up into his dark, handsome face and gulped. The intensity of his gaze was quite unsettling, and the gentle smile he usually reserved for her was gone, replaced by an extremely obstinate-looking grimace. But his complaint caused instant concern, and she forgot her fears in the face of it. "There is a bench, just there. Sit down and rest and determine the extent of the damage. The little imps ought to be locked up until they are old enough to behave with decorum."

"Then you would still be in a cage, my dear." Rhys took her advice and the bench, pulling Melanie down with him. "And the rest of the world would be a dull place. We cannot all be alike. For some of us, the differences are enchanting."

Melanie gave him a swift glance to determine his meaning, but looked away again in confusion at the emotion she detected in his usually impassive face. "You have grown staid and stodgy, Rhys Llewellyn. I can remember a time when you were not so."

"We all change with time, some more than others. I'm sorry if I have disappointed you, but I have only behaved for your own good. There has never been a time when I haven't acted in your behalf. Do you think you can ever understand that?"

"No." Sulkily Melanie plaited her fingers together. "How can you know what is for my own good without consulting me? I am not an empty-headed child, you know."

"Never empty-headed, but until recently still a child. You're not a child any longer, however; you're a lovely young woman with a mind of your own. I was wrong to pretend otherwise."

Melanie's head came up with a jerk and she turned to face him. "Do you mean that? you will admit that you were wrong? Everyone still treats me as a child."

"You have a child's effervescence and charm, and we've all watched you grow up for so long, we hate to admit that you're no longer a little girl. But if it weren't for those little scoundrels running about in the bushes right now, I'd be tempted to show you that I mean what I say. With your permission, I'd like to court you as a proper suitor should. I know I cannot offer all that your other—"

Melanie's cry put an end to his usual argument, and her arms thrown about his neck prevented any turning back. With nowhere else to put his hands, Rhys wrapped them around her slender waist, and in a moment he was doing what he had promised himself he would not do.

Lucy and Davie halted in the shrubbery, shook their heads in disgust, and returned to chasing their straying charges.

"Galen, we cannot—" Arianne's breathless words broke when her suitor proved that they could. Pressed backward against the rolled arm of the divan, she surrendered to his ardent caresses, pulling Galen's head closer to better learn the heady passion of his kiss.

When his hand began to stray, she struggled, but it was only a moment's work to learn there were some things she could not resist. The new sensations to which Galen introduced her were among them, and she gave a small cry of loss when his lips moved from hers to stray across her cheek and downward.

"Say yes, Arianne," he murmured as his mouth moved seductively closer to her ear.

"Yes, Arianne," she whispered wickedly, welcoming this momentary respite, returning her hands to press at his waistcoat instead of entangling in his hair, although she knew she could not win against him.

"So agreeable. Now say, 'Yes, Galen.'" His fingers located the frail edge of her low-cut bodice and lingered there.

"I've granted you your one wish for the night. It's too late to ask for another." Arianne's attempt to push him away was weak even in her own eyes. She wanted to feel his kiss again. It was as simple as that.

"If I'm allowed one wish a night, then I know the one to ask tomorrow. I would suggest you have your bags packed before I ask it, though, for once it is granted, I'll not stop for anything."

"Galen, we cannot—" This protest ended where the earlier one had. Arianne's fingers curled in his already disheveled cravat as Galen's lips sought and conquered hers without a fight. The sensation sent her head spinning. How did one think at times like these?

"If you do not like Scotland, I'll buy a special license. I'm quite determined, Arianne. I've been going about only half-alive until now. Now that I have found the missing part of me, I will not do without any longer."

"You just wish Papa's Titian as a wedding gift," Arianne teased when he drew back once more. She was fully aware that he could press his ardent attentions further and she would not be able to stop him, would not wish to stop him. But Locke held himself to a limit that he had set in his own mind, certainly not society's limit, but one that he seemed in grave danger of exceeding at any second. He made her feel small and fragile lying here, something no man had ever done. She would not surrender the feeling for propriety.

"It will look splendid in the library," Galen agreed unmercifully. "But then, your father will feel right at home with it. If he means to clean and catalog every oil in this mausoleum, he will be with us a very long time."

Arianne laughed lightly and traced the strong lineaments of Galen's face with the tips of her fingers. "What you propose is impossible. If my father moves in here, so will the rest of my family. Your father will undoubtedly go into a severe decline, and there will be no room for us. It won't do at all."

"My father is having the time of his life arguing with your father, because he wins them all by default. And I don't mean for there to be room for us. Not just yet. I want you to myself. I mean to make you the toast of London first. Then, perhaps when there is a family to think about, we can consider returning here. We could have the whole east wing to ourselves and never see anyone else if we don't wish to."

Such solemn talk shattered the light banter of earlier, and Arianne instantly sobered, gazing up into the crystal gray of Galen's eyes with uncertainty. "How will it ever work, Galen? Please don't say these things because you think you have to. I don't wish to marry because you feel obligated. It would hurt me above all else. But you keep me so confused . . ."

He stroked her hair from her brow and whispered kisses down the line of her nose before replying. "I want to keep you confused. I want to keep you in such a swirl that you cannot think. I'm terrified that if I allow you to consider, you will find me unsuitable. I know I will make you a good husband, and I think I can teach you to love me as I love you, but I cannot bear to let you escape in the meantime. I'm being selfish, aren't I?" His last words were sorrowful as he pushed himself upright.

Arianne became aware of her wanton position with his movement, but she did not immediately move to right it. She had never been the recipient of a man's hungry gaze before, and she would be less than womanly if she did not appreciate the desire in Galen's eyes now as he looked on her. The power he had instilled in her with his look was almost as great as the one given by his confession. She wasn't entirely certain what to do with it, but her heart seemed to be beating excessively at the thought.

She held out her hand to him to be helped upright and found herself in his arms again. It seemed right to be sheltered against Galen's broad chest, resting her head on his shoulder. Had anyone told her a month ago that this would be so, she would have thought him touched in the head. But she could not imagine being anywhere else ever again.

"I don't think it's selfishness," she answered slowly, still uncertain as to how to reply to his amazing declaration. "I think I understand what you are saying, but it is all happening so fast, I'm a little frightened."

Carefully, not daring to hope, Galen lifted her chin

so he could look down into her eyes. They were such beautiful eyes, in all the colors of midnight. He would rather just kiss her senseless and let matters take their course, but that would be unfair to her. "Do you think . . . ? Is there any chance that you might learn to love me in return?"

Dreamily Arianne closed her eyes and let the touch of Galen's fingers open the box that she had kept so tightly fastened inside. It felt good to just let the sensations drift out, to not worry and fret about what the next minute, the next day, would bring. If she could just live forever in this moment . . .

"I've never been in love before, Galen. How will I know it's love? Does it have something to do with being happy when one is with someone, and feeling all confused and empty inside when he is gone? Is it listening for a certain footstep, a particular voice, until that someone returns? Can just talking and laughing and feeling comfortable with someone have anything to do with love? Does it . . . ?" Arianne lowered her voice as Galen pressed her head against his shoulder and began to scatter kisses against her hair. "Does love have anything to do with thinking about someone all the time and wondering what it would be like to have his children?"

Galen responded gravely, crushing her close. "All that, and more, my darling. There's no defining it, I fear. Do you feel like that, Arianne? Can I make you happy?"

The bliss enveloping her shone in Arianne's eyes as she looked up to him. But before she could speak, a mournful howl developed somewhere outside, followed by shrill screams, and the words were struck from her tongue. She stared at Galen, who had begun to scowl horribly. Then, with a resigned lift of his lips, he brushed a kiss across her brow and pulled her to her feet.

"Will our children be any better behaved than your siblings?" he inquired calmly, pulling her through the darkened conservatory toward the door.

"It's doubtful," Arianne answered honestly, running to keep up with him.

"Good, I wouldn't have them any other way." Grinning, he propelled Arianne through the rear door to the garden, where the entire household seemed to be converging in nightdress.

Lucinda was hopping up and down sobbing. Davie was down on his hands and knees sneaking through the shrubbery toward some goal as yet unseen by the others. Melanie and Rhys came dashing down the walkway, stopping and looking guilty upon seeing Arianne and Galen emerging from the house. From another door came Ross Richards and the earl in slippers and hastily tied robes. Various and sundry servants were stumbling down stairs and from the stables as Lucinda's cries grew more frantic.

Turning to see Galen and Arianne, Lucinda ran babbling toward them. "Oh, Lord Locke, you must save Puddles. Hurry, please. I'm afraid Davie will get bitten. They're fighting. It's awful. Please." She tugged impatiently at his hand, dragging him toward the scene of the crime or whatever awful horror had brought the entire household out into the middle of the night.

Not certain who was fighting whom, since Davie was obviously all alone beneath a bush, Arianne rushed to keep up with them. It didn't escape her notice, however, that Rhys was now grinning as hugely as Galen and his arm was wrapped proprietarily around Melanie's waist as they sauntered closer to the nocturnal activities causing such a commotion.

Galen arrived first, grabbing Davie by the neck of his nightshirt and removing him from the shrubbery before passing him on to his father, who looked somewhat dazed to be receiving such a burden at this hour of the night. The howling and yapping continued without interruption somewhere in the center of the spreading evergreens.

Galen caught Lucinda by the shoulders and propelled her in Arianne's direction despite the look of betrayal the girl directed at him. Signaling one of the grooms, he gestured toward the howls. "Grab them when they come out of there, and don't let either of them loose again, if you value your life." At the questioning lift of Arianne's brow, he offered with a wry smile, "A lovers' spat, I fear. If we're to keep the family together, we'll have to marry, or you will have poor fatherless puppies on your hands. A bucket of water will cool them off directly."

The earl gave a snort of disgust, took in the fully dressed but disheveled states of the young people, and muttered something about calling the bishop in, come morning, before stalking back to his bed.

Ross Richards, still holding firmly to his son's shoulders, gave Arianne's mussed hair and clothing a knowing look and pierced Galen with a steely glare. "You can have the Titian as a wedding gift, but my daughter goes back to London in the morning. I'd recommend you stay here until the date is set."

There was an abrupt interval as a servant ran up with the requested bucket of water and poured it on the animals in the shrubbery. The ensuing howls and chase disappeared into the further part of the garden. Lucinda quit fighting Arianne's hold and wandered hand in hand with Davie toward the house, wearily leaving the adults to carry on the task.

Through all this, Galen sent Arianne a questioning look, and the reply he found in her smiling gaze allowed him to give the proper response when the noise died down. Holding out his hand to Richards, he said, "The sooner, the better, as far as I'm concerned. How long will it take to have the proper sort of gown made up?" He threw this last to Arianne and Melanie.

"Months!" Melanie replied eagerly.

"A week," Arianne said overruling her calmly. "One gown should take no more than a week."

"But, Rainy, you need *lots* of gowns! I will help you pick them out. And Rhys can come along with us and it will be great fun . . ."

Rhys firmly regained Melanie's waist and hauled her toward the house. "Rhys will do no such thing. Rhys will come and call on you and your family properly, and attend the proper functions, but he will not . . ." The words faded into the night as they disappeared around the corner.

Arianne relaxed and leaned back into Galen's embrace as they both met her father's approving gaze. "I need only a week," she murmured. "And I don't need to go all the way back to London for a gown. I'm certain there will be one in Bath that will be quite satisfactory. Since everyone is already here but Evan and Daphne, it seems foolish to go traipsing about the countryside."

"For once, your logic is compelling, my dear. A week it is then. Mr. Richards?" Galen looked questioningly to his prospective father-in-law.

Ross had found another focus for his thoughts. Seeing his daughter and her intended silhouetted against the night sky, he nodded absently. "I rather fancy Beechey to do the job. An outside setting, I believe. I will speak to him when I return to London." And turning away, he wandered back toward the house, leaving the young couple laughing silently behind him.

Epilogue

"WE CAN GIVE them puppies for their wedding gift!" Lucinda danced excitedly from the kitchen, her best dress already smudged and her ribbons hanging askew as she ran down the hallway.

The couple watching her approach turned to each other with mutual laughter and understanding as their gazes met with love made stronger by the passing of three months of bliss. Anyone watching would have thought them the couple about to seal their vows, but Lucinda was accustomed to their mushy exchanges by now and waited stalwartly for them to remember her presence.

" 'Tis a pity they are not quite ready to be weaned yet. I think it would be most appropriate if we brought them to the church with us."

Arianne giggled at the mischievous light in her husband's eyes. Even after three months she was not quite accustomed to seeing the lighter side of things, but Galen was rapidly teaching her. She had worried that the painting they had chosen for Rhys and Melanie's new home would not be suitable. The idea of wishing a couple of brand-new puppies on a newly married couple made her concerns incongruous.

"Rhys would never forgive you. Don't you dare. He is trying very hard to act the part of proper baron and settle all the scandal for Melanie's sake. Turning their wedding into a riot would do no one any favor."

Galen graciously acquiesced, but only after tweaking the curl dangling by his wife's ear. "Does that mean my consequence is such that it was quite all right when little sister here beat Davie over the head with her bouquet before you even walked down the aisle at our wedding? And that your father spent the ceremony examining the stained glass while Evan and Gordon argued over who had the ring I gave them to carry? If Rhys had not been the only stable fellow there, I would have to disagree with you, my love.''

Arianne's laughter wafted through the halls of the London town house, where relatives were beginning to gather prior to the ceremony. In the library, the Earl of Shelce and Ross Richards were glaring at each other over a miniature of Melanie's parents that the earl meant to present to the couple as a wedding gift. The argument over the quality of the artwork ceased momentarily as the laughter reached them, and when his opponent's eyes grew misty and his attention drifted off, Shelce snorted and set the miniature aside.

The couple just arriving so they might travel together with Galen and Arianne to the ceremony heard the laughter and stopped in the foyer to exchange glances. Evan smiled and lightly touched the rounding of his wife's abdomen, bringing a smile of pleasure to Daphne's lips as her thoughts retreated inward. She tugged her husband's hand until he bent downward to place his head near hers.

"Don't tell anyone, but I think your cousin has an announcement to make when this is all over," she whispered in his ear.

Evan tweaked an eyebrow upward. "You have become an expert in this field already, have you?"

As Arianne and Galen approached to greet them, Daphne nodded knowingly at the glow on Arianne's face and pinched Evan when Galen protectively caught his new wife in his arms when she exhibited a slight unsteadiness on the last stair. Evan chortled and held out his hand to his friend.

"Welcome to the family, old man. May we both have sons to look after each other, for heaven forbid that one be female."

Arianne blushed heatedly and Galen looked momentarily taken aback that their carefully guarded secret had come undone, but then he grinned proudly and accepted the offered hand. "We'll send them off to school together."

"No, you won't," both Arianne and Daphne murmured demurely together, causing both their husbands' attentions to swerve back to their respective spouses.

As three little boys came screaming down the back stairs to the kitchen, a mile ahead of the maid meant to watch over them while their elders attended the wedding, the women exchanged warm glances.

"We mean to have only girls," Daphne announced firmly, and Arianne's laughter seconded the idea.

Geoffrey Ashe is well-known for his Arthurian studies, notably *The Quest for Arthur's Britain*, which he edited, *Camelot and the Vision of Albion*, and *King Arthur's Avalon*. His researches have led him into the wider field of what have been called 'collective mystiques', and it is from this interest that have come such books as *The Ancient Wisdom*, *The Virgin* (a study of the cult of the Virgin Mary), and his new book, *Miracles*, which is also to be published in Abacus. He is the author of a novel, *The Finger and the Moon*.

Geoffrey Ashe lives at Glastonbury on the Tor, in the house formerly occupied by the magician Dion Fortune, now a rendez-vous for travellers and researchers.